D0349987

Discover why everyone's falling in love with Happily Inc!

You Say It First

"Delightfully flirtatious and deceptively easy dialogue... Mallery excels at creating protagonists who grow individually as well as together on the way to their destined happy ending."
—*Publishers Weekly*

"The first in ever-popular Mallery's new Happily Inc series has the author's signature blend of humor, poignancy, and small-town charm."
—*Booklist*

"There's a lot to like about this first book in Mallery's new series, Happily Inc, about a California desert town that's known as a wedding destination. The romance is sweet and hot, the writing is quick and easy... A great choice for a weekend read."
—*Kirkus Reviews*

Second Chance Girl

"A heartfelt and genuine friends-to-lovers story fraught with emotional trauma that makes the happily-ever-after satisfyingly sweet... Sharp, well-drawn characters and a naughty beagle add depth to the story."
—*Publishers Weekly*

"You can always count on Mallery to deliver warmhearted and quirky stories featuring emotionally dented individuals doing their best to survive and hopefully thrive.... A truly unforgettable read! Mallery is one of a kind!"
—*RT Book Reviews*, Top Pick!

"Mallery's second title in the new Happily Inc series features her typical mastery of the romance format, with another quirky small town and a set of characters for her fans to love, complete with a mascot animal. The potent and prolific Mallery delivers again."
—*Kirkus Reviews*

Why Not Tonight

"Verdict: Soul-crushing revelations and old resentments are tempered by whimsy, sass, and belly laughs in a scrumptiously sexy, playful story from one of the genre's best. Touching, refreshing, and fun."
—*Library Journal*

"Full of blissful, sigh-inducing scenes and surprisingly complex characters."
—*Woman's World*

"Delightful… Natalie is a charming, funny, and beautifully human heroine, and her chemistry with Ronan is genuine. A wedding destination hot spot in California is the perfect romantic setting for this tender story."
—*Publishers Weekly*

"Susan Mallery hits all the romance sweet notes… *Why Not Tonight* arrives blissfully at the kind of happy-ever-after that every romance reader treasures."
—*BookPage*

"Sexy, connected, emotional and fun."

—*Kirkus Reviews*

Not Quite Over You

"Second chances, long held secrets and dreams come together in this wonderful, warm romance."
—*Night Owl Reviews*

"A heartbreaking but uplifting story about how when you find your one true love you can get a second chance to rekindle that relationship and that secrets, when finally revealed, can bring two people closer together."
—*Fresh Fiction*

SUSAN MALLERY

meant to be yours

HQN™

ISBN-13: 978-1-335-14637-3

Meant to Be Yours

meant to be yours

meant to be yours

CHAPTER ONE

Jasper Dembenski could accept an idiosyncratic GPS, the blown tire and the five hailstorms he'd driven through yesterday. It was the lack of coffee that was going to do him in.

He shook the empty coffee can, as if the action would magically produce results. Not shockingly, no coffee appeared. He was going to have to head to the grocery store, which was easier said than done, given that he was driving a thirty-six-foot RV. Or maybe there was coffee up at the main office. If he could grab some there, he could put off having to shop until later in the day.

Jasper was on the last leg of a three-month book tour for his latest suspense novel. Rather than trying to convince him to deal with dozens of flights, rental cars and hotels on the multicity tour, his publisher had enticed him with the idea of traveling via RV. Jasper didn't mind driving long distances, he enjoyed the solitude and time to think, and the RV parks were actually pretty decent.

He was about eleven hundred miles from home. Once he joined up with Interstate 10, it was a straight shot back to Happily Inc. All he needed was a large cup of coffee. He would find a Walmart or Target close to the interstate and get enough food to see him through the next two days.

He walked out into the warm September morning and started for the main office. Along the way, he nodded at people who waved or called out greetings. RV parks were friendly places. As he wasn't one for unnecessary chats, he'd learned to keep moving while offering a brief wave. Otherwise, he might get trapped in a lengthy and tedious conversation about the viability of a certain back road or a discussion about the best kind of bait for catfish.

"You git, you hear me? Go on out of here or I'll get my shotgun."

The angry words came from his left. Jasper instinctively went on alert, his body tensing as he spun in that direction. Using the RV he'd just passed for cover, he backtracked so he could come around from behind and see what was happening.

"You heard me," the man yelled. "Get out of here."

Jasper stayed close to the RV as he circled around and then stepped into view, prepared to get between some jerk and whoever he was threatening. Only the short, round, old man wasn't taking on his kid or his woman, instead he was raising his hand to a dog. An old dog with ribs showing through dirty fur. A dog who flinched and backed away.

"Problem?" Jasper asked, using his *tell me your story before I kick your ass* voice, the one he'd perfected during his time with the military police.

The old man glared at him, as if wanting to take him on, then seemed to think better of it. "It's nothing. Just that dog who's been hanging out here for a few weeks. Somebody dumped him. If you don't want a dog, just shoot him. That's what I say."

The kindness of strangers, Jasper thought grimly. Or lack

thereof. He knew there were more good people than bad, but every now and then he was forced to question his faith in humanity.

The dog—some kind of Lab-shepherd mix—looked at him with sad, knowing eyes, as if he didn't really expect better of life. He stayed out of reach and, despite the heat, shivered a little. He was obviously starving and might be sick. Who would just dump a dog at an RV park?

"He begs for food," the old man added, his tone defensive. "I don't have time to deal with him."

Jasper thought about the coffee he hadn't had yet and the eleven hundred miles between him and home. He thought about the book he was trying to write and how slowly it was going. He thought about the nightmares he often had and that there were still enough bad days to keep him humble. The absolute last thing he needed in his life was some old dog.

"If you were him, you'd beg for food, too," Jasper said. "Don't shoot him."

"You don't get to tell me what to do."

Jasper sighed before squaring his shoulders and staring down at the old man who was maybe five-five to Jasper's six foot three.

"Seriously?" he asked. "You're going to go there with me?"

The old man shook his head. "I'm just saying…"

"I know what you're saying. Don't shoot the dog."

Jasper walked to the office. Sure enough, they had a huge carafe of coffee that he used to fill his travel mug. While he drank down the dark, hot liquid, he asked about the dog and confirmed it was indeed a stray. A few attempts had been made to catch it, but no one had been successful.

Jasper headed to his RV. He would spend no more than fifteen minutes looking for the dog. If he found it, he would lure it back to his RV with food. Once it was inside, he would take it to a local vet and have it checked for a chip. If there wasn't one, he would drop it off at a shelter and be on his way. It would take him two hours, tops.

Or less, he thought as he approached his RV and saw the dog sitting outside the side door.

"Good morning," Jasper said, opening the door.

The dog jumped inside and made his way to the small refrigerator, where he sat again.

"Somebody's messing with me," Jasper grumbled.

He pulled out lunch meat he was going to use for a sandwich and gave that to the dog, who gulped it down. Jasper quickly scrambled a couple of eggs. Less than ten minutes later, the dog was stretched out on the sofa, completely relaxed and nearly asleep.

Jasper looked up the closest vet's office and called to explain the situation. The perky receptionist told him they'd just had a cancellation and could see him right away.

"Of course you can," he muttered.

The drive was easy, there was parking for his RV and damn if the dog didn't follow him inside the vet's office with no problem.

Jasper explained the situation to the smiling older woman with a name tag that read Sally. When he got to the part about him giving the dog to a shelter, her smile faded.

"You don't want to keep him yourself?" she asked.

"Ah, no. I'm not really a pet person."

Both she and the dog stared at him. Jasper shifted uncomfortably. He wanted to explain that he wasn't being cruel— rather his reluctance was realistic. He'd been in a really bad place when he'd gotten out of the army. After tons of therapy, medication and stumbling onto the one thing that could get him halfway back to being able to exist in polite society, he was healed enough to pass for normal. But he knew the truth—he would never fully get there. More than one thera-pist had warned him he was broken beyond repair.

They hadn't used those exact words—they were too pro-fessional for that. But the truth had been clear enough all the same.

But the woman in front of him wouldn't want to hear that and he certainly didn't want to tell her.

"I'd like him checked for a chip and maybe given an exam to see if he's all right," Jasper said.

"Sure. Let me take you to one of the rooms."

He and the dog followed her. She paused by a floor scale and motioned for the dog to step on it.

"Come on, boy. Right here."

The dog obliged. He was forty-eight pounds. Sally winced.

"He should be closer to seventy-five pounds," she said. "He's really skinny. Poor guy."

Jasper and the dog went into an exam room.

"I'll get one of the techs to come in and scan him. If there's a chip, we'll take it from there. If there isn't, we can talk about whether you want to pay for an exam when you're just going to take him to the shelter."

Her tone was pleasant enough but Jasper heard the judg-ment, all the same. Instead of speaking, he nodded. The woman left and he was alone with the dog.

They both sat and stared at each other. Jasper looked away first.

"You can't stay on your own," he said, shifting uneasily in his chair. "Look at you. You need someone to take care of you. A shelter would mean three squares and a bunk, right? And you'd find a family of your own."

Without wanting to, he recalled reading somewhere that older dogs had trouble getting adopted. Which wasn't his problem.

"I've never had a pet," he added, glancing at the dog, who still regarded him steadily. "I don't know how to take care of you."

He supposed there were books on the subject. Plus, the old guy wasn't a puppy. He would know how to deal with humans. Between the two of them, they might be able to get it right.

"I'm not a good bet," he added in a low voice. "I was in the army for eight years and I saw things. Sometimes I have flashbacks and I just... I'm better off alone."

The dog's head dropped as if he realized what Jasper was trying to say. As if he'd given up hoping and had accepted he was going to be abandoned—again.

Jasper stood up and glared at the dog, who still didn't look at him.

"I didn't want any of this. It's not my fault. I'm not the bad guy."

The dog didn't move—he sat there all hunched, as if the weight of the world was just too much for him.

Jasper thought longingly of his quiet house, the sameness of his life when he was home. He had friends, but on his terms. He had relationships with women. Sort of. He just wasn't like everyone else and wanting to be different didn't change the truth.

The dog raised his head and looked at him. In that moment when their eyes met, Jasper would swear he saw down-to-the-bone sadness and despair. It was so real, so visceral, that he felt the anguish as actual pain.

The door to the exam room opened and a petite, pretty, gray-haired woman in a white coat entered.

"I'm Dr. Anthony," she said with a smile. "For once all my techs are busy and I'm free." She crouched down and gently patted the dog's back. "Hey, old guy. How are you? Where'd you find him?"

"At an RV park a few miles from here. They told me he was abandoned a few weeks ago. Apparently he's been avoiding people, except to beg for food, but he came right into my vehicle."

Dr. Anthony petted him a little more, before running her hands up and down his legs and along his back as if gently checking for wounds or injuries.

"People can be cruel," she said as she stood. She pulled a handheld device out of her coat pocket and turned it on. "All right, let's see if you have a chip."

Jasper found himself tensing, not sure if he wanted the dog to have one or not. Dr. Anthony ran the reader back and forth a couple of times, checking him closely, then straightening and shaking her head.

"No dice," she said. "I didn't think so. Someone who cares enough to get a microchip doesn't walk away from their pet. Sally said you were going to take him to a shelter?"

Jasper hesitated.

Dr. Anthony gave him a sympathetic glance. "Look, it's better for him to be there than on the streets. We have a good one nearby. They'll take care of him. He's not your responsibility. You did the decent thing, bringing him in. That can be enough."

Which sounded like permission to do what he knew made sense. Great. He would take the dog there and be on his way.

He opened his mouth to ask for the address, but what he said instead was, "What if I wanted to keep him?"

"You sure?"

Jasper looked at the dog, who stared back at him. He thought about his house up in the mountains and how every now and then, the quiet got to him. He thought about the loneliness he'd seen in the dog's eyes.

"No, but I think giving him a good home is the least I should do."

Dr. Anthony smiled. "Okay, then. Are you from around here?"

"California. I'm heading home today."

"Then I would suggest a brief exam to make sure he's relatively healthy. I can give you a collar and leash and food that will be easy for him to digest. When you get to your place, find a vet and get him a more thorough exam. You and your vet can discuss what to do as far as vaccinations. He'll need a few chew toys, maybe a ball and a bed of some kind. He's an old guy, so he's going to want to take things easy. Still interested?"

"I am."

"Good. Now why don't you put him on the exam table there and we'll get started."

"It might just be okay," wedding coordinator Renee Grothen murmured softly to herself as she surveyed the wedding reception. She wouldn't risk admitting everything had turned out as planned until the last guest had left, but four and a half hours in, things were going really well.

Jim and Monica Martinez were a sweet couple with a fun firefighter theme for their big day. There was a long tradition of firefighters on both sides of the family and plenty of cute touches in the wedding and reception.

Monica's dress laced up the back and instead of white ribbon to cinch her gown, she'd used bright red. The centerpieces were ceramic boot vases painted to look like firefighter boots, filled with red, orange and yellow flowers. There was even a walk-through fountain at one end of the reception area, created with fire hoses, a pump and a lot of engineering.

Renee walked around the perimeter of the indoor reception space, looking for problems. So far, so good, she thought with cautious optimism. The cake had been cut, the bar service was about to end and the tone of the party had faded from raucous to comfortably tired—exactly as it should. With a little luck, things would wrap up on time and without a crisis. This was Monica and Jim's day—Renee wanted it to be as perfect as possible. While she always took care of her clients, she tended to unleash her mother bear instincts for her special couples and Monica and Jim certainly qualified.

She spotted Pallas Mitchell, her boss, walking toward her. It was nearly ten on a Saturday night and Pallas, a pretty brunette only recently returned from maternity leave, yawned widely. When she spotted Renee she held up her hands, palms up.

"What can I say? I've been home with an infant. These wild late-night hours are going to take some getting used to."

"No one's judging," Renee told her. "As I said at seven, at eight and again at nine, *go home*. I can handle this. You're barely back and you need to give yourself time to adjust to the schedule."

"You've been running things for nearly six months. You need a break."

In truth, Renee *was* a little ragged around the edges, but she'd loved handling Weddings Out of the Box while Pallas had been gone. She'd enjoyed the challenges each unique wedding presented and watching all the details fall into place on the big day.

"I had lots of help," Renee pointed out. "Hiring college students on summer break was a good idea." And what they'd lacked in experience, they'd made up for in energy and enthusiasm.

"Now that I'm back, things can return to normal," Pallas said, covering another yawn.

"Go home," Renee urged. "Please. I can handle things here. I promise."

"Okay. I will. Thanks. Don't you dare come in tomorrow." Pallas's voice was firm. "For once, we don't have a Sunday wedding. Enjoy the break."

"I will." Renee would probably pop in to do a little paperwork, but she wouldn't stay long. "Are you coming to The Boardroom on Monday night?"

In a wedding destination town, the rhythms of the residents were determined by weekend weddings. Happily Inc's workweek started on Wednesdays as the businesses geared up for the dozens of nuptials that occurred in multiple venues. Which meant the town's Friday night was actually on Monday.

The Boardroom, a local bar, hosted game nights on Mondays. Board games ruled and tournaments were heated and fun as friends crushed each other at everything from Candy Land to Risk.

Pallas shook her head. "I'll admit to being a bit of a worrier. When we went a couple of weeks ago, I couldn't stop thinking about Ryan. He's only five months old. It's too soon to leave him at night."

Renee held in a smile. "Sure. I get that."

"I know you don't, but thank you for pretending. Have fun for me, too. Oh, Jasper's back, so tell him hi, if you think of it."

Jasper was back? Renee hadn't heard. She liked knowing he'd returned from his big book tour. Not for any reason in particular, she amended hastily. Sure, he was nice, but there were a lot of nice guys in the world. There was just something about Jasper. Maybe it was because in addition to being good-looking and just a little dangerous, he wasn't a forever kind of guy.

"I saw that!" Pallas grinned. "I totally saw that. You did the predatory smile thing I was never good at. You want to use him for sex! Did I know this?" She stomped her foot. "Did this happen while I was on maternity leave? What else went on while I was off having a baby?"

Renee laughed. "You're reading way too much into my smile. I'm happy he's home from his book tour. That's all."

"I don't believe you."

"Jasper and I are not involved. I doubt we've had more than a three-sentence conversation."

Not that it took many sentences to ask *Your place or mine?* And while the description of predatory was nice, it gave her too much credit. Would she stalk him and pounce? Not even on her best day. Would she say yes if the man asked? She smiled again. Oh, yeah, she would. Definitely. Okay, probably. *If* she was feeling brave. Because while she worked her butt off to give her couples their perfect happily-ever-after day, she knew it was never going to happen for her. Those who could—did. Those who couldn't became wedding planners.

Avoiding relationships might be the smart choice, but it was also a lonely one. She knew Jasper was into the long-term, monogamous, not-serious kind of thing and she was pretty sure she could handle that. Assuming she was his type and he was interested. They could have some laughs, lots of sex and walk away completely unscathed in the heart department. Where was the bad?

"There's something going on and you can't convince me otherwise," Pallas said. "You have depths. I'm very impressed.

Okay, use Jasper and then tell me the details because hey, he's got to be great." She yawned again. "I'm such a lightweight. I'm leaving now."

"Good night. Hug Ryan for me."

"You know I will."

Pallas walked out of the reception hall. Renee continued to circle the space, looking for any forgotten handbags or phones, and noting how long it would take the cleaning service to return the huge room to order. Doing her job and not thinking about the fact that Jasper was back—that was her.

A loud whoop got her attention. She turned and saw three teenaged guys running through the fountain at the far end of the big, open room. Each of them jumped, trying to touch the arc of water dancing overhead.

The younger brother, she thought as she made her way toward them. And his friends. No doubt they were bored after so many hours with not very much to do. Regardless, she was not going to have them disrupt the reception when it was so close to being over.

As she approached the running, jumping teens, she saw both sets of parents, along with the bride and groom, still dancing. They swayed in time with the music, oblivious to the fountain and the idiots messing with it. Then several things happened at once.

The younger brother started an extra long run toward the fountain. Jim let go of Monica and spun her out the length of their arms. Monica bumped her mom, who stumbled a little. Dad grabbed Mom, moving all of them closer to the fountain and the younger brother running, who had to swerve suddenly to avoid them. As he swerved, he lost his balance and slipped, tumbling into the fountain mechanism. One of the hoses broke free, wiggling and spraying water everywhere.

Renee saw it all happening and knew there was no way

she was going to allow her beautiful bride to get soaked. She lunged for the hose, caught it and held it tightly against her chest as the bride's father rushed to turn off the water to the hose. It took only seconds, but by then the entire fountain had spilled over and Renee was drenched, shivering and had water up her nose even as she wondered if she looked half as ridiculous as she felt.

The new Mrs. Martinez hurried over. "Renee, are you all right?" She turned on her brother. "How could you? This is a wedding, not a water park."

Aware that end-of-wedding exhaustion could easily lead to emotions spiraling out of control, Renee quickly faked a smile.

"Monica, it's fine. Don't worry. Keeping you and the rest of the wedding party dry was my only concern." She glanced at the water draining onto the floor and realized part of the fountain was still pumping out water. That couldn't be good. If she couldn't get everything turned off, she was going to have to call in one of those companies that took care of disasters like flooding. "Really. It's no problem."

"You're dripping and the water's rising. My dad went to find the main shutoff."

Renee wrung out her hair and hoped her makeup wasn't too badly smudged. Then she realized the water level in the reception hall was indeed climbing and hoped Monica's father found the shutoff soon.

She was just about to go help him when he returned.

"All turned off." He glanced at the mini flood. "Sorry about this."

"It's fine," Renee lied, her tone soothing, because that was part of her job. To pretend all was well even when they needed to be figuring out how to build an ark.

The rest of the guests were heading out. Nothing like

the threat of an unexpected flood to get people moving, she thought, trying to find the humor in the situation.

"I'm so sorry," Monica told her as she held her dress out of the water and slipped out of her shoes.

"Don't be. You had a wonderful wedding and reception. Why don't you and Jim start gathering your things? I have a spare set of clothes in my office. I'll get changed, then help you make sure you have everything."

As she spoke, she noticed the water seemed to have settled at about the six-or seven-inch level. Yup, she was going to have to call someone. No doubt she would be here all night. Oh, joy.

"I'm really sorry," Jim said. "We thought we'd planned for every contingency." He glared at his new brother-in-law. "Except for stupid." He turned back to her. "Let us know the cost of cleanup. We'll pay for it."

"Thank you. I think the deposit should take care of it but I'll let you know if there's a problem. Now if you'll let me go get changed, I'll be back with you in ten minutes."

Monica nodded.

Renee slipped out of her shoes and walked through the ankle-deep water. When she reached her office upstairs, she carefully closed the door behind her before undressing, then slipped on jeans and a T-shirt. No exactly professional, but she wasn't going to worry about that right now. Before she returned to her bride and groom, she looked up the local disaster cleaning service. The number was in her files, but wasn't one she had had to use before.

They picked up on the first ring.

"Happily Inc CleanUp. This is Hilde. How can I help you?"

"Hi. I'm Renee Grothen at Weddings Out of the Box. We had a firefighter wedding tonight with a big fountain. There was an accident with one of the hoses and now our main re-ception hall is flooded."

There was a pause. "Um, did you say firefighter wedding? Never mind. How much water?"

"About six inches."

"That's a lot."

"It was a big fountain."

"Give us thirty minutes and we'll be there."

"Thank you."

Renee hung up, gave herself a second to catch her breath, then headed back to deal with the bride, the groom, the flood and anything else that might happen tonight. Because with a wedding, it was always something.

CHAPTER TWO

Six days into pet ownership, Jasper had no idea how he was doing. He and Koda—a name that had just kind of shown up in his brain and seemed to suit the dog—appeared to be getting along okay. Koda had slept most of the drive back, waking up for meals and for easy walks while they both stretched their legs. Along the way, Jasper had bought dog beds, some toys and more food. Koda's appetite was good and he looked better every day.

Once they'd reached Jasper's mountain home just outside of Happily Inc, Koda had explored the house before quickly settling into a routine. When let out to do his business, Koda didn't stray far from the house and he seemed to prefer to be inside rather than out. They took a couple of walks a day, going slowly, Koda sniffing and Jasper thinking. Koda slept quietly while Jasper worked. When they left the office together, Koda brought his favorite toy—a stuffed rabbit—with him.

From Jasper's point of view, Koda was pretty easy company. He slept on his dog bed in Jasper's bedroom at night.

Once, Jasper had awakened from a familiar nightmare, to find the dog on the bed, pressed hard against him, as if offering comfort. As Jasper got his bearings and was able to slow his breathing, Koda hopped down and returned to his own bed where he quickly went to sleep.

Jasper had installed an electronic doggie door so Koda could come and go as he wanted without Jasper having to worry that local wildlife could also wander into the house. Koda had figured out how to work the doggie door in about ten minutes. They had a vet appointment later in the week and Jasper had downloaded a book on having a dog as a pet to make sure he had it all covered.

He still didn't know why he'd brought the old guy home— nor did it matter. Koda was here now and Jasper would take care of him. He had to admit, the quiet company was nice.

"I'm going into town," he told Koda as he set out the bowl of kibble mixed with canned food. "It's Monday night and I like to hang out at The Boardroom. It's a bar that caters to locals. On Mondays they have board game tournaments. Most of my friends go."

He had no idea why he was explaining any of this to the dog—it wasn't as if Koda could understand him. Still, he couldn't help going on.

"I won't be that late," he continued. "You have water and your bed. I'll leave the radio on that classical station you like. There's the doggie door if you need to go out." He paused, not sure what else to say.

Koda finished his dinner, then looked at Jasper, as if processing the information. After a couple of seconds, the dog retreated to his bed in the family room and lay down.

"All right." Jasper put his food bowl in the sink. "I'll see you when I get back."

He got in his truck and started down the mountain. The

road was familiar and when compared with the RV he'd been driving, the 4X4 truck was practically sporty.

The thought made him smile. The long book tour had been good for him. The RV had given him a home base. Although his publisher had offered to rent a fancy bus with pop-outs and an onboard washer and dryer, Jasper had decided to buy an old, used RV instead. He'd thought he might want to use it again, for a tour and maybe a trip of his own. He'd liked being on the road.

As he headed into town he wondered if Koda would enjoy another trip or if he'd been too traumatized by what had happened to him in San Antonio. He supposed he could take an overnight trip and see how it went. Although any time away would have to wait. He was getting back into his book and had a deadline looming. For the next few months, his primary focus would be getting the story right, then getting it down on paper. Well, not paper, exactly. He used a computer, but the concept was the same.

He reached the main part of town and turned into The Boardroom's parking lot. He saw plenty of familiar cars and smiled. His friends would be there, as would other local residents. He would kick a little ass on the board game front, have a beer and a burger, talk to his buddies, then head home. A perfect evening.

Four years ago, if someone had told him he would settle in this quirky wedding-based town, he would have said that person was crazier than him, but here he was—doing better than anyone could have expected. Forward progress, he thought as he made his way inside. It beat getting left behind.

"Jasper! You're back."

"Hey, stranger. How was the book tour?"

"When'd you get home?"

The calls came from every corner of the bar. Jasper nodded at his buddies, waved at a few people he knew by sight and scanned the room, looking for an open spot at the tables set up for four.

Mathias Mitchell, an artist who worked with glass, walked past him, a beer in one hand and a glass of wine in the other.

"Hey, man, you made it. Good to see you." Mathias nodded toward a table. "Come sit with us. Carol's friend, Renee, is hanging out with us, so you'd make a fourth."

"Will do."

Jasper walked around for a few minutes, greeting his friends and giving a brief account of his three-month book tour. When a gong sounded, giving the ten-minute warning before the game started, he walked to the bar and ordered himself a beer. He figured he would get the burger later.

As he took his drink, he glanced around the room and caught sight of a petite redhead talking to Carol, Mathias's wife. Renee Something, he thought. The woman Mathias had mentioned. She was maybe five-one. Despite her slight stature, there was something powerful about her. As if she would do whatever was necessary to get what she wanted.

He held in a grin. Right. Because he was just that good at assessing women. The truth was he knew nothing about her, which was fine. Even though it had been nearly a year since he and Wynn had ended their not-quite relationship, he wasn't looking for anything else right now. Still, there was something about a woman with long hair. Especially long, *red* hair.

As if aware of his scrutiny, Renee turned toward him. For a brief second, their eyes met. Jasper was about to offer a wave when Renee surprised him by flushing slightly and looking away. As if she'd been caught doing something she shouldn't.

He glanced around, trying to figure out what could have caused her discomfort. When nothing obvious showed itself, he figured he'd simply misinterpreted the situation. Hardly a surprise—he wasn't just a guy, he was a guy who knew diddly about women. A fact proven by his inability to create a love interest for the hero of his latest novel. He knew the guy needed a woman in his life—it was a great way to wrap up the series—but he had yet to figure out who she was and how she fit into the story. Or how to write her. So far the only sentence he'd managed to write and then not delete was: She was tall, with short, blond hair. Oh, yeah, the royalty checks were going to roll in on that one.

He was still chuckling when he approached the table. Carol rose and hugged him.

"You made it back! Welcome home. Did you miss us?"

"I did."

Mathias held out his hand. "Good to see you. How was the tour?"

"Good. Long. Plenty of stops."

"And adoring fans?" Carol asked, her voice teasing.

"There were some." Jasper turned to Renee. "Mind if I join you?"

She smiled and waved to the empty chair. "Please. Your reputation precedes you, so I'm happy to be on the same team."

Whatever weirdness had existed before—or hadn't existed—was obviously gone.

He raised a shoulder. "I haven't played board games in a few months. I'm probably rusty."

"I doubt that," Carol said as she sat down. "Speaking of rusty, I want to warn everyone that this is my first night away from Devon. I've been away during the day, but never at night."

Jasper wanted to ask how one was different from the other, but knew there was no point. Her reasoning might be based on the fact that her baby was maybe five months old, or it might be a female thing, or it could be something everyone else understood intuitively.

Mathias reached across the table and squeezed her hand. "You know she's fine, right? And it's not like she's with someone we don't know."

Renee smiled and leaned toward Jasper. "Pallas and Carol share a nanny. With their kids only ten days apart in age, it makes sense. The woman is terrific and does a great job, but they're both uncomfortable being away from their babies." Her tone softened. "You know what new moms are like."

He nodded rather than say something along the lines of "not really." He knew even less about young mothers than women in general. His stint in the army had given him a range of skills that could be useful in a wartime situation but they hadn't been much on training him for life with regular people. As for that small town where he'd grown up…well, that was eight lifetimes ago.

He studied Renee, taking in her freckles and the cute way her nose turned up a little at the end. She had green eyes—although hers were more gray than his. There was something about her smile he liked. If he were to describe her in a book he would probably mention her long bangs and…

And what? Her height? Her eyes? The shape of her mouth? Did anyone care about that kind of crap? Dammit—he was a number one *New York Times* best-selling author and he couldn't describe a woman? His career was obviously over.

He pushed that thought away. He would dwell on his inability to write later. Tonight was about having a good time.

"What's the game?" he asked as several of the servers started passing out board games. "Ah, Monopoly. Excellent."

Carol picked up the piece of paper that had been left on the table. "Traditional rules," she read. "Whoever has the most money at the end of an hour goes on to the next round. After that, rounds are thirty minutes." She glanced at her team-mates. "That sounds easy enough."

Renee nodded and turned to Jasper. "While you were gone, we had a Monopoly Junior tournament and odd number rolls didn't count. Things got quite heated."

"I'll bet."

Her conversation was completely normal. He must have imagined whatever had happened before. Only was she leaning toward him or was he imagining it?

They unpacked the game and chose tokens. Mathias counted the money and passed the right amount to everyone, then they rolled to see who would go first. As usual, Jasper rolled the highest number and got to start. He rolled double sixes, followed by a five. He bought the Electric Company property, then collected two hundred dollars from the Community Chest card he drew from the top of the stack. Carol was on his left, so he handed the dice to her.

She stared at him. "I'd forgotten what it was like to play against you. I don't think I like it."

He flashed her a smile. "What can I say? I'm a lucky guy."

She made a huffing sound and rolled a seven. "How did the cleanup go yesterday?" she asked Renee.

"We are back to normal. The water is gone, everything is dried out and there's not really any serious damage." She glanced at Jasper. "We had a little accident at the firefighter wedding on Saturday night. Someone bumped the hose fountain and nearly flooded the place."

"What's a firefighter wedding?"

She took the dice from Mathias and rolled. "Weddings Out of the Box does theme weddings. In this case, the theme was firefighters. The wedding colors were red, yellow and orange. The flower girl carried flowers in a fireman's helmet. That sort of thing."

"People do that?"

Renee grinned. "Jasper, you've driven by Weddings Out of the Box. One side of the building looks like a Tuscan villa and another looks like a castle. What did you think was happening there?"

"I thought Pallas was quirky."

"Theme weddings are big business," she told him. "There are the usual ones. Princess, pirate, weddings based on books or movies. This fall we're having a Halloween wedding, a football wedding and an apple wedding."

"What's an apple wedding?" he asked.

"They're apple lovers." She laughed. "It's kind of hard to explain."

An apple wedding? Was that really a thing? He felt as if there was a whole world out there, about which he knew nothing. First women and now weddings. He needed to work on his life skills education.

Mathias rolled the dice and then moved his token. "I'm going to make a quick call to our nanny," he said, then shrugged sheepishly. "Like we said before, it's the first time we've left Devon at night, so…"

"You should absolutely check in," Renee told him. "You'll feel better."

Carol watched him go. "It's funny. All the things I worried about before we had Devon haven't been a problem. Instead there are so many *other* things to worry about. Like leaving her alone."

Renee patted her arm. "It will get better. You're a terrific mom. She's lucky to have you."

"Thanks."

Jasper looked at Renee. "Do you have kids?"

"Me? No. I'm not married." She flushed slightly. "Not that you need to be married to have children. I wasn't saying that.

Or judging. I just mean…" She cleared her throat, lowered her gaze, then looked at him. "Um, no. You?"

He shook his head.

Okay, there was *something* going on with her. He was sure of it. Fairly sure. Reasonably sure, at least. He really had to get out more. He hadn't felt the need before, but being around people again made him aware of his solitary state. Not to mention the lack of sex in his life.

He looked at Renee. She was small, but everything was in the right place. She had a sense of humor and he liked her smile. What were the odds she was looking for a brief but satisfying fling that would go absolutely nowhere?

Mathias returned and took his seat. "Everything is fine," he told Carol. "Devon's asleep and nothing is wrong."

Their eyes locked. "I want to go home," Carol said softly.

"Thank God. Me, too." Mathias sprang to his feet. "Sorry about this, but it's a baby thing."

Renee waved her hand toward the door. "Go be with your beautiful baby. Great progress was made tonight. Next time you'll stay the whole first hour."

Carol laughed. "Thanks for understanding. See you at lunch tomorrow."

"You will," Renee told her.

Seconds later, they were gone. Jasper looked at Renee. "I guess the odds of one of us heading to the finals just went up."

"They did."

She held his gaze a second past what he would consider normal, friendly interaction, shifting them into the *maybe I'm interested* category. Or was that just wishful thinking on his part? He really had to get this whole man/woman thing figured out. At sixteen, being socially awkward could be considered a little charming. At his age, it was pathetic.

"Monopoly is less fun with just two players," he said. "Could I buy you a drink instead?"

Renee told herself there was absolutely no pressure. Jasper had invited her for a drink and she had said yes. Big whoop. Men and women met for drinks hundreds of times a day and it was all completely normal. Boring even. Only sitting across from Jasper wasn't anything she would describe as normal, and it could never be boring.

For one thing, the guy was hot. He was tall, with broad shoulders, but more than that, there was an air of casual strength about him. As if he could handle himself in any situation. Should scary-looking bad guys burst into the place, Renee knew Jasper would handle the situation. She, on the other hand, would run screaming into the night. Or hide. Or faint.

He also had that hint of slightly wounded male about him. He'd been damaged in his past and it showed. It took a stronger woman than her to resist that kind of yumminess. Although this was just a drink, she reminded herself as Jasper walked over to small corner table they'd moved to. He set a cosmo in front of her and before taking a seat across from her and picking up his gin and tonic.

He took a sip, studying her over the glass. She had no idea what he was thinking, nor did she know what to say. Nerves gripped her tightly, making her feel awkward. She hadn't been on a date since moving to Happily Inc, and before that she'd been getting over a shattered heart, and before that she'd been in a nearly three-year relationship, and before that...

"So, how was your book tour?" she asked brightly, hoping the question and his answer would distract her brain. "You were gone a long time."

"I was. My publisher tried something new, sending me out in an RV."

"I'd heard something about that but I thought maybe people were kidding. You really traveled the country in an RV for a month?"

"Three," he said with another one of his sexy smiles. "Before that I spent a few weeks in Europe. Traveling more conventionally."

"You must have a lot of fans. I knew you were a successful author, but you're internationally famous."

She meant the words to be teasing, but didn't think they came out that way. Probably because she hadn't actually put together who Jasper was. In her mind, he was the slightly mysterious, former military guy who kept to himself and provided plenty of *take me now, big guy* fantasies. Apparently he was a little too close to, say, Chris Pine territory for her purposes.

Not that she was going to smile brightly and offer a night of hot sex. Because while everything went fine in her head, in real life, there were serious pitfalls. Hysterical laughter followed by a look of extreme pity. Not that Jasper seemed like the hysterical laughter type. But the pity was a real possibility. Or revulsion. That would be depressing and she wasn't looking for another boy-girl setback.

The smart decision would be to enjoy the drink, pretend she'd never once undressed him with her eyes and retreat to her charming apartment where she would tell herself she didn't care that she was never going to have sex with a man again.

"I've been lucky," he said easily. "The books have to work for people, of course, but there are a lot of authors who struggle in obscurity. I had breaks early on."

"Like I said—internationally famous. What's touring like? Is the Europe part different from the US part?"

"Very, especially with the RV. Here I was able to drive from place to place. I'd park near a big city, then head in for the events. Sometimes I'd do a morning show, or drive-time radio. I might have media interviews during the day or drop in to a few bookstores and sign stock. In the evenings I would have organized book signings where I'd talk for a few minutes, take questions, then sign books. Then back to the hotel or RV and start it over in the morning."

"That's less glamorous than I thought. What about in Europe?"

"That's a different schedule. I would arrive in a city, usually in the morning, have lunch with whomever the publisher wanted me to meet, do media, then have a signing, followed by a late dinner. Get up in the morning and drive, fly or take the train to the next city and do it all again." He flashed her another smile. "All while not speaking the language. It's an endurance sport."

"It sounds like it. What's the best part?"

"Meeting the readers. It's hard not to like people willing to line up to tell you how much they love what you do."

"I hadn't thought of that. I get the occasional thank-you note, but there's never been a line." She picked up her drink. "Anyone creepy? Didn't Stephen King write a book about a crazed fan?"

"Yes, and we're not going to talk about that." He chuckled. "There are fans who know way more about my books than I do and want to talk themes and what I could do instead. Sometimes readers want to give me story lines, which I have to sidestep because of potential legal problems."

"Your life is really interesting."

"No, it's not. Ninety percent of the time I'm sitting at a computer, trying to figure out what to say next. It's a lot of hours by myself, sometimes with swearing."

She liked him, she thought with some surprise. She hadn't really spent time with him before, so had filled in the blanks with her own fantasies, which were more about his body than his personality. It was nice to know there was an actual person behind the gorgeous eyes.

Funny how she'd been thinking about him on and off for the past couple of days and tonight he'd walked into The Boardroom and sat down at her table, as if fate were stepping in.

"Tell me about the apple wedding," he said, leaning toward her. "No one dresses up in an apple costume, do they?"

She laughed. "No. I promise, nothing like that. An apple wedding is more like a Christmas wedding. The theme inspires the decorations and the colors, not the clothing. Let's see. The bridesmaid dresses are apple green, there are crab apples in the bouquet and the floral arrangements on the tables. The signature drink is an apple martini. That sort of thing."

He stared at her, his expression blank. "I have no idea what you're talking about."

"What's confusing?"

"All of it. I get the bridesmaid dresses. I've seen women in those before. But the rest of it? You're speaking a foreign language."

"What about all the weddings you've been to?"

He took another sip of his drink. "I haven't. I joined the army when I was eighteen. None of my friends were even thinking about getting married then. I got back for a few visits, but no weddings. After my dad died—it was always just the two of us—I never went back. My military friends went home to get married and I usually couldn't get leave."

Now he was the one speaking a foreign language. "You've never been to a wedding?"

"Nope."

"That's not possible."

"It's no big deal."

"It's a rite of passage. It's how this town supports itself. Happily Inc is a wedding destination town and you have actually never been to a wedding?"

"Pallas and Nick got married in Italy and I was gone when Carol and Mathias got married."

She stared at him. "Come by Weddings Out of the Box sometime and I'll show you a video," she told him. "They're all variations on a theme, so once you've seen one, you'll be wedding literate."

"But not fluent?"

His voice was low and teasing. It sent ripples down her spine and made her wish she was the kind of woman who could look a man in the eye while inviting him back to her place. But she wasn't and she couldn't. She might want a *let's get naked* night with Jasper, but the truth was she'd never once had sex with a man she wasn't half in love with and it seemed unlikely she could find the skill set to change that now.

"I think fluency is a ways off," she said lightly, hoping he couldn't hear the disappointment in her voice. As he had no idea what she was thinking, the emotion would only be confusing and misleading. Man, even without a relationship, the whole boy-girl thing was really hard to navigate.

"You help brides plan their weddings, right?" he asked.

"Yes, although it's better when the groom is involved, too. Weddings Out of the Box is a wedding venue. We specialize in theme weddings. We've done princess weddings and cowboy weddings and apparently the world's greatest alien wedding based on a computer game, but that was before my time."

"Interesting."

She wasn't sure it was, but it was nice of him to say it.

They looked at each other, then away. Silence stretched

between them, grew awkward, got bigger and started making Renee uncomfortable. Crap, crap, crap, this wasn't going to work. Who was she kidding? She was only confident in limited situations—like work. She was never going to be the kind of woman who could tell a guy she thought he was attractive and ask if he would like to have his way with her. Which left her sad and depressingly aware of the fact that she might never do the deed again, which made her want to stomp her foot. Or cry.

Neither response would go over well in public, so it was definitely time to go home. She looked at Jasper.

"It's getting late. Thanks for the drink. I had a nice time."

He studied her for a second before nodding. "I did, too. Let me walk you to your car."

They went out into the night. It was mid-September, so still warm, but they'd passed through the burning heat of summer. In a few more weeks, there would be an actual nip in the air. At least in those hours close to midnight. It rarely got cold-cold in Happily Inc.

They walked to her black Mini with the white racing stripes on the hood. A silly car, to be sure, but one she loved as much as she could love a car. It was cute, it was zippy and with the back seats down, it held as much as she needed.

"This is me," she said lightly.

Jasper glanced from the car to her and back. "It suits you."

She smiled. "Thank you. I try to be worthy of its sassiness, but I don't always succeed. I suppose that's a metaphor for my life. I want to be wild, but I'm not quite sure how."

"You mean that?"

She looked up at him. Literally. With them both standing, she was aware of how tall he was, how strong. He exuded power and confidence. He was all things male and maybe that should have scared her, but it didn't.

"Renee?"

"What?"

"You didn't answer the question."

"There was a question?"

One corner of his mouth turned up. "I may be reading this all wrong, but just in case I'm not…"

He put his hands on her waist and pulled her toward him. The move was unexpected and she would have instinctively resisted, only there was something about the feel of his hands and her growing sense of anticipation. Because he was holding her exactly like a man holds a woman he means to kiss and kiss well.

She looked up to confirm her theory, which gave her exactly half a second to prepare herself for the impact of his lips on hers.

Her first impression was of heat. His mouth was warm, as was his body, but she was on fire. Need erupted long before he deepened the kiss. Just pressing against him, having him hold her and holding him back was unbearably arousing. When he actually got busy with the kissing part, she wasn't sure if she was going to melt, scream or fall apart right there in the parking lot.

His tongue stroked her bottom lip. She parted, then groaned when he slipped inside. They circled and danced and explored. She raised herself on her tiptoes to get a better angle. He nipped her lower lip, then ran his hands up and down her back.

Everywhere he touched blazed with hunger. She was nearly shaking with need. He might not know much about weddings, but he sure could kiss and right now that was the superior skill.

But just when she was really getting into it, Jasper pulled back. He was breathing heavily and looked slightly dazed.

"That was unexpected," he murmured.

"Good unexpected?"

He cleared his throat. "You have to ask?"

"Just checking."

They stared at each other. Here it was, she thought. The moment of reckoning. She could wimp out and walk away or she could be strong and self-actualized by asking for what she wanted.

"Come home with me."

The words came out more question than statement, but she'd said them, so good for her. Unless he said no. Then she would die—right there in the parking lot. They would find her stiff body in the morning and no one would know what had happened.

Jasper raised an eyebrow. "You sure?"

She hunched her shoulders. "I've used up all my courage, so I can't ask again."

He chuckled. "I'm not looking for you to repeat the question. I'm confirming this is what you want."

She looked at him, starting at his very large feet and working her way up. It was too dark in the parking lot for her to be sure, but she was fairly confident he had an erection. She took in his broad shoulders, his handsome face and then thought about how sad and lonely her girl bits had been.

"This is what I want," she told him.

That corner of his mouth turned up again. "How far is your place?"

"About six minutes from here."

"Then we'd best get going."

CHAPTER THREE

Seven minutes and maybe twenty seconds later, they were in her small apartment. Renee managed to turn on the lamp by the door and kick off her shoes before Jasper reached for her. Their lips clung even as he tugged at the hem of her T-shirt. It was impossible to pull off her shirt while kissing, but they tried before finally breaking apart.

"Bedroom," she said, thinking of the box of condoms she had in her dresser. A box she'd bought when she'd moved to town and never had the opportunity to open until now.

Movement out of the corner of her eye caught her attention. She turned and saw Jasper had pulled off his shirt, leaving his broad chest bare. He was muscled and male and she couldn't help moving closer and pressing her mouth to his warm skin.

She'd barely had a chance to do more than register the slightly salty taste of him when he was unfastening her bra and reaching around to cup her breasts. The feel of his fingers against her hungry flesh was perfection. He caressed her curves before brushing against her tight, sensitive nipples. At the first stroke, her breath caught. At the second, she cried out as pleasure burned through to her center. She was already wet and swollen. In seconds she shifted to downright desperate.

"Bedroom," she said weakly, still thinking of that condom and him inside of her and oh, please could they get on with it.

"You *are* focused on getting up there," he said, his voice teasing.

She managed to open her eyes and look up at him—a challenging task considering how he was playing with her nipples, rubbing them between his thumb and fingers and then squeezing just tightly enough to make her groan.

"Unless you walk around with protection in your pocket which, I confess, will make me think less of you, we should head to the bedroom."

"Well, damn. You're right."

Before she could say anything, he shifted, bending over and then scooping her up in his arms. She shrieked at the sudden loss of control and grabbed on to him.

Renee couldn't remember the last time she'd been carried. She assumed she'd been maybe eight or nine. Yes, she was small, but she was mighty and she didn't take kindly to being—

He lowered her onto her bed. Before she could complain that she did not enjoy being picked up like a sack of potatoes, he lowered his head and drew her left nipple deeply into his mouth. He flicked his tongue against the taut skin before sucking hard enough to make her writhe with need and delight. Heat poured through her. Wanting grew until she couldn't think about anything else. Even as he shifted to her other breast, she was unfastening her jeans and pushing them off.

He drew back and watched her. "That much of a hurry?"

"It's been decades."

"You're not old enough for it to have been decades."

"It feels like decades." She pointed to his jeans. "Take your clothes off."

He grinned. "Yes, ma'am."

He stood and quickly did as she requested. Renee gave herself a moment to study his naked body. The man looked good and was, ah, well proportioned.

"Condoms?" he asked.

She rolled over to get them out of the far nightstand drawer. When she shifted back, Jasper returned to the bed.

"How would you like this to go?" he asked.

"Fast."

He chuckled. "What I meant was you're kind of small and I'm a big guy. Until we figure out what works best, do you want to be on top?"

She had a brief image of impaling herself on his erection, sliding down until he filled her all the way.

"Done," she said, tossing him the box. "Hurry."

"You're bossy."

"Yes, I know. It's part of my charm."

He put on the condom, then motioned to his covered dick. "Whenever you're ready."

She supposed she should spend a minute thinking about the fact that she barely knew the man, yet here she was, naked and prepared to do the deed. While she'd never been particularly prudish during sex, she wasn't exactly wild, either. Maybe it was because there was no emotional risk, or maybe she was simply that horny, or maybe it was Jasper himself. At this point, she genuinely didn't care.

She straddled him and positioned herself over him, then closed her eyes as she slowly lowered herself. He was long and thick and filled every inch of her in the most delicious way possible. She shifted that last bit all the way in, then let her body remember what all this was about.

Jasper swore. She looked at him.

"What?"

"You." He swore again. "You're naked, sexy as hell, all-in with how it feels and I'm just supposed to lie here without losing it like some kid? I'm not sure I have that much willpower."

Really? *Really?* She smiled. "So this is arousing?" She wiggled a little, then contracted her muscles.

He inhaled sharply. "That is not a game you're going to win. Not if you want what I think you want."

He had a point, but she couldn't help teasing him with another squeeze. He groaned.

She laughed. "Okay, I'll stop, for now. What if I do this?"

Without thinking, she slipped her fingers between her parted thighs and found her swollen clit. She'd only meant to tease him with a quick show of her touching herself, but the second she rubbed herself, her need climbed from desperate to unbearable. The combination of her touch and the fullness of him inside of her was too much to resist. She told herself she had to stop, that she couldn't do that kind of thing in front of him, but the sensations building inside of her were powerful and amazing and...

"Don't stop," he said quickly. "Renee, don't stop. Please."

She looked at him and saw him intently studying her. His pupils were dilated, his body stiff. He moved his hands to her hips, guiding her up and down in the rhythm designed to take them both over the edge.

Still watching him watch her, she rubbed harder, faster, with each circle, she brushed against the base of his erection, she felt how hard he was, how ready.

"Tell me it's not going to take long," he breathed.

"It's not."

She was so close already. Her orgasm was just there, on the fringes. Still holding his gaze, she moved up and down faster and faster. She could feel her breasts bouncing, her face flushing, her release getting closer. Need built and built until she was overwhelmed and had no choice but to give in to her orgasm. She cried out, her body contracting around him, forcing him over the edge. His hands tightened on her hips, holding her still as he pushed in even farther, pressing against the very heart of her and groaning as he came.

Renee stayed where she was for a few seconds. Reality returned and she had to face the fact that she was naked, straddling a man she barely knew and his penis was still inside of her.

Just as her afterglow was about to crash and burn in a sea of humiliation, Jasper smiled at her. It was a very self-satisfied male smile that spoke of his own pleasure at everything that had happened.

"You're not all that," she said, shifting off him and standing. Her legs were a little shaky and she'd been stretched every which way, but she had to admit, she felt good. Better than good.

"I'm all that and so are you."

He got up, as well. They cleaned up and went looking for their clothes. Once they were dressed, Renee braced herself for the speedy departure. It was what guys did, or so she'd been told. This was her first one-night stand. No regrets, she told herself. She wasn't looking for anything but easy sex. She was a disaster at romantic relationships and knew the smartest decision was to avoid them completely. Jasper had given her everything she'd wanted.

"Got any beer?" he asked when he'd tugged on his T-shirt.

"I do."

She moved toward the kitchen. As she passed him, he reached out and lightly stroked her arm. They paused to stare at each other. One corner of his mouth turned up in a boyish half smile that left her feeling oddly...floaty.

She grabbed a bottle for each of them and they went into the living room. So he was going to stay for a bit. That was unexpected, but nice. Really nice.

He settled on the sofa. She hesitated a second before sitting in the chair opposite. While snuggling next to him sounded appealing and something she could get into, she didn't actually know him that well. The truth of the statement nearly made her laugh.

Sex?

Why, yes, thank you. Now what was your name again?

"Something funny?" he asked.

"Um, no. Just thinking about stuff."

He studied her for a second. "You know I'm not the marrying kind, right?"

She'd nearly taken a sip of her beer. Grateful she hadn't, so she wouldn't choke to death, she set the bottle on the coffee table between them and stared at him. So much for feeling floaty.

"What are you talking about? The marrying kind? Why would you say that? Why would you think it? Who do you think I am? I don't want to marry you. It was just sex. It was good sex but it wasn't in the—" she held up both hands and made air quotes "'now we have to get married' category."

She didn't know if she should stand up for emphasis or just glare convincingly.

Jasper grimaced. "Sorry. I didn't mean to upset you. It's just, you plan weddings for a living."

"That is my job, not who I am. You write about people getting murdered. I don't assume you're planning to murder me. Not the marrying kind. No wondering you're not in a relationship."

"Hey, don't judge."

"That line deserves judgment."

"Can I have a do-over?"

"Sexually or conversationally?"

An eyebrow rose, as his expression shifted to slightly preda- tory. "Give me a few minutes and you can have both."

"You wish." Although in truth, she thought it was a good idea, too.

"I kind of do."

They smiled at each other. There was a moment of silence, but this time it was comfortable.

"How'd you end up here?" she asked. "You don't strike me as a Happily Inc kind of guy."

"My car broke down. I was living in LA and I had just driven to New York to visit my publisher and agent."

"You drove from LA to New York and back? Why didn't you fly?"

"I didn't fly well back then. I still don't like it, but I can do it."

Why wouldn't he fly well? Oh, right, she thought. While she didn't know the details, she'd heard rumors about his time in the military and how he'd escaped without physical injury but still had suffered from significant PTSD.

"So you were stuck in town while they fixed your car?" she asked.

"I was. It was an old clunker and it took a while to get the parts shipped in. I stayed at one of the hotels."

She picked up her beer and grinned. "Oh, please, please tell me you stayed at the Sweet Dreams Inn."

"Why would you care about that?"

"I want to picture you hanging out in one of the themed rooms. The princess room or the Heidi room or the wood- land creature room."

"There's a woodland creature room? Why?"

"It's fun. I'd love it."

He shuddered. "That must be a girl thing. For what it's worth, I was in the pirate room."

"I know that one. It's nice."

When she'd first taken the job in Happily Inc, she'd made it a point to visit all the local businesses that supported the wedding industry. She wanted to be able to offer recommendations because she knew what she was talking about. To that end, she'd toured all the rooms at the Sweet Dreams Inn, so she knew the pirate room was actually fairly masculine, with a huge sailing ship doubling as a bed.

"But still—no little woodland creatures to keep you company?" she asked, her tone wistful.

"I'm afraid not. Argh."

She laughed. "Okay, I'll accept the pirate room. So you were stuck in town and decided to stay?"

"I didn't have a plan. I drove around to kill time. The people were friendly enough. I was here over a Monday night, so the clerk at the front desk suggested I head to The Boardroom for game night."

"And you were hooked?"

"I was intrigued." He shifted so he rested his bare feet on the coffee table. "I contacted a local real estate agent about places on the market. I knew I wouldn't want to live in town, so I wasn't expecting much. My house is the first place we saw. I looked at a half dozen more, realized I'd already found what I wanted and made an offer."

"And here you are."

His gaze locked with hers. "Here we both are."

She felt the tension rising between them. It was nice. Sexy and insistent. Inside, heat began to build.

"So I'm not looking for a relationship," she said. "I haven't

ever had good luck in the romance department." Which was
putting it mildly, she thought. Her love life had been a disaster, and while she wanted to say it was her mother's fault, in
truth there were other reasons.

"Giving up on your own happily-ever-after?" he asked.

"Pretty much."

He lowered his legs and rested his feet on the floor, then
put his beer on the table. "But a woman has needs."

His tone was low, sexy and intriguing. Renee felt herself
flushing. Stupid red hair, she thought with a sigh. "A woman
does. As does a man."

"Yes, that's true."

She kept her gaze on his, even though she desperately
wanted to look away. "But, ah, I've never really done anything like this before."

"Had a sex-only relationship?"

She winced. "Could we not call it that?"

His voice turned teasing. "But you *do* want me to be your
booty call."

In for a penny and all that. "Yes."

He nodded slowly. "So you'd be using me for sex?"

"I could say the same thing about you."

"I didn't ask you to be *my* booty call. I don't know." He
raised and lowered his shoulders. "I've never been anyone's
sex toy before."

"You didn't really just say that."

He dropped his gaze to the floor. "I feel used."

"Just stop it. No one believes that for a second."

He looked at her again and grinned. "Sex without the
promise of anything more," he said. "I'm in." His smile faded.
"Having said that, I'd like to keep things exclusive. Otherwise it gets confusing. Unless you want to invite one of your
friends to join us."

"What?" she shrieked.

He stood and pulled her to her feet. "I'm kidding. I know them too well. Worse, I know the men in their lives. It would be weird. So just you and me, for as long as it's good for us, then when it's over, we walk away. No regrets, no bad breakup."

It sounded so mature and modern, she thought. And was exactly what she wanted. And while she was fully aware that it could all end horribly, because her boy-girl things always did, at least she was starting from a position of clarity and honesty.

"Agreed," she said firmly, raising herself on tiptoe so she could kiss him. "Now, if it's been long enough, I think I should let you use me for sex. To keep things fair."

"I like how you think."

He pulled a condom out of his jeans pocket and tossed it onto the coffee table. "I grabbed that from your bedroom. I say that so you don't think less of me." He grinned. "Your sofa is very comfortable. Why don't we start here and see where things go."

Renee had been healed. Despite her lack of sleep and the generally achiness from unused muscles getting a workout, she felt happy and energized and just a little bit weightless. It was amazing what a night of great sex could do for a woman. And with a little luck and some schedule planning, it was exactly what she intended to experience again and again. Yup, she would be enjoying her booty call bonanza for as long as it lasted.

Jasper had left around two in the morning. Even though she technically could have slept in, she'd been awake by six, happy and practically humming with the glory of the day. After clearing up her work emails, she'd gone to the grocery store for ingredients for one of her favorite pasta salads. She'd fixed that, showered, done a little more paperwork, then just before noon she headed for Willow Gallery, where she would meet her girlfriends for lunch.

She had a large group of friends in town. Their schedules were complicated and everyone was busy, so the weekly lunch was a priority. They rotated locations and whoever hosted provided an entrée. Everyone else brought whatever they were in the mood for. Mostly the menu worked out but every now and then they ended up with three veggie plates. Still, Renee was far more interested in the conversation than the food. She enjoyed the chance to hang with other women. In the past, she'd worked hard to keep herself a safe distance from the people around her. But since moving to Happily Inc, she'd realized it was safe to connect and fit in. She could relax here and that felt good.

Willow Gallery, a beautiful venue close to the river, housed amazing art pieces. Happily Inc was home to several successful artists. Renee had moved to town in time to see her friend Natalie grow from struggling unknown to rising star. Natalie had been able to quit her office manager job to concentrate on her art full-time.

Renee pulled in next to two familiar cars. Pallas and Carol were both already inside, and if previous lunches were anything to go by, they would have brought their babies with them.

Just as difficult as accepting she would never have love in her life, was the realization that she would never have a traditional family. While children weren't an impossible dream, if she wanted kids, she was going to have to go it alone, and being a single mom wasn't an easy road. Renee had watched her own mother deal with being both parents while raising a child and it had been hard for her. On the flip side, Renee also knew what it was like to be left by a father and that was a pain that didn't go away. So while she could have a child on her own, she didn't want to go that route, and what with her finally accepting she was never going to trust her heart to a man again, she was stuck.

"I'm not going to think about that," she said aloud as she got out of her car. She'd had great sex the night before, she was going to enjoy hanging with her friends and she would hold Devon and Ryan as much as she could until the other women wrestled the sweet infants from her arms.

She was still smiling as she walked into the gallery. Natalie already had Ryan, so Renee dropped her tote on the buffet table set up by a display of a massive blown glass garden filled with exquisite glass flowers.

"How's my best girl?" she asked, gently taking the sleeping baby from Carol.

"I'm fine," her friend said drily. "Thanks for asking."

Renee grinned. "Good to know." She gently rocked Devon, enjoying the weight of her and admiring her rosebud mouth and velvety soft skin.

"We need more babies around here," Pallas said as she unpacked Renee's insulated tote. "Pasta salad. At some point I need to get off carbs, but I'm not quite ready. What's in this?"

"Cheese tortellini, bacon, tomatoes, diced cucumber, broccoli all tossed with an avocado ranch dressing and sprinkled with cheese."

Pallas raised her eyebrows. "That's a lot of work, young lady."

Renee thought about her early start and good mood. "I was inspired. It's a recipe my mom used to make, only she used regular ranch dressing."

"Sounds delish. I brought brownies," Pallas said with a sigh. "It's the carb thing. I can't help it."

Silver and Bethany walked in together. Silver dumped her container on the table and headed for Natalie.

"Hi, everyone. Pass him over."

Natalie reluctantly passed Ryan to Silver.

"I guess we really do need more babies," Natalie admitted, pushing up her glasses.

"You first," Silver, a pretty platinum blonde and the owner of a mobile bar called AlcoHaul, told her with a grin.

"Not me." Natalie shook her head. "I want another year at least before I get pregnant. I'm working on my art and enjoying being married to Ronan. I'm more interested in aunt status right now."

Renee looked at Bethany, expecting her friend to hurry over and claim Devon, but Bethany stayed by the buffet.

"Hi, everyone," Bethany said with a wave. "The lunch looks great. I brought a veggie plate."

Pallas made a face, then forced a smile. "It's always good to have something healthy on the table."

Renee lowered her voice and whispered, "Liar."

Pallas took Devon from her. "I meant it. Sort of."

Wynn arrived, a plate of brownies in her hand. "Sorry. I got on a call with a client and he was a talker. How is everyone?"

As she spoke, she set down the brownies and reached for Devon.

"Go hug your own baby," Wynn said with a smile as she cooed at Devon. "Mine is way too old to rock."

Renee felt an unexpected stab of guilt and worry rip through her. Jasper and Wynn had once been a couple. Sure, things had ended nearly a year ago, but still, they'd been involved. Wynn was her friend and did that make things awkward?

Renee told herself she would talk to Wynn after the lunch—there was no way she was going to discuss it in front of everyone. Not when it was new and she had no idea what having a man available for a booty call actually meant.

The still-sleeping babies were placed in their car seats and the friends filled their plates before sitting at the table that had been set up in the center of the gallery.

"How's everyone?" Silver asked. "Bethany, weren't you and Cade planning a trip to El Bahar next month?"

Bethany, the adopted daughter of the king of El Bahar, looked startled by the question. "Nothing is finalized. We're still figuring it all out. Leaving the horses for that long is always difficult."

"Don't you have a manager and several people helping out in the stables?" Renee asked.

"We do, but it's still complicated."

Not exactly an answer that made sense, Renee thought. She looked at her friend and wondered if something was going on. Bethany didn't seem like herself.

"I can't find anything better than an appletini for the apple wedding," Silver said. "I've tried a bunch of different cocktails and I'm not sure our bride is going to love any of them."

Pallas looked around the table. "We have an upcoming apple wedding. The bride wants appletinis but the groom's mother wants a different apple-based drink. So far they've been unable to agree on anything. We have one final tasting this week."

"This whole thing is putting me off apples," Silver grumbled. "And I like apples."

"Give yourself an apple-free month and your love will be restored," Carol told her.

Everyone laughed.

Conversation flowed easily. Renee remembered the first time Pallas had invited her to the girlfriends' lunch. She'd been nervous and not sure she would get along with the women, but they'd welcomed her and now were an important part of her life. She knew that her friends would be there for her. She liked being a part of something—belonging. She hadn't had that in a while. Certainly not in high school where the other girls had mostly avoided her. College had been a little better, until someone had figured out the truth about her mother.

Nothing she had to worry about now, she reminded herself. She was keeping Verity far, far away from Happily Inc.

"Great salad," Wynn said, waving her fork at Renee. "There are just enough vegetables to make me feel righteous."

Renee smiled and ignored the guilt. She would talk to Wynn later and get any issues resolved. It was the right thing to do.

But ninety minutes later, all Renee wanted to do was bolt. Instead, she forced herself to walk out with Wynn and ask if they could talk for a moment. Wynn looked surprised, but immediately agreed.

"Want to go grab coffee or can this be talked about in the parking lot?"

Renee glanced around. Everyone else had already left and the gallery was closed on Tuesdays, so customers would not be arriving.

"I just need a second," she said, not sure how to begin. Or what to say. Or… "I had sex with Jasper."

Wynn, a gorgeous woman with curly, dark hair, raised her eyebrows. "Interesting."

"Sorry. I didn't mean to blurt it out like that. It's just you two used to, you know, be friends, and now you're not and I wasn't sure if you were still, um, thinking about him and if it was all right that I…"

"Had sex with him?" The corners of Wynn's mouth twitched. "Aren't you asking a little late? The deed is done."

"I know, but it was unexpected, so I didn't really have time to text you."

Wynn grinned. "That would have been a really noteworthy text for sure." Her expression turned serious. "Our relationship ended last year. We're completely done and what he does with you is great with me." The smile returned. "I mean that in a not awkward way."

Relief erased the guilt. "You're sure?"

"Very. Jasper and I weren't right for each other. He's a great guy, but not *my* great guy."

"Oh, this isn't serious," Renee said quickly. "Neither of us is looking for that. This is very much a no-strings kind of thing." No way she was going to mention the booty call aspect of things.

"That's how it always starts." Wynn tilted her head. "Just as an FYI, Jasper isn't as broken as he thinks. You might want to be careful about that."

Renee had no idea what she was talking about. "Meaning?"

"Most normal guys eventually reach a place where they want more. If you're sure that's not in the cards for you, great. But Jasper just might want to change the rules."

"I can't see that happening."

"Maybe I'm wrong." She smiled. "I'm glad you two found each other. It's nice to be a part of something."

"What about you?"

Wynn shook her head. "Yeah, I'm not really that girl. I try to be, but I'm not."

CHAPTER FOUR

Jasper thought about throwing his laptop out the window, but as always, talked himself down. The urge occurred fairly regularly and so far he'd resisted destroying his computer. No good would come of it, he reminded himself. It wasn't as if getting rid of the piece of equipment would solve the problem. It wasn't the keyboard's fault that he couldn't write for shit.

"Dammit," he growled, pounding on the table.

Koda raised his head, as if asking what was wrong.

"Sorry," he told the dog. "Go back to sleep. I'll be more quiet." Jasper saved the pitiful three sentences it had taken him the entire morning to write and leaned back in his chair.

"I can't write women," he told the dog. "Never knew it was a problem. After six years of being published, you wouldn't think that would be news, but it turns out I've never tried to write a woman before. Not one who isn't a victim or a one-night stand."

He rested his head in his hand. "Please don't repeat that to anyone. It makes me sound like a misogynistic asshole and I'm not. It's just my detective had been single through the entire series and now that I'm wrapping things up with him and moving on to another character, everyone thinks I need to leave Vidar in a better place, and that means involved with a woman."

His editor had suggested the idea more than once, and Jasper knew she was right. But who was the woman and how did they meet and when they met, what did they talk about? So far all his dialogue had been stilted and unrealistic. Book dialogue was not like normal human-to-human conversation. It was high points and information and moving the plot forward. In real life...

He smiled, thinking about the conversations he'd had the other night with Renee. Now those had been fun. Especially the parts where she'd gasped "More" or "Harder." Neither of which was going to make it into his book. Writing a woman was difficult enough—no way he could write sex. He wrote about serial killers, and unless sex was part of the ritual murder, he absolutely was not going there in his novel.

Jasper looked at Koda. "I am one sick guy," he admitted. "I need help."

Koda got up and stretched, then picked up his stuffed rabbit and carried it over to Jasper.

"Thanks," Jasper told the dog, before tossing it across his office. Koda trotted over and picked up the rabbit, carrying it back to Jasper, who threw it again.

They played the game for a few minutes before Jasper gave up pretending to work. He stood and headed for the door, Koda at his heels. They both went outside. Koda headed off into the woods to take care of business while Jasper looked around, wondering if there was any inspiration to be had or if he should simply accept his limitations and hope his career continued despite them.

He was deep in self-flagellation when he heard a familiar

voice calling his name. Hunter Beauchene walked around the side of the house.

Wynn's son was thirteen now, and getting taller by the day. He was at that awkward stage where his arms and legs didn't fit with his torso. His voice was in the process of changing and every now and then, Jasper caught glimpses of the man he would eventually grow to be.

"Hey, you," he said, holding out his hand. Hunter did the same as they greeted each other with their elaborate hand-shake, a ritual that had been established nearly two summers ago. Back when he'd first started seeing Wynn.

Not that she'd introduced him to Hunter. Instead she'd insisted their sex-only relationship be kept secret—especially from her son. If Hunter found out, it was over. Well, Hunter had figured it out almost immediately and had wanted to be friends with Jasper. The kid knew the rules and wanted to keep their hanging out time off his mom's radar. Jasper had resisted at first but eventually Hunter had won him over and they'd started hanging out. He supposed his willingness to break her only rule had been a sign they weren't going to make it as a couple. Ironically, as soon as they'd broken up, she'd stopped minding if he hung out with her son. Yup, women were confusing as hell.

"Is it afternoon already?" Jasper asked, glancing up at the sun. It felt earlier.

Hunter looked at him. "It's barely eleven. I have the day off. The teachers are doing some training or something. You really don't know what time it is?"

"I've been working."

Hunter nodded, getting the explanation. He was used to Jasper's odd ways.

Koda broke through the trees and raced toward Hunter. The teen dropped to his knees to greet the dog. In a matter of seconds, they were on the ground, tumbling over each other. The combination of happy yips and human laughter comforted Jasper. At least this part of his world was as it should be.

"You hungry?" Jasper asked, when the two broke apart.

"Got any cookies?"

Jasper and Hunter shared a weakness for Cheryl's Cookies, and Jasper ordered them frequently. They agreed that the sugar cookies with buttercream frosting were the best.

They went into the kitchen and Jasper pulled four cookies out of the freezer. Hunter poured himself a glass of milk while Jasper refilled his coffee mug. Koda settled in his bed in the kitchen where he could watch everything going on.

The dog was doing well, Jasper thought. Putting on weight, sleeping and settling in to his new life. He was good company.

"How's school?" Jasper asked as he opened the plastic wrap around the first cookie. "Classes going okay?"

"Jasper, you always ask that."

"I'm interested. So answer the question."

Hunter rolled his eyes. "I'm doing fine. I get good grades."

"You better."

"Or what?"

Jasper grinned. "You want to go there with me, kid?"

Hunter laughed. "No, I don't. But in a couple of years I'll be able to take you."

"In your dreams."

"Mom says this year if you hire some guy to teach you a new fighting style I can come to the lessons. As long as they're after school." Hunter's expression was hopeful. "So maybe you could think of something really cool for the book you're writing."

Jasper found it easier to write about something if he could actually do it himself. He'd learned to throw knives and use fighting sticks for previous books. And shoot a crossbow.

Hunter had begged to be a part of the lessons, but while Jasper was willing to cross some lines, there were others that needed to stay in place.

"I will think of something cool," he said, "but I will also run whatever it is past your mom."

"She really did say that."

"I believe you." He flashed a grin. "Sort of."

Hunter laughed and tossed Koda a piece of cookie.

"So what's going on for the rest of your day off?"

Hunter finished his second cookie and picked up his milk. "I'm going to go over to a friend's house."

"You ride all the way up here?"

"I got a ride partway from a park ranger."

Jasper thought about the pages he hadn't written. He was behind on his book and if this morning was any indication— and so far, it was—without doing something drastic, he was never going to make forward progress on his story. Maybe he needed a change of scene and a chance to observe women in their natural habitat.

"I'm heading to town," he said. "We can throw your bike in the back of the truck and I'll drive you to your friend's house."

"Thanks."

Thirty minutes later Jasper stood in the center of town and tried to figure out what he was supposed to do now. Walk around and watch women going about their lives? That wasn't going to be good for anyone. He wasn't some crazed stalker guy and would watching a random female do grocery shopping or walking her baby get him any closer to solving his problem? He honestly didn't know where to start. Or how to start. Or what he wanted to do.

He walked over to a bench by the river and sat down. Detective Vidar needed a love interest. He didn't want the woman to be a cop, so not anyone he worked with. Which was limiting because Vidar, like Jasper himself, didn't have much of a social life. Dating a victim seemed tacky. Plus, most of Jasper's killer's victims ended up dead. So someone involved on the fringes of the crime? Or what? A neighbor? A…

He stood up. This was ridiculous. He knew women. Lots of women. All he had to do was talk to one of them. He looked around and saw the large wall that defined the boundaries of Weddings Out of the Box. Renee. He would go see Renee. Not only could they talk about his book, he would get to see her smile and that alone was worth a trip down the mountain.

"We can do an assortment of different kinds of apples to hold the place cards," Renee said, scrolling through photos of apples on her computer. "That adds variety. However if you want consistency and to be in line with your color palette, then I would say stick with the Granny Smith apples."

She paused and glanced at the speakerphone. There was a moment of silence, followed by the sound of breathless female laughter.

"I've hit a wall," Stacey Treadway said. "I can't make one more decision. I just can't."

"Someone has to," Renee said gently. "And it's not going to be me."

"And I thought apples would be easy. Let's do the Granny Smith apples for the place cards. They'll go with the glass towers we'll have around the space and it will look nice."

"Done and done," Renee said, studying her list. "Stacey, I don't want to scare you, but I think we're finished."

"Really? So no more decisions?"

"Not today."

Stacey laughed. "Let me guess. You're not making any promises."

"Nope. But we're really close and your wedding is going to be beautiful. I'm very excited to see everything turn out."

"Thanks, Renee. You've been so wonderful to work with."

"You've been great, too. Just remember, I'm here for you. Call me if you need anything and I'll do the same. Otherwise, we are good to go."

"Wow. It's getting close. I guess I'll see you soon."

"You will."

They hung up. Renee wrote up the notes from their phone call, entering the information on her computer where it would automatically feed to her tablet. A happy wedding day was all about keeping track of the details.

She'd barely hit the save key when Jasper walked into her office.

He looked good, she thought as she felt a bit of tingling low in her belly. Tall and a little rugged. She hadn't seen him since their night together and wasn't sure what to say now. Or think. Or how to act. Unexpected nerves tightened her throat and chest and she had the strangest urge to both bolt and throw herself at him. She settled on doing neither.

"Hey," he said as he paused by the door. "Is this an okay time?"

"It is. What's up?"

"I was in town and I wondered if we could talk for a second."

"About?"

He motioned to a chair in front of her desk. She nodded and he sank down, then looked at her.

"I have no idea," he said.

"You have no idea why you're in town or you have no idea what you want to talk about?"

"Both."

"Okay. Do you want to take a minute and collect your thoughts?"

Instead of answering, he glanced around at her office. "You plan weddings, right?"

"I do."

"What does that entail?"

Not the question she was expecting. She smiled. "Are you asking for yourself?"

"You know I'm not."

"Just checking. You might have met your one true love in the last few days."

His gaze turned knowing. "I had someone on my mind, so no. Tell me what you do?"

"When a couple decides to hold their wedding here, I help them with as much of the wedding as they want. We provide a full service venue. We can arrange catering, bar service, flowers, an officiant and anything else they might want. In addition we have the unique ability to create nearly any kind of theme wedding the happy couple is looking for."

He nodded. "Say I want a movie wedding. *American Graffiti*. Do you know it?"

"I've seen it before. It's what, the 1960s? I'm kind of picturing the movie *Grease*, so I'd have to watch *American Graffiti* again to get the details right. We'd take liberties with the clothing. Some kind of poodle skirt bridesmaid dresses could be cute. We could do food from a diner for sure. Maybe a play on burgers and fries. Silver could come up with some fun cocktails—all variations on classics. You'd want a cutout of that white Thunderbird for guests to take pictures in. 1960s music, for sure. Oh, we could get a bunch of 45 records and use them in lots of different decorations. Maybe around the base of the centerpieces, or hanging from the ceiling. I think themed custom cookies would be terrific, too. If the groom was willing, we could really play on the poodle skirt idea and have poodles made out of flowers. And a soda fountain would be fantastic. Oh, we could do ice cream–based adult beverages. That would be unique and the guests would love it."

He stared at her. "You came up with all that in a minute."

"Probably more like five, but yes. Jasper, that's what I do. I might know what a bride wants before she comes in but often I don't. I need to be able to think on my feet." She leaned toward him. "Once we picked a direction, we would discuss who's providing the vendors and where she is in her process. Oh, we also need to know how long we have. Less time makes things frantic, but more time means decisions get changed again and again and that can be stressful for all of us."

She paused. "I can keep talking, but I'm not sure what you want to know."

"Me, either. You've given me a lot to think about. Thanks."

"You're welcome. This is for your book, isn't it?"

"Yes. Maybe. I don't know. I'm having some problems with one of the characters." He frowned. "Why aren't you married?"

She hadn't seen that question coming. "Excuse me?"

"Why aren't you married? You're smart, you're sexy and—" He glanced over his shoulder and lowered his voice. "I happen to know you're dynamite in bed."

She felt herself flush. "Thank you and that is off-topic."

"Too personal?"

"A little, but also confusing."

"I don't get women," he admitted. "I have this character and I can't figure her out. I can't even make her close to real. Why do women do what they do? What are they thinking?"

He got up and closed her office door, then returned to his seat. "That night at The Boardroom. Why me? Why then? I served for eight years and when I got out of the army I was so screwed up in the head. I've made my way back a fair amount but we both know I'll never be normal. I'm okay with that. But you're not damaged. So why aren't you with some great guy, popping out babies and living the American Dream?"

She could see he was genuinely confused, which was kind of appealing. Later she would think about how casually he talked about being damaged. According to Wynn, he wasn't as broken as he thought, but that was for another day.

As for his question about her single status, she wasn't sure what to say. There were a lot of reasons and many of them had to do with her mother. No way she was going to talk about that. So maybe something safer. And lucky for her, it was the truth.

"I've had two serious relationships," she began. "In college and then a few years later. My last one lasted almost three years. He was a little older, established. Nice. That's what I liked most about him. He was just plain nice. A thoughtful man who paid attention to the little things."

"I hate him already."

She smiled. "Don't bother. He's not worth the energy. Things were going great until they weren't. We were seeing each other regularly, when we could. He traveled. I thought we were in love and mentioned marriage. He said he needed time. He loved me but didn't see himself committing to one woman for the rest of his life." Her mouth twisted as she remembered the long talks. "He said if he was ever going to marry someone, it would be me."

Jasper looked concerned. "Did he cheat?"

"Not in the way you're thinking." She sucked in a breath and looked at him. "It turns out he was already married. With three kids. When I found out and confronted him, he admitted he totally adored his wife and his family and had no plans to leave them, but he loved me, too, and hoped we could just go on the way we had been."

Jasper swore under his breath. "You kicked his ass to the curb."

"I did. I felt stupid. Did he play me or did I allow myself to be played? And did it really matter?"

She still couldn't answer that question. She'd taken over a year to come to terms with his deception and her own foolishness. Falling for someone married after the disaster with Turner and their broken engagement, she'd realized love simply wasn't going to happen for her. Whether it was because she chose the wrong guy or because there was something fundamentally wrong with her, the end result was the same. Relationships ended. Men left—like her dad, Turner. Or they were total losers. Regardless of the how and why, she always found herself alone and shattered. She wasn't going to do that ever again.

"You weren't wrong to give your heart," Jasper told her. "You didn't know what he was doing. It's not your fault."

"I still feel stupid and ashamed. At least I did. Now I've moved on. Anyway, that goes in the column of reasons why I'm not married. I take issue with your assuming that a woman has to—" she made air quotes "—be married and pop out babies to be living the American Dream."

He nodded. "Yeah, I kind of figured that one out on my own. The woman thing is hard. Any suggestions on how to do better?"

She thought for a second. "Movies. Watch movies." She started writing on a piece of paper. *"Two Weeks Notice, Brooklyn, Juno, Steel Magnolias."* She wrote down several others. "These are all strong women in great stories. Watch them, then we'll talk."

He took the list and stood. "Thanks, Renee. I appreciate it. I'll start watching them today."

Before she could answer, he was gone. Just like that. No offer for a lunchtime quickie or even some idle chitchat.

"You are such a guy," she murmured, before turning back to her computer. Which, she had to admit to herself, wasn't really a bad thing at all.

Jasper watched the movies Renee suggested and a few more. He made sure he fed Koda on time and took the old guy for a walk every day. Otherwise, he was pretty much glued to his TV or tablet. He watched movies while jogging on his treadmill, while preparing and eating his meals. He fell asleep watching movies, then started fresh in the morning.

Several days later, he surfaced, realizing he'd watched all the ones Renee had suggested, and several more, and he still had questions. After checking the time on his phone and re-alizing it was barely seven in the evening, he texted Renee.

You around?

A bit later, she responded. Are you asking what I think you're asking?

He picked up his phone and called her.

"I was asking if we could talk," he said when she answered. "I watched all those movies you suggested and I have a lot of questions." And an interest in seeing her because it had been a few days and even while watching the movies, she'd been on his mind.

"Oh. Okay. I wasn't sure."

"What else would I be asking?"

"I thought maybe a polite version of 'u up.' You know—the texting question about a booty call."

"I didn't know that." He paused. "Maybe I knew that, but I wasn't thinking about that."

She chuckled. "Apparently we need a code word. And to be honest, some foreplay, because I would need more than 'u up' to get me in the mood."

"I can be all about foreplay. What would you like?" Because while he had wanted to ask her some questions, they could wait until after. "Or I could come over and figure it out."

"I can't. I have my period and I feel awful. And while that probably falls under the category of TMI, it's true."

"I'm sorry. Can I do anything?"

"I wish, but this is my problem. However, I am available to school you on the mysterious ways of women. Did you really watch all those movies?"

"Yes, and a lot more. You sure you're up for company?"

"I would appreciate the distraction. Just ignore the soft whimpers."

"Would ice cream help?"

She sighed. "Actually, it would help a lot."

"I'm on my way."

CHAPTER FIVE

Renee spent the time between the phone call and Jasper's arrival alternating between wanting to see him and wishing she'd told him tonight wasn't going to work for her. She just plain didn't feel good and she wasn't sure trying to make polite conversation was going to go well. Only the second she opened her front door and saw him standing outside her apartment, she had the strongest urge to throw herself into his arms and be held in a strong, powerful, *I'm here for you* hug.

What was up with that? she wondered as she stepped back to let him in. Her hormones must be more out of whack than she'd realized.

"Hi," Jasper said, holding up a small white bag. "I didn't know what you liked, so I brought three different flavors."

"That's very thoughtful. Thank you."

He stepped inside and shut the door. She peeked in the bag and saw there where three containers of different flavors of Ben & Jerry's ice cream.

"Cherry Garcia is my favorite," she said, pulling out the pint. "What would you like?"

"The cookie dough one."

She got out bowls and served them each a generous portion, then led the way to the sofa. She curled up in the corner by where she'd plugged in her heating pad. It wasn't glamorous, but when the cramps got bad, the heat helped. Right now she was only dealing with a low ache, but that could change at any moment.

He sat at the opposite end and angled toward her. "You really up to this?" he asked. "I could just eat my ice cream and leave."

She grinned. "I notice you're not willing to abandon your ice cream."

"I can if that would make you feel better."

"Sweet, but not necessary. So you watched the movies. What did you think?"

He took his time answering, as if considering his words. He was so large, so masculine, that he seemed out of place. She'd never thought of her apartment as girly, but with him sitting on her gray sofa, with all the throw pillows, and the pale mauve walls, she had to admit, the space had a decidedly feminine air.

Funny how last time she'd been so intent on getting him into her bed, and into her, that she hadn't noticed the absence of maleness.

"I liked nearly all the movies I watched," he said. "*Juno* was great. I never thought about what it must be like for a girl in high school to have to deal with a pregnancy. It's not easy."

He put down his ice cream and gazed at her intently. "*Steel Magnolias* was unexpected. Not what happened with Shelby but how the characters impacted the story. The guys were in the background while the women carried the plot."

She smiled. "Now you know how we feel a lot of the time."

"I can see that. I watched *Gilmore Girls*."

"The series?"

"I started with the one that covers a year in their life and then went back and watched a couple of seasons."

He was determined to figure out his female character, she thought, impressed by the time he was willing to put into his project.

"What did you think?"

He picked up his ice cream again. "I was confused. What happened to Rory? In the original series, she was strong and driven. In the later one, she had no direction. She was a character who always overprepared so to show up at that interview with nothing didn't make sense. That's not who her character was. And the ending." He shook his head. "If I did something like that, my readers would hunt me down. Actually they wouldn't have to. My editor would have already killed me."

He sounded passionate and engaged in the characters. "Did you like it or not?" she asked.

"I don't know. I was unsatisfied but I can't stop thinking about it. So there's a lesson in that. Plus, I liked how strong the women were in the movies. It's like in my books. The stronger the villain, the stronger the hero has to be to defeat him."

"Or her."

He sighed. "Yes, or her. Although statistically, there are very few serial killers who are women."

"That's because they don't get caught."

He flashed her a grin. "Touché."

"Thank you. So you're thinking a strong woman for Vidar?"

"I think that would work best with him. Not a cop. If she was on the force, he would have met her already. And a transfer seems too convenient. Not that it matters—I don't like the idea of a work relationship. He wouldn't do that."

"What about someone he meets locally? He goes to that

coffee shop by his apartment," she said, trying to think of who else Vidar ran into regularly in the books. "She could work there, or have just moved to the neighborhood. They could accidentally grab each other's to-go cups."

Jasper looked surprised. "You've read my books?"

She laughed. "Of course I've read your books. You're a local author and the only writer I've ever met. Why wouldn't I read your books?"

"I didn't know."

He sounded both sheepish and pleased, which oddly enough made her feel a little teary, which was craziness on a stick. Hormones, she thought again. They were powerful little creatures.

He cleared his throat. "I like the idea of someone local. She works in an office, she's a dog walker."

"I don't see Vidar as a real dog kind of guy. He's too focused on what he does. I'm not sure he'd be a good pet parent."

"He could do it. He just hasn't had a chance."

Her lips twitched. "You're defending someone who doesn't exist?"

"Yes. He's my guy."

"Fine. He could love dogs." She held in a smile. "Or cats. What if he meets a crazy cat lady?"

"No. Definitely no."

"What about just one cat? I've always wanted a cat. They're so beautiful."

"No on the cat."

She smiled. "Okay, she owns a restaurant, she's a plumber, she works in a bar, she's a teacher, she's a…" She tried to think about what kind of career would make sense for Vidar's lady friend.

"What if she's a wedding planner?" Jasper asked.

Renee finished her ice cream and licked the spoon. "Really? That's both flattering and creepy at the same time."

"It makes sense. You're creative and resourceful. She could be, too."

"How would they meet? Vidar goes to a wedding?"

"He could. Someone from the force. Or a friend."

"Not family," she said. "He doesn't have any. I don't know—a wedding planner is nothing like what he does. Would they even get along? And while we're not on the subject, where did you come up with his name? Vidar. It's unusual."

"I found it in a baby name book. It's based on Norse mythology. Vidar is the son of Odin and a giantess named Grid. He's silent and known to be strong. I thought it suited him."

"I can't get past his mother's name. Grid? Really?"

"It was different back then."

"Still. 'This is my mother, Grid'?"

"You're not helping."

Renee laughed. "Okay. Vidar, son of Grid. Oh, wow, I just realized that Pallas's name comes from Greek mythology." She paused. "Or Roman. I think Greek. We have two mythologically based names in town. What are the odds? And back to your girl. She could be a florist, an artist. Oh, make her a glass artist. You could totally hang out with Mathias and Ronan and learn the trade. It would be very method acting. Or writing, I guess."

"You're feeling better."

She smiled. "I am. The ice cream cured me, at least for the moment. Thank you for bringing it."

"Thanks for helping me with my book."

"We didn't accomplish anything."

"I have a lot to think about. That's progress."

"If you say so." She thought about all they'd discussed and

how he'd watched all the movies she'd suggested plus more she hadn't. He was good at his job, doing the work and then some. He was handsome, funny, godlike in bed and successful.

"So why aren't you married?" she asked. "Why the serial monogamy?"

"You proposing?"

"Not today."

He grinned. "Okay, you answered my question when I asked it, so fair is fair. You know I was in the army."

She nodded.

"Before that I was just some small-town guy. I grew up in Montana. I liked the usual outdoor stuff, had a girlfriend in high school. There weren't a lot of opportunities and I wasn't excited about college so I joined up right after I graduated."

His gaze shifted past her, as if he was seeing something she couldn't.

"I got into the military police and that was good for me. I liked my work and I was serving my country. Some days were more difficult than others." He shifted his attention back to her. "I had several tours in Afghanistan. They got harder and by the time I was ready to rejoin the civilian world, I found myself physically intact but mentally and emotionally messed up."

"PTSD?" she asked.

"Among other things. I had nightmares, anxiety, sleeplessness. I couldn't focus. Some days I couldn't stop shaking. I went through all of it. Therapy, drugs, group counseling, halfway houses. Everything helped a little but nothing helped very much. After a while I figured out I was never going to be whole. Not the way I had been. The doctors I saw talked about managing my symptoms. One day we were given an assignment to write about how we were feeling. I started writing and couldn't stop. Two years later, I'd finished a book that had nothing to do with the war and everything to do with someone else's problems. That was the first Vidar novel."

She thought about what Wynn had said—that he wasn't as broken as he thought—and wondered if it was true.

"So you're too wounded to love anyone?" she asked lightly.

"Something like that. It's okay. I've got a pretty decent life." He grinned and got to his feet. "I never thought I'd be a writer, that's for sure."

He moved close, bent down and kissed the top of her head. "Thanks for talking to me tonight. I hope you feel better soon."

"I will. The first twenty-four hours are the worst for me. By the morning, I'll be fine."

"I'm glad." He touched her cheek. "I'll show myself out. See you soon."

She nodded and he left. When he was gone, she stretched on the sofa and thought about all they'd talked about. Jasper was an interesting guy. Under other circumstances, she just might want to test her friend's theory about his condition. But as things were, she would be foolish to even try. Love was not happening—at least not for her. Given her past, she was going to have to go it alone. But for this moment in time, Jasper was exactly right.

Renee hung up the phone and did a little shimmy in her chair. Having the disparate elements of a wedding start to come together always made her happy. When a seemingly impossible item—like a request for half the chairs at the reception to be black and the other half to be white, while all of them had gold cushions—worked out, she felt as if she could achieve anything. At least when it came to weddings. Ride in on a hot air balloon? Done. A vegan cake so delicious no one would guess its lack of dairy and eggs? Easy-peasy. Talking dolphins? Renee winced. Best not to go there, she thought, entering the information about the chairs on her computer and saving it so it flowed through to her tablet.

She was about to call yet another vendor about yet another challenging request when Jasper walked into her office and smiled at her. Her body reacted immediately, reminding her that it had really liked this man and the things he'd done to her and hey, her period would be over soon so maybe they should set up a date or something.

Instead of going down that path, she settled on the more conventional and safe, "Hi."

"Morning. You have a minute?"

If he was willing to take off his clothes and have his way with her, she had several, she thought dreamily, only to remember they were in her office and she should probably play just a little harder to get.

"I do," she told him, motioning to one of the chairs in front of her desk. "What's going on?"

"I've been thinking about what we talked about last night. I want Vidar's love interest to be a wedding planner. It gives her access to a lot of people he wouldn't normally come in contact with and it gets him out of the station. He was in there a lot in the last book. We both need a break."

She was still processing his announcement so could only ask, "You and Vidar need a break?"

"Uh-huh. I thought I could follow you around for a few weeks, learn about the business and—"

"No," she said firmly, as all thoughts of them having another close encounter faded from her mind. "You're not getting your serial killer cooties on my weddings. I'm a big believer in keeping the energy positive and flowing forward. Do you know what a serial killer would do at a wedding?"

Jasper stared at her, his gaze intense. "That's what I was thinking. I want the serial killer to be a wedding crasher."

"No," she said firmly. "Just no."

"No what?" Pallas asked, walking into the office. "Oh, hi, Jasper. Did I know we had a meeting with you?" She frowned. "You're not getting married, are you? I mean of course you could if you wanted, I just didn't think you were seeing anyone right now. Are you?"

Renee tried to act normal. She had no idea what he would say to that question and was incredibly grateful when he simply smiled and said, "I'm doing research for a book. I want to give my hero a love interest in the last book of the series and I'm thinking she'll be a wedding planner."

"Oh, Vidar's going to fall in love?" Pallas sighed. "That's so great. I love that. He needs a woman for sure. He's way too alone all the time and with his dark thoughts and all. A wedding planner would be perfect. Weddings are positive and upbeat and happy." She smiled at Renee. "Are you going to help him? That's a terrific idea. Let him follow you around and stuff. Jasper's the kind of writer who gets the details right."

Renee held in a groan.

"If it's not too much trouble," he said, smiling winningly at Pallas. "I'd really like to follow her around and get to know the business."

"Sure. Whatever you need." Pallas turned to Renee. "I'm assuming you're fine with it. Being married to an artist, I know how important it is to go with the flow when they get an idea in their head. So we're good?"

Renee sighed. "We're good." She waited until her boss left before glaring at Jasper. "If I didn't know better, I would swear you'd planned that."

"You know I didn't." He leaned back in his chair and rested his ankle on his opposite knee. "Sometimes I get lucky."

"I'll say," she muttered, ignoring the potential double entendre.

"You could have told her no," he pointed out. "You could have said I would be in the way and you didn't want me around to taint everything with my serial killer cooties."

An excellent point. She could have and she hadn't so this was partially on her. While Pallas might not have understood Renee's reluctance, she would have respected it. So why had she just sat there like a lump? Did she want to spend the time with Jasper? Did she want to help with the book? Did she not want to have to think about that question right now?

"I'm not in a place to discuss that," she told him firmly. "So let's set some ground rules. Weddings are incredibly stressful for everyone involved. It is a special day for the bride and the groom and no matter what, they come first."

"Agreed."

"You will not offer suggestions or opinions, make faces or otherwise indicate you think what they're doing is anything but magical."

"I'd never offer an opinion."

"You say that now, but when Wendy and William want to get married while riding the prize pigs they both raised, you might find yourself with a thought or two."

"Prize pigs?"

"It's an example." She glared at him. "I'm serious, Jasper. For you this is work, for them, it's their lives. They will remember their wedding forever. You can't get in the middle of that."

"I know that, but why do you think I'd want to get in the middle of anything?"

"You get involved in your research. You learn by doing. I've heard about the fighting sticks and who knows whatever methods you use to figure out how to do stuff. I don't want you getting into that level of detail with my weddings."

"You're really protective of them."

"Of course I am."

He put both feet on the ground and leaned toward her. "Renee, I give you my word that I won't get personally involved in any of your weddings. All I want to do is observe you and learn about what you do."

"It all sounds fine," she grumbled.

"You don't believe me?"

"Oh, I believe you mean what you say now. But I don't trust you not to change the rules."

"That will never happen."

"Sure. You go to hell for lying, same as stealing."

He grinned. "I haven't heard that one in a long time."

"The point is still valid."

She knew she was going to regret allowing him into her world and at the same time she was oddly excited about the idea of Jasper learning about what she did. Later, she would have a serious talk with herself and figure out what exactly was going on with her brain. But until then...

She unlocked a drawer in her desk and pulled out a tablet and charger.

"You'll need the tablet to keep up with what's going on with the various weddings," she told him. "I have a firm 'you break it, you bought it' policy, so respect the property."

He studied her. "You're tough."

"Yes, I am. You need to respect that, too."

"Yes, ma'am." He picked up the tablet and turned it on, then waited while it booted. "How did you get to be a wedding planner? Is it something you study?"

"Not exactly. I was a marketing major in college." After her attempt to get into fashion had failed spectacularly, she thought sadly. "I liked marketing but I didn't love it. On a whim, I applied for a job as a wedding planning assistant in Bel Air."

"Fancy."

"It was. I discovered I had a flair and one thing led to another. After I learned the business, I started looking for a different location. That led me to here."

His gaze settled on hers. "I'm glad it did."

The quivers in her tummy were unexpected but very nice. "Me, too."

He glanced at his tablet. "It's ready." He looked again. "How many weddings are in this thing?"

Renee picked up her own tablet and glanced at the index. "We average one and a half weddings a week or about seventy-five a year. We can hold as many as three a week—Friday night, Saturday and Sunday—but we try not to. Everyone gets too tired and cranky."

He shook his head. "That's a lot of weddings."

"It is. Most of the weddings we're doing these days are multiday events. With the entire wedding party coming into town from somewhere else, it makes sense. We can host a rehearsal dinner on Friday night and a brunch on Sunday morning with the wedding as the main event on Saturday. As soon as bride and groom sign with us, they have their own file. You'll see their names listed in alphabetical order, bride first."

She looked at him. "We usually have the most contact with the bride. If we have two men getting married, or two women, we list under our point of contact. All right, click on Jackson/Kincaid."

Jasper did as she asked, then looked at the display. "I get it. There are tabs for every category. Guest list, flowers, catering, decorations. Huh." He touched the display. "So the calendar tells you what needs to be done when. Green means it's good, yellow is pending and red is trouble?"

"Exactly. I can easily print the calendar. I can also print out a to-do list for each wedding. Every week I print out a master list, so I know where we are on each wedding and what needs to be done and the status on pending orders. Because Happily Inc is a wedding destination town, our vendors work with us all the time. I don't have to worry that Silver won't show up with the bar, or Gary won't deliver the right number of chairs. In some ways, we're able to pass on some of the work directly to our vendors, which keeps costs down."

She showed him a basic contract and talked about the various weddings coming up in the next few weeks.

"I'd like to go to one," he said.

"You're not crashing a wedding. It wouldn't be right."

"Could I work at one?"

Renee pulled up her wedding calendar, then tabbed through the various menus. "The apple wedding is coming up. The drinks are all premixed, so you could talk to Silver about helping her. If you know how to be a waiter, then you could talk to the catering company."

"I'll go see Silver," he said. "I think I'd do better with drinks than food."

"There *is* less to go wrong."

He flashed her a smile. It was a good one that had her toes doing a little curl in her sensible pumps.

"What other themes do you have coming up?"

"Can't get excited about the apple wedding?" she asked, her voice teasing.

"I'm going to see it for myself, and that will be plenty."

She looked at the calendar. "It's fall so we have some that are just seasonally based. There's a Halloween wedding, which should be interesting, and a football wedding." She looked at him. "It's more Dallas Cowboys–based than generic football. I was a little nervous, but it's turning out beautifully. The wedding colors are the silver and blue. The bridesmaids are all in silver and the dresses are gorgeous. I'm getting excited about it. We're also doing a Scottish wedding. That couple lives in Sedona so we have most of our meetings in person. With the other couples, most of the meetings are teleconferences."

She paused, not sure what else he wanted to hear about. Before she could ask, he said, "What's wrong with the Halloween wedding?"

"Nothing. Why?"

"Your voice was different when you mentioned it. As if you didn't approve or something."

"What? No. It's fine. There are a lot of fun elements. The best man is the bride's dog."

His gaze didn't waver. "There's something, Renee. I can hear it."

How could he have guessed? Was it a writer thing or was she not hiding her feelings? She bit her lower lip.

"It's not anything," she said slowly. "At least it's not anything I can define. I just don't..." She glared at him. "This is just between us. You can't tell anyone or put it in your book."

He set down the tablet. "I won't betray you."

For a second she wondered if he meant something else by his words, or had a different meaning. She told herself not to be ridiculous.

"I don't have a good feeling about them," she admitted. "I can't explain it beyond that. Sometimes, when I'm working with a couple, I get a sense of whether or not they're going to make it. Maybe it's how they treat each other. I don't know."

"They're not going to make it?"

She hesitated before shaking her head. "I don't think so. I hope I'm wrong. I hope they live long, happy lives together."

"But you don't think so."

"No."

"It's okay. People have intuition about different things. This is your area of expertise. You've seen a lot of couples come and go. Of course you'd have a sense of them."

He rose. "Thanks for all the information. I'm going to head home and process it. I promise not to show up again without giving you a little notice."

"That would work."

He surprised her by closing the door, then circling around her desk and drawing her to her feet. When she was standing, he cupped her face in his large hands and kissed her.

"Thank you for your help," he murmured, his mouth moving against hers.

"You're, ah, welcome."

He chuckled, kissed her again, then walked to the door.

"I'll be in touch," he promised.

"I look forward to it."

And then he was gone. Renee sank back in her seat and pressed a hand to her chest. The man had skills. With nothing more than a very fleeting kiss, he'd made her heart race.

Work, she reminded herself. She had to focus on work. She glanced at the tablet and saw she'd pulled up the Halloween wedding. Instantly her good mood vanished. She did not want to be right about Andrew and Asia, but she was afraid she was.

Intuition, he called it. She could accept that. At least she wasn't doing anything crazy like claiming she could see ghosts or talk to animals and wasn't that a good thing?

CHAPTER SIX

The nightmare began as it always did—on the edge of a road, with the rocky, brown hills behind him. Everything was familiar, but even though he knew what was going to happen, he couldn't stop his heart from racing as he braced himself for the unfolding chain of events.

The open pickup rounded the corner. Jasper walked toward the driver to check his ID. Jasper's men were already inspecting the truck. The details were all there—the chill in the winter air, the scent of distant cooking fires, the crunch of his footsteps on the gravel.

Even as he went through the motions, he tried to stop himself, warn his dream-self that there was danger. That there was going to be an explosion and—

A soft whine broke through his dream. Unexpected weight shifted on the bed, drawing him back to the present. He opened his eyes and found himself in his darkened bedroom, Koda stretched out beside him. The dog watched him anxiously.

"Hey you," Jasper said, feeling his heart pounding and the

sweat on his body. The physical manifestations of the nightmare weren't that bad this time. Koda had awakened him before the really bad stuff started. Before everyone died.

He reached out and rubbed the dog's head, then sat up so he could catch his breath. It was nearly dawn. Getting up made more sense than trying to sleep again. Safer. He leaned his head against Koda's strong back and told himself it was just a nightmare. It wasn't real—not anymore.

"When do you close on the house?" Jasper asked several hours later.

Garrick McCabe stretched out his long legs, picked up his beer and shrugged. "In ten days. I've never bought a house before. My real estate agent tells me it's going really well, but I have to admit the amount of paperwork is staggering. Weren't we supposed to be a paperless society long before now?"

Jasper grinned. "Try being self-employed. When I bought this place, I thought the bank was going to ask for a blood sample or something. I was lucky—I'd just signed a great deal with my publisher, so I dumped my advance into the down payment and that helped."

"Makes sense. At least I have W-2s from the city to flash around. Plus, I think being a cop makes me a decent bet. The odds of me taking off and not making my monthly payments seem unlikely."

Garrick was with the Happily Inc police department. Jasper knew he'd been born in the area and had grown up here. He'd moved to Phoenix to go to ASU and had taken a job with the Phoenix Police Department before moving back two years ago.

He and Garrick had gotten to know each other over games at The Boardroom. Jasper had asked for his help with a couple of details for one of his books and since then Garrick had been a part of the cadre of people Jasper called on to get it right for his characters. Just before the book tour, he and Garrick had gone off to a weekend conference in rural Virginia where cops came from all over to learn about new kinds of weaponry and body armor.

The front door to Jasper's house opened and a familiar voice called, "Sorry I'm late."

Koda stood and watched, his hackles raised.

"It's just Cade," Jasper told the dog. "You remember him, don't you?"

Koda stayed on alert until Cade appeared. When he saw the tall man, his tail wagged and he walked over for a greeting.

"Hey, big guy," Cade said, dropping into a crouch and petting the dog. "You're looking good. You've put on more weight. Another month or so and you'll be where you should be."

He stood and nodded at his friends. "I see you started the party without me."

"Go grab a beer and join us," Jasper said, hoping he didn't sound as nervous as he felt. He'd invited his friends over to read pages from his new book. Normally he only needed help with new fighting skills or police procedures, but this time was different. This time he had to deal with *Mandy*.

Vidar's love interest, whom he'd named Mandy, was going to be the death of him. So far he'd written and rewritten their first scene eight times. In half, they already knew each other and in the rest, they didn't. None of them had gone well. He really hated to send his agent crap if he didn't have to so he was hoping his friends could give him some insights.

Cade returned from the kitchen, beer in hand. He sank into one of the oversize chairs and glanced at Garrick.

"Close on the house yet?"

"In ten days."

"Let me know if you need help moving."

"Me, too," Jasper added.

"I'm good. The place I've been staying is furnished, so I only have a few boxes of personal things. I'll live on a futon for a few weeks, then figure out what I need."

Cade grinned. "A futon? You're such a guy. Come on, man. Grow a pair and buy a big-boy bed."

"In time, in time."

Cade shook his head. "You losers. You both need a woman in your life."

"We're not going to share," Jasper said mildly.

"Fine. You *each* need a woman in your life." Cade sipped his beer. "Being friends with a writer is a pain in the ass."

"You love being on the fringes of my fame."

"Fame?" Garrick chuckled. "Is that what we're calling it now?"

Jasper wanted to continue the banter, but he was too concerned about his story. "So," he began, then cleared his throat. "I have some pages I'd like you to read. For the new book."

He told them about the plot—as far as he knew it—and explained that Vidar would be finding a love interest as Jasper wrapped up the series.

"That's new," Cade said, studying him. "You don't put women in your books."

"Not unless they're being killed," Garrick added. "Or they're a one-night stand for Vidar. Even in bars and stuff, the walk-ons are nearly always men."

"They're not," Jasper protested before wondering if it was true. Given the trouble he was having writing Mandy, it made sense that he'd avoid the whole "female" thing. Write what you know and all that. Which said what about him? That he was so uncomfortable with half the species that he avoided them, even in his books? Was that what he wanted with his life or who he was? He tried to tell himself he'd had a relationship with Wynn, only it hadn't been much more than someone to have sex with. And how well did he know Renee? So far he liked her a lot, but it had only been the one night.

"Jasper?" Cade's voice was soft. "You okay?"

"What? I'm fine."

Both his friends were watching him with studied concern.

"I'm fine," he repeated. "I'm not having a flashback or anything. I was just thinking." Damn—the problem was worse than he thought.

He pointed at the pages in the center of the coffee table. "That's them. Make notes if you want or just set them on fire. Either way, I'd like to know what you really think. No holding back. Being nice isn't going to be doing me any favors."

With that, he rose and called to Koda. "We'll be outside. Let me know when you're done."

With that, he walked out of the family room, through the kitchen and toward the back door. Koda followed, his nails clicking on the hardwood floors. Once they were clear of the house, Jasper found a good-sized stick and threw it as hard as he could. Koda raced after it, returning it a few seconds later. He politely dropped it at Jasper's feet for him to throw again.

While he didn't know exactly what his friends were going to say, he was pretty sure there wasn't going to be any praise for what he'd written. He simply didn't understand Mandy enough to write about her. He couldn't get in her head or imagine her dialogue. She was as much a mystery to him as the moon.

He liked that she was a wedding planner and, based on what he'd learned from Renee, he'd been able to figure out where Mandy worked, but he needed more details. What did a wedding planner talk about with her clients? What was the happy couple interested in and where did his serial killer make his appearance?

After throwing the stick a few more times, Jasper set off with Koda at his heels. They did a quick circuit in the forest. As always the combination of movement, nature and quiet did its thing and his mind calmed.

Obviously he was going to have to follow Renee through one of her weddings. Go to meetings, watch the decision-making process, meet with the bride and groom. That would clarify the work aspect of things. He would also have to observe women more closely. He needed to figure out how they talked. Maybe he could record some conversations to get the right word usage and cadence.

He and Koda headed back to the house. Cade and Garrick were sitting on the back porch, beers in hand. Both of them tensed when they saw him.

"That bad?" he asked, deliberately keeping his tone light.

His friends shared a glance before Garrick looked at him. "In my version, Mandy's part robot, part Soviet general during World War II. She's barking out orders and telling people to be calm."

"The bride was nervous," Jasper started, then told himself to shut up. He was here to learn, not justify.

"She wasn't sympathetic," Garrick told him. "And the way you describe her walking was just plain weird. Do authors really talk about how a person walks? Don't we just picture what we want in our head?"

"Sometimes a walk shows character," Jasper muttered, hoping he didn't sound defensive. "Thanks for the info."

"I made some notes on the page." Garrick shrugged. "I was honest."

"I appreciate it." He looked at Cade. "You must have read the kiss scene then."

Cade shifted uncomfortably. "Yeah, well, that wasn't a kiss. Damn, Jasper, up against the wall and sucking out her lungs? Where did you come up with that?"

Jasper couldn't remember the last time he'd been this embarrassed. He wanted to remind them both he was a number one *New York Times* bestselling author. Several hundred people lined up at his book signings. He was successful and a hell of a writer. Or at least he had been.

He swore silently. "I was trying to show passion."

"It was either rape or porn. I couldn't decide which. Sorry, man."

"No, I need to hear the truth." He absently patted Koda. "It's just tougher than I thought it was going to be. Women are hard."

Cade sighed. "Actually women are soft and they smell good. Not knowing that might be your problem."

Jasper laughed along with his friends, but deep inside he felt a cold knot of worry. He was totally and completely screwed and he had no idea how to fix the problem.

Renee didn't know how to tell Jasper that with her period finished, she was more than ready to have another night of whatever he wanted to do with her. A phone call was out of the question. How exactly was she supposed to start *that* conversation? The same with texting. It would just be too weird.

On the bright side, she had an appointment with him this morning, so maybe she could work it into the conversation somehow. She could mention she was feeling much better. *Much*, much better. Although she shouldn't be too enthused. She didn't want him to think they were going to do it in her office. But their meeting was at eleven, so maybe when they were done talking, they could head to her place for a noontime quickie.

She cleared her emails and confirmed everything she needed to get done for the week, all the while doing her best not to think yummy Jasper thoughts. He strolled into her office right on time, looking all tall and Jasper-sexy.

"Hi," she said, trying not to sound too excited. Interested was appealing. Desperate didn't look pretty on anyone.

"Hey."

She waited for the obligatory "How are you?" to which she was going to say something like "Much better," as per the plan, only instead of saying anything like that, he paused for a second, then blurted, "We need to talk."

Nooooooooooo! She mentally stomped her foot. She didn't want to talk. She wanted hot kisses, big man hands and him having with his way with her, none of which she was comfortable sharing so she wasn't sure what to say, which turned out to be fine because he spoke first.

"I can't figure out Mandy."

Mandy? There was a Mandy? Disappointment and a bit of hurt formed a powerful knot in her stomach. "Who's Mandy?"

"Vidar's love interest. I finally named her."

Okay—she was fine with women who weren't real. "You mean you don't understand her character?"

"I don't get anything about her." He walked to her desk and sat down. "I can't get a handle on any part of her. Not her background or how she talks or what she's thinking."

"Do you have to be in her point of view?"

"I don't know. I think so. At some point she's going to be alone with the killer, so we'll have to know what's happening. Unless I did it from his point of view, but that seems like cheating." He glanced up at the ceiling and then back at her.

"I think it would help if I could be more involved with a wedding."

Coldness settled on her. "What, exactly, does that mean?"

"I need more details about Mandy's work. Your work. I think if I followed a couple from concept to ceremony, it would make a difference. What are the decisions being made and why? What do they fight about? Where could the serial killer come in? Is he with catering? Is he the officiant? The groom's father? A guest? I've been considering—"

"No."

She spoke the word firmly, meeting his gaze with as determined a glare as she could muster.

"Just, no. You are not going to get involved in one of my weddings."

"Why not? I'm following you around anyway. How is this different?"

"You're following me around in general. Now you're asking for something specific. Sitting in the corner while I'm on a teleconference is very different from being involved. You're asking me to insert you into a wedding where you'll be in all the meetings and possibly influencing the bride and groom so you get what you want rather than them getting what they want."

"I wouldn't do that."

She stared at him without speaking.

"I wouldn't," he repeated. "I don't want to be in the wedding party. I just want to be on the fringes."

"And if you decide that changing the colors from yellow and green to gold and silver would help your plot, you wouldn't say anything? Oh, please. Of course you would—in a hot second."

All her soft, gooey, sexy feelings disappeared, leaving behind a protective anger she was going to put to good use. She didn't know Jasper very well, but she understood he was a man who was used to getting his way. Only not this time.

"We are talking about the most significant day in a couple's life together. Weddings often take a year of planning. I'm willing to show you what goes on behind the scenes and you're already going to help serve drinks at an upcoming wedding, but you will not get involved in the process. The wedding isn't about you or your book, it's about the bride and groom. You don't get to mess with that."

"I wouldn't be messing with anyone. I don't understand. I learn by doing. I need to do this."

She rose so she could better make her point. "Jasper, let me be clear. I will not have you destroying a beautiful wedding with your serial killer research."

He looked completely baffled. "I wouldn't do that. I'm kind of famous. They might be honored."

"Or horrified."

He stood—all six-foot-whatever of him—and looked down at her. "You really willing to take me on?"

"Oh, please. I'd take on you and the devil himself to protect my clients. My job is to give them the wedding of their dreams and I will do everything in my power to make that happen. Standing up to you is nothing."

She spoke with conviction, aware that, with each word, she was most certainly putting an end to any afternoon delight on the Jasper front. On a purely *I enjoy a man-induced orgasm as much as the next girl* basis, everything about this pissed her off. But none of that really mattered—not when it came to her couples. She could always get a vibrator and a supply of batteries. Her brides and grooms had only one shot at their wedding day.

He started to respond, then simply shook his head and walked out. When he was gone, Renee sank back into her seat and drew in a breath. She'd done the right thing—she knew that down to her bone marrow. But doing the right thing often came with a price and this time that price was Jasper himself.

★ ★ ★

Jasper started toward his truck, then changed course and went looking for Pallas. He had a feeling she would be more reasonable than Renee.

He had to admit—he hadn't gotten the reaction he'd been expecting. Yet more proof that he knew less than nothing about women. Were all guys this clueless or was he more lame than most? A question he would have to answer another time, he thought grimly as he stepped into Pallas's office and looked around.

She wasn't there and, based on the fact that her computer was off and her desk was clear, he would guess she wasn't in the building either. Probably for the best, he told himself, as he headed back to his truck. Going over Renee's head was kind of weaselly on his part. She'd been very clear on her feelings and while he didn't understand them, he had to respect them. And her. She'd been fired up for sure.

Now, away from the situation, he had to admit she'd been kind of sexy when she'd been yelling at him. She hadn't been intimidated by him at all. She'd been willing to take him on, no matter what, to protect her clients.

He reached his truck and slid onto the seat, but instead of starting the engine, he pulled out a pad of paper he kept in the glove box, along with a pen and began scribbling notes. He described how Renee had looked as she'd taken him to task—the fire in her eyes and the determined set to her body. Small but mighty, he thought. She was a woman who wouldn't take crap from anyone—at least not when it came to one of her weddings. He wondered if she was that brave on her own behalf.

Mandy would be the same way, he thought absently. Strong and willing to take on the world. He wasn't sure a wedding disaster would resonate with his readers but there had to be something… Did she have a baby sister who needed… Did she have a kid?

He looked out the window but instead of the wall of Weddings Out of the Box, he saw Mandy walking a little boy to school. No, a little girl. Mandy would take on the world for her. She would be fearless and determined. And if she was a single mom, getting involved with Vidar would mean higher stakes. She couldn't bring just anyone into her daughter's life. Plus, at the end of the book, when her life was in danger, the stakes would be even higher—she had to stay alive for her daughter.

Jasper scribbled notes as quickly as he could, all the while feeling that sense of rightness he got when he finally figured out a problem with his book. He was barely aware of a car pulling in next to his truck until the doors opened and the conversation drifted to him.

"We have to finalize the colors today," the young woman said with a laugh. "If we don't, Renee is going to fire us for making her crazy."

The man with her smiled at her across the roof of the car. "I don't think a wedding planner can fire the people who hired her."

"Did you read the entire contract, word for word? I'm guessing there's a 'they make me crazy' clause for situations just like this one."

Jasper set down his notepad. The man was maybe thirty, about five-ten and wearing a suit. The car was a late model BMW. His bride-to-be was only a couple of inches shorter, with blond hair and a curvy build. They looked successful, happy and in love.

Even as he told himself a smart man would respect what Renee had told him, he was getting out of the truck and closing the door behind him.

"Morning," he said. "You're here to meet with Renee, right?"

They looked at him. "We are."

"Great. I'm Jasper Dembenski."

The couple exchanged a glance. "I'm Hanna and this is my fiancée, Graham."

They both looked faintly puzzled and a little concerned as if they were wondering if he was going to try to steal away their business or tell them something bad about Weddings Out of the Box.

He offered them an easy smile. "You're going to love working with Renee. Her weddings are magnificent."

Hanna smiled. "That's what we've heard. We've only started and we're on a tight schedule, but so far, so good." She tilted her head. "Wait, you wouldn't be *the* Jasper Dembenski would you?"

"You mean the author?" He raised a shoulder. "I am."

"Really?" Hanna turned to Graham. "I love his books. They're the ones you read, too. What are you doing here? Are you getting married? You should so have your wedding here. You'll love working with Renee."

"No wedding, at least not the way you mean." He glanced at the building and knew there would be hell to pay, and yet he was going to do it anyway. "But I am writing a book."

Hanna's eyes widened. "A new one? A new book?" She clutched her hands together. "Are you doing research? Is that why you're here? Say yes! Please say yes."

Jasper chuckled. "You guessed it. My serial killer will be involved with a wedding. I don't have all the details yet."

She waved Graham closer and grabbed his hand. "Do you need to research a specific wedding?" She looked at Graham. "Is it okay if he uses ours?"

"Sure. Can one of us be the serial killer?"

Hanna jumped up and down. "Yes! Pick me. Or Graham. Or my dad! He loves your books, too. We're doing a Scottish-themed wedding. Does that work for you? Do you want us to change something?"

Because they would, he realized. They would do pretty much anything he asked, which was exactly what Renee had been worried about. That he would turn their wedding into his.

"What I'd like is to observe," he said. "Just stay in the background and take notes. Maybe ask questions."

"Anything," Hanna said. "This is so exciting. I can't wait to tell my dad. Come on. You have to meet Renee. She's the best. She's going to be so thrilled."

Reality landed like a sucker punch to his gut as Jasper realized Renee was going to be many things, but thrilled wasn't one of them. Less than twenty minutes after she'd shut him down, he'd managed to get exactly what he wanted. He was still trying to figure out how he was going to explain himself when they walked into her office.

"Hi," she said, coming to her feet. Then her smile collapsed when she saw him. "What are you doing—"

"You'll never guess," Hanna said happily. "This is Jasper Dembenski. He's an author."

"Oh, I know exactly who he is," Renee said, staring at him. "You three know each other?"

"We just met in the parking lot," Graham said. "Jasper's writing a book about a serial killer at a wedding and he needs to do some research."

"He's going to use our wedding as the backdrop." Hanna clapped her hands together. "I really hope one of us can be the serial killer."

Renee's gaze sharpened as she stared into his eyes. He saw anger and frustration but what hit him the hardest was the disappointment. Then she blinked and the calm, organized wedding planner Hanna and Graham knew was back.

"A serial killer bride would be interesting," she said pleasantly. "Now about your wedding—let's go into the conference room and review where we are. As I recall, we were going to have our color choices made by today. How are we coming on that?"

Jasper stepped back so Renee could lead the way. He followed Hanna and Graham down the hall. He knew she was mad now, but it would be worth it. At least that was what he told himself. Whether or not he believed it was another story.

CHAPTER SEVEN

Renee got through the meeting with Hanna and Graham by focusing on them and pretending Jasper wasn't in the room. A reality made difficult by Hanna deferring to him on every decision. On the bright side, they'd chosen medium blue and mauve as their colors and they'd set up meetings to discuss food, drinks and decorations.

With all that decided, Renee printed out the details and handed a copy to Hanna and Graham before reluctantly passing one to Jasper.

"I'll be in touch next week with the information we're waiting for," she said as they prepared to leave. "We're on a tight time frame, so we need to get going on everything."

"This is so wonderful," Hanna told her. "I can't thank you enough." She turned to Jasper. "You have our email addresses, right? So if you need anything you'll be in touch?"

He looked faintly uncomfortable as he shook hands with them. "You know I will be."

Renee was hoping his uneasiness came from the fact that he had to now face her. She hoped he was feeling like the worm he was, but she had her doubts. If he cared about anyone but himself, he wouldn't have done what he did. It wasn't a lesson she wanted to learn, but better early in their nonrelationship.

Hanna and Graham left. Renee half expected Jasper to duck out with them to avoid her, but he stayed where he was. She waited until she was sure the other couple was out of earshot before turning her attention on him.

"That was lucky timing," she said, careful to keep her voice calm when she really wanted to throw a chair at his head. "It took you what, fifteen minutes, to go behind my back?"

"Renee, it's not what you think."

"It's exactly what I think and you know it. You understood everything I was saying and when you didn't agree, you did what you wanted. You never gave a thought as to why I felt as strongly as I did. You didn't care that I would be upset or feel betrayed. You wanted what you wanted and that's all that matters to you."

She closed her tablet. "Your book is nowhere near as important as their wedding. It's their day, not yours. You were thoughtless and selfish and you have proven that I was a fool to think we could be friends or that I could trust you. Neither is true. Now I would like you to leave."

"I don't get to say anything? What about my thoughts on what just happened?"

"Your opinion doesn't matter at all to me, Jasper. Not anymore."

When he made no move to stand, she got up and walked out of the conference room. She went to her office, where she closed and locked the door. While it was unlikely he would follow her there, she wanted to make it clear she was done talking to him.

She leaned against her door and closed her eyes for a second. Disappointment didn't begin to describe what she was feeling. While their relationship was never going to be about more than sex, she had thought he was a decent guy and now that was ruined forever. He was just some thoughtless jackass who had wormed his way into one of her weddings and there wasn't a damn thing she could do about it.

"I'll be there at the end of next month, Mom," Renee said as she turned on the road that would take her to the animal preserve. Her friend Carol had asked her to stop by, without saying why. A reason to be concerned, Renee thought, hoping everything was all right.

"I'm glad we'll get a few days together," Verity Grothen, Renee's mother, said, her voice perfectly clear over the car's speakers. "I've found a lovely little spa in the neighborhood. Let's have a girls' day out."

"I'd like that, Mom."

"Then it's a date. You take care, sweetie."

"I will. You, too."

They hung up. Renee breathed a sigh of relief that her mother hadn't mentioned visiting Happily Inc. There had been a few murmurings when Renee had first moved here, but she'd claimed she was too busy to have anyone visit and had instead promised a trip to her mother's place in San Diego.

Not that she didn't love her mother—she did. Verity was the only family she had. It was just having her mother around was complicated. Especially here, she thought as she parked at the animal preserve.

The Happily Inc Animal Preserve was on the outskirts of town—by the dump and recycling center. Carol's father and her uncles, Ed and Ted, had bought the dump and all the surrounding land years ago. After establishing a healthy savanna, they'd brought in nonpredatory animals such as zebras, gazelles, giraffes and a water buffalo.

The nonprofit was supported by donations and a trust that had been established the previous year when artist Ronan Mitchell had donated several glass pieces that were sold at auction.

Whenever Carol hosted a girlfriend lunch, she had it at the preserve, weather permitting. While everyone else enjoyed being outside and catching sight of the animals roaming free, those lunches always made Renee nervous. She preferred to live her life wild animal–free. Not that she didn't love nature—she did. Just from a safe distance that was definitely out of earshot.

A cat would be different, she thought wistfully. She liked cats. At least she thought she could, if she was ever brave enough to get one. But whenever she considered it, her mind reminded her of all the potential disasters that could follow.

Renee pushed those thoughts away and instead wondered why Carol had asked her to stop by. As Carol was happily married and the mother to an adorable baby, Renee didn't anticipate them having to discuss a problem.

At least not a problem of Carol's, Renee mentally amended as she walked toward the main offices. She, on the other hand, was still fuming from her encounter with Jasper two days ago. His complete disregard for her job, her clients and her specific request that he not get involved in a wedding had made it clear he was a definite candidate for jerk of the year. Her only regret was that she'd ever thought he was a decent guy. Obviously her ability to find the worst guy in the room was still alive and well. Note to self—avoid men forever.

Easy enough, she told herself firmly. She wouldn't look, wouldn't date and certainly wouldn't touch. Any attempt to get along with a man on a romantic or sexual level would only lead to disaster. It was just…she'd really liked him. And now she couldn't and that made her both pissy and sad.

Pushing all thoughts of Jasper and his dickishness from her mind, she walked into the main building and was surprised to find both Carol and Bethany waiting for her.

"Hi," Renee said, smiling at her friends.

Carol and Bethany both rose and hugged her. Carol was a pretty, down-to-earth redhead who favored cargo pants and T-shirts. Bethany, a gorgeous blonde, was equally casual in her dress code. While Carol worked with the grazing animals that roamed the Happily Inc savanna, Bethany and her husband, Cade, were co-owners of a horse ranch outside of town. Bethany's claim to fame was that she was the adopted daughter of the king of El Bahar and therefore an honest to goodness princess complete with tiaras and bodyguards. While she was in Happily Inc, she lived pretty much like everyone else, but when she returned to El Bahar, she was living the princess life.

"So what's up?" Renee asked, then paused as the two women exchanged a glance. Her first thought had been maybe some kind of group party they needed help planning, but now she was thinking it wasn't anything like that at all.

Her stomach clenched as she braced herself for bad news. Was someone sick? Was it worse than that?

"Let's go back to my office," Carol said, leading the way down a short hall.

They went into her small, messy office and she shut the door behind them.

After clearing files off chairs, they all found a seat. Renee looked at each of them.

"Just say it," she told them. "I can handle it."

"It's nothing bad," Carol said quickly. "I'm sorry. We didn't mean to scare you."

"It's actually good news." Bethany offered a fake smile. "Really."

"Uh-huh. Why don't I believe that?"

"I have no idea." Bethany sucked in a breath. "I can't do this."

"You have to," Carol said gently. "The news is going to come out eventually and the more people you tell, the better you'll feel."

"I'm not sure about your logic," Bethany muttered before looking at Renee. "I'm pregnant."

Renee blinked. She hadn't seen that coming. "You are? That's wonderful. But you're not happy. Is there something...?"

Bethany quickly shook her head. "The baby is fine. It's not that. I'm thrilled, Cade is over the moon. We're both so excited. It's just..."

Renee had no idea what she was talking about. If they were happy and the baby was healthy, then what could possibly be wrong? They were going to be parents. There would be a new generation and—

"Your parents," she said flatly. "You have to tell your parents."

Bethany dropped her head. "I'm having the first grandchild of the king and queen of El Bahar. My brothers are still kids, so it's going to be years before any of them gets married, let alone has a kid. My mom will be excited, but my father is going to ruin everything."

She looked at Renee. "He'll fly over and wrap me in bubble wrap himself. He'll want me monitored and protected and life as I know it will never be the same." Tears filled her eyes. "What if he orders me back to El Bahar?"

"Can he do that?"

"He's the king. He can do anything he wants when it comes to his family. I wasn't born in the country, so I'm not in succession to the throne and neither is my child, but that won't matter to him. He's going to want to make sure his first grandchild is taken care of from conception, or from the second he knows I'm pregnant."

Renee grinned. "He's going to be a grandfather. Of course he'll be excited."

"He's a grandfather with superpowers. There's a difference."

Renee glanced at Carol. "Am I here to offer advice?"

Carol nodded. "You're the most honest, sensible, pragmatic person we know." Her mouth curved up. "I mean that in a good way."

"Then I'll take it that way." Renee touched Bethany's hand. "Tell your parents. This is their first grandchild and they deserve to know. Plus, you're making yourself miserable keeping it from them and that's not fun."

Bethany scowled. "That's it? That's your advice?"

"Not quite. Before you call, take some time to come up with a phrase that defines how you feel and how you want to be treated. For example, something like, 'Dad, I appreciate that you're worried about me, but right now I need to focus on taking care of myself and our baby. I need to stay calm and centered and the best way for me to do that is to be with Cade in Happily Inc.'"

Renee shrugged. "Or whatever your version of that is. Then you write it down and keep repeating it until he gets the message. Oh, and have a point of compromise ready. Let him fly over a doctor or invite him to listen to the baby's heartbeat or something. Ask for what you want, then offer him something he wants that you can live with."

Bethany stared at her. "That could work. I like what you said." She turned to Carol. "Can I have a piece of paper and a pen? I want to write that down. It was perfect. And you're right about offering him something. I'll say no to everything first, then compromise later. That way he feels as if he's win-ning."

"I told you she'd be good," Carol said as she handed over a pad and pen.

"It comes from years of working with feuding wedding par-ties," Renee said, her voice teasing. "Sometimes what Mom wants and what her daughter wants are not the same thing." She smiled at Bethany. "I think I forgot to say congratula-tions. I'm so happy for you."

"Thanks. We're both thrilled. There's just the big royal thing to get over and then we'll be fine. Now tell me again what you said."

Renee worked with Bethany to get the statement how she wanted it. They talked for another thirty minutes or so, then Renee drove back to her office. On the way, she thought about how lucky Carol and Pallas were to have their babies. Now Bethany was pregnant. She would guess it was just a matter of time until Natalie and Silver were pregnant, too. She and Wynn were the only ones not married and Wynn had her son, Hunter, so she wasn't totally alone.

It was hard to be left behind, Renee thought sadly as she waited at a light. She wanted it all—husband, kids, a normal life—and she couldn't have it. She'd thought just sex might be enough but even that had gone spectacularly wrong. The universe was trying to tell her something and she should probably listen. When it came to a happily-ever-after, she was doomed to nothing but disappointment.

Jasper was willing to admit that he'd reached the virtual bottom of guydom. He wasn't sorry about what he'd done, but he was sorry Renee was upset with him. The moral equivalent of not regretting the crime while disliking the consequences.

In the three days since it had all gone to hell with Renee,

he'd emailed with Hanna three times, getting more details about their wedding, along with several stories about how they met and two pictures of their cat. They were a cute couple and he knew they would be a great resource and he should have been happy only he wasn't. He felt guilty and possibly ashamed, although he wasn't ready to admit the latter. Not yet. And if all the emotional angst wasn't punishment enough, he couldn't write.

This wasn't the *I don't understand women so Mandy is a one-dimensional cliché.* Nope, he actually couldn't put words to paper.

He'd been trying. He had lots of ideas. He'd worked on the plot, had developed Mandy's character a little more, all of which went fine, but when it came to writing the story, he sat in front of his computer and thought about how he'd screwed up with Renee.

Not that he was going to take it back. He wasn't. He needed Hanna and Graham to help him. Plus, he wasn't going to mess with their wedding. Not in a serious way. They were excited to be a part of his book, so it was possible he'd added to the wedding. They were special and didn't everyone want to be special?

None of which helped with the lack of writing, so he finally gave up and drove to town. He went up and down the main streets, circling closer to Weddings Out of the Box but never actually getting there. At the last minute, he made a left turn and found his way to Wynn's print shop. He parked and went inside.

He had no idea what he was going to say to her or why he was even here, which turned out not to be a problem. She took one look at him and called for one of her workers to man the front desk, then motioned for him to follow her into her office.

"What?" she demanded when she'd closed the door behind him. "What did you do?"

"Maybe I didn't do anything."

She put her hands on her hips and glared at him. "Really? Then why are you here?"

She had the whole mom-stare down cold—no doubt due to years of practice. She looked good in black pants and a multicolored short-sleeved sweater. Her hair was long and curly, her eyes were dark and thickly fringed with lashes.

Funny how he'd never noticed her lashes before. Should he talk about Mandy's lashes in the book? Did guys notice lashes? He hadn't until just now, so probably not, although—

"Jasper!"

He returned to the present moment. "What?"

"Tell me what's going on." Her gaze narrowed. "It's Renee, isn't it? Do not tell me you've messed that up already."

"What? No. How did you know about Renee?"

"She told me you two had gotten together and wanted to make sure I was fine with it."

Damn—women really did talk about everything. Renee had told Wynn about their night together? He hadn't said a word to anyone. Not that he was keeping a secret—it simply hadn't occurred to him to say anything.

Wynn's sharp expression softened. "I told her it was okay. You and I were over months ago."

There was something in her tone. At least he thought there was. "What aren't you telling me?"

She smiled. "Nothing."

He didn't believe her but wasn't sure he really wanted to know. The whole woman thing was so much more complicated than he'd ever realized.

"I'm sorry about before," she told him. "When we were going out. I was wrong to be so arbitrary about Hunter."

"You mean telling me he and I couldn't be friends? You *were* wrong."

She laughed. "Yes, I was. I was scared of you becoming too important to him and then us breaking up. I should have seen that you would stay friends with him no matter what."

He didn't know what to do with that. While the apology was nice, he had a feeling it wasn't free. There was something else coming—he was sure of it.

"So you don't mind Hunter and I hang out now?"

"It's good for him. You were right. He needs a man in his life. As much as I want to be everything to him, that's not realistic."

"Maybe you'll meet someone and get married."

She rolled her eyes. "No, thank you. I'm not interested in anything permanent."

They'd had that in common, he thought. He knew his reasons—he'd been damaged in the war and would never be healed enough to fall in love—but what about Wynn? What were her demons?

Before he could ask, she said, "This conversation is not about me. You're the one who showed up on my doorstep."

"I didn't know where else to go. Do you really think you're going to be alone for the rest of your life?" Did Mandy? Did she want more? And if she didn't, why not?

"Sometimes love isn't practical," she told him. "It's not about wanting or not wanting, it's about what can be. You assume you can't fall in love because you're too broken from what happened in Afghanistan."

"I was warned it was a likely outcome."

"Maybe then, but you've changed a lot. When you first moved to town, you kept to yourself. We barely saw you. Then you started making friends. We got together. It was nearly a year, Jasper. That's a big deal."

"It didn't work out."

"It was the best we could do at the time. My point is you've come a long way. Hunter said you even have a dog."

"I didn't plan on getting a dog."

"You still have one, even without a plan. You're getting better by the week. I think you're a lot closer to normal than you want to believe. Now tell me what happened with Renee."

He wanted to say that she was wrong, that he hadn't healed as much as she claimed, that he would never be right and he was okay with that. Only he didn't want to fight with her and suddenly the need to know what to do about Renee seemed more important than anything else.

"I told her I wanted to be involved with one of her weddings. Sit in on the meetings, understand why the bride and groom were making the decisions they were, listen to them pick out stuff."

Wynn frowned. "Why on earth would you want to do that?"

"In the book I'm writing Vidar's love interest is a wedding planner and the serial killer is somehow involved with the weddings."

"Oh dear God, you're not subtle, are you?" She rubbed her temple. "Let me guess. Renee said no way, no how because she would never agree to that." She looked up at him, her eyes wide. "Tell me you didn't go behind her back and charm some couple into letting you get involved."

He shifted his weight, then shoved his hands in jeans pockets. "Maybe."

"You are the dumbest of the dumb. She must be furious with you. Personally I'd hire someone to beat you up and then set you on fire. How could you? And don't tell me you needed it for the book. Yes, it's how you make your living, blah, blah, blah. We're talking about the woman you were sleeping with. We're talking about a friend. You dismissed her feelings and violated everything she cared about. She let you into her world, she trusted you, and you betrayed that trust and her."

He opened his mouth to say it wasn't like that at all, only before he could speak, he realized it was exactly that. He'd done those things and more. He'd acted as if what she thought didn't matter. He'd treated her badly, then he'd rubbed her nose in it.

"I see the light bulb," Wynn said.

"I was terrible," he breathed. "I messed up everything."

"Yes, you did."

She opened the door and pushed him into the hallway.

"What are you doing?" he demanded. "We have to talk. You need to tell me what to do to fix this."

"Sorry. That's not my problem. I suggest you go home and think about everything you did wrong. Revel in your wrongness and when you feel you understand it fully, wallow just a little more. Only then can you go and apologize to Renee."

Before he knew what was happening, she'd pushed him out onto the sidewalk and turned and walked away. Jasper stood there, the self-loathing growing by the second. He felt awful and he had no idea what he was supposed to do now.

CHAPTER EIGHT

Renee hadn't seen Jasper in nearly a week. She'd passed through the stages of grief at least three times and then kept circling back to anger. Probably because it was such an energizing emotion. She was dealing with all her weddings, enjoying her work with only occasional flashes of how much she really disliked him when he surprised her by walking into her office at two in the afternoon.

She glared at him, ignoring the huge bouquet of flowers he placed on her desk. Flowers didn't come close to making up for what he'd done.

They stared at each other. Renee was determined not to speak first. She might have to deal with him on the Scottish wedding, but she wasn't going to make it easy. She wondered if it was still possible to have someone tarred and feathered and if so, what that entailed. Could you buy feathers in bulk and did they have to be a certain kind?

"I'm sorry."

Renee allowed her face to shift from unreadable to disbelieving.

Jasper sat across from her. "Renee, I mean it. I apologize for what I did. I was wrong. You told me you didn't want me involved in a specific wedding and instead of listening, I went behind your back. I betrayed your trust. I get that."

"Do you? Or is this where you tell me it was worth it because you have a book to write?"

He drew in a breath. "You told me these are people's lives. That they'll remember their weddings forever and I have no right to get involved in that. You were right and I was wrong and I'm sorry."

"But?"

His gaze locked with hers. "I was wrong."

She felt the first crack in the emotional wall she'd erected, followed by a second crack and a few bricks tumbling down.

"I'm going to contact Hanna and Graham and tell them I won't be bothering them anymore."

"It's too late to do that. They're both excited. If you back out now, you'll disappoint them so I'm stuck and you get what you want."

He looked a lot more miserable than triumphant, which almost made her feel better. Almost.

"I didn't want to hurt you," he said.

"You didn't care about hurting me."

"I didn't, but I do now." He put his hands on her desk. "For me, writing is capturing the movie I see in my head. It has to be clear to me before I can get it on to the page. When it's not going well, I'm constantly scrambling to solve the problem and when I get into problem-solving mode—"

"You don't give up."

"I don't."

"We need a safe word."

His eyebrows shot up. "We do?"

She did her best to keep from smiling. "Not for that. For

when you get too involved in your story. I need a word or a phrase that will remind you to stop being a crazy writer and start being a human being again. I can't work with you if I can't get through to you."

"I know. I'm sorry."

There were more cracks and more tumbling bricks until the wall was pretty much gone and she was left with wanting to tell him everything would be fine. Only she didn't because while she believed him, she wasn't totally sure she could trust him.

As if reading her mind, he asked, "Am I forgiven?"

She wanted to say he was, only she wasn't all the way there yet. "That's going to take some time and work on your part."

"Fair enough. Are you sure about keeping me on the Scottish wedding?"

"Yes. Just don't try to influence them. Let them do what they want to do." Her voice was sharper than she meant it to be and she sighed. "Let them have their wedding."

"I will. You have my word."

"Are you sure you want to offer that?" she asked. "If you break your word, you're leaving me with nothing."

She tried to keep her tone light so he wouldn't guess how close her statement was to the very heart of the problem. She liked Jasper, she wanted to keep liking him, but if he broke his word again, she couldn't. And there wouldn't be a third chance. She just didn't have that in her.

"I give you my word I will not knowingly influence Hanna and Graham. What I ask in return is if I accidentally start down that path that you kick me in the shins to help me remember."

One corner of her mouth turned up. "You've seen my shoes. You sure you want to risk that?"

"Yes."

"Okay. Kicking it is." She pulled a file out of a stack on her desk. "The apple wedding is this weekend. By now I assume Silver's been in touch about that."

He frowned. "You're going to let me help at the apple wedding?"

"I was always going to do that, Jasper. I was pissed but I'd said you could."

He grimaced. "You're saying you don't go back on your word."

"Something like that." She opened the folder. "You know what to wear. You'll be walking around with a tray of premade drinks and that's all. Respect the wedding and the participants. Don't initiate conversation with anyone. You've been to fancy parties and events before. The servers are invisible. Observe all you want but don't engage. Agreed?"

"I'll be a ghost," he told her. "I really am sorry."

"I believe you."

She did believe him. But trusting him—that was something else entirely.

Jasper arrived at the apple wedding a full two hours before the ceremony started. He was still feeling guilty about his behavior, which he didn't like, and figured the only way to make things better was to let his actions show Renee he wasn't a total loser.

He parked at the far end of the parking lot, as instructed, and made his way toward the Airstream trailer set up by the gate on the property.

He could see into the open, outdoor area of Weddings Out of the Box. Dozens of round tables had been set up on the grass. The chairs were a stained light brown, the linens a bright apple green and white. Flowers and some kind of small apple made up low centerpieces at some tables while others had tall clear vases filled with Granny Smith apples. Place cards were attached to apples, continuing the theme.

He'd been reading up on weddings and receptions and had even bought a few bride magazines. He'd ordered those online so he wouldn't have to explain himself to a grocery clerk he would have to face again when he bought groceries.

He knew about place settings and charger plates and the issues with votives (they burn out quickly) versus tapers (tall candles were an inherent danger, what with people brushing up against them). Stacey Treadway and her fiancé, Felix, had chosen votives but instead of using a traditional holder, they'd place them in hollowed-out apples.

He spotted the table where the cake would be set up and wondered what kind the bride and groom had chosen. Something apple-y, he would guess.

He still wasn't sure who his serial killer would be. Not the bride and groom—that he knew for sure. It seemed too complicated. From what he'd read, both would be extremely busy on their wedding day. Plus, they couldn't be a bride and groom over and over, which made being a serial killer more complicated. The same could be said for the family members, which left the catering staff, the officiant and anyone else who worked around weddings, such as the cake baker or florist. He was also still considering a random stranger who crashed the party.

But this was not the time for him to be thinking about that, he reminded himself. He was here to work. He made his way to the Airstream, where he would report for duty. Silver Lovato, a platinum blonde with great business skill and some serious attitude glanced at him before pointing to a stack of aprons on a small table by the rear wheels of the trailer.

"You're early. That's encouraging. Put on an apron and

then wash your hands. You can help me set up. We'll start with martini glasses."

As instructed, he'd worn a white long-sleeved shirt and khakis. He rolled up his sleeves and washed his hands, then began pulling out trays of martini glasses from storage lockers in the trailer.

The Airstream had been converted into a traveling bar—in keeping with Silver's business name: AlcoHaul. The previous year she'd taken on her now-husband, Drew, as a business partner and they'd expanded from a single trailer to a total of three, allowing them to grow the business. From what his friend Drew had shared, these days Silver was more into overall management than handling specific events, but every now and then she worked a wedding.

Silver showed him where to stack the glasses.

"We have two hundred guests," she said. "The drink list is simple. Appletinis and beer. There will be champagne for the toast, but the catering staff is handling that, so not our problem. There is nonalcoholic apple cider for those who want it. Water, iced tea and soft drinks are also handled by the catering staff. If anyone asks for that, point them to the far side of the room. That table there will have pitchers of water and iced tea along with tubs filled with canned soda."

He nodded, wondering if he should be taking notes.

"There is a dishwasher in this trailer," she continued, her blue eyes staring intently into his. "You will load it the way I tell you. You will check with me before starting it. The wash cycle is fifteen minutes. We will need to run the dishwasher continuously for the second hour of the reception. I brought four hundred glasses. That will not be enough."

He stared at her. "We'll go through more than four hundred glasses?"

Her expression turned pitying. "You really don't know

what you're doing, do you? According to Renee, there aren't children at this wedding. That means two hundred adults. I always assume two drinks in the first hour and one drink per hour after that. Assuming the usual five to six hours, that's at least eight hundred glasses, not taking into account people leaving their glasses somewhere, or changing their mind about what they want."

"Eight *hundred*?"

"Uh-huh. Back in the day, we washed them by hand." She flashed him a grin. "Be glad you're not going to have to do that."

She motioned to the large portable bar she'd set up in front of the trailer. "I'm cheating. I'll be premixing batches of the appletinis and storing them in pitchers in the refrigerator. When we get the high sign that the ceremony is nearly over, we'll pour them into shakers, add a little ice and start filling glasses. The first twenty minutes will be the worst. However many drinks we have ready, it's not enough."

She pointed to the kegs sitting in ice. "I have more helpers coming. They'll handle that. No guests touch the keg. If you see it happening, come get me." Her eyes narrowed. "Do not take on a drunk guest yourself. You don't know what you're doing and you'll only escalate the situation. Do I make myself clear?"

Jasper thought about pointing out not only didn't he work for Silver, he, in fact, wasn't getting paid. He was helping out to learn about weddings. But as her gaze held his, he thought maybe that was not the smartest thing in the world to be saying right now.

"Yes, ma'am."

"Good." She started toward the building. "Let's get our update."

He had no idea what she was talking about, but obediently

followed her toward the main building. When they were in the paved courtyard, Renee stepped out, tablet in hand.

He'd seen her dressed for the office, but not working a wedding. He was used to tailored dresses and suits, but there was something about the short-sleeved dark green dress she had on. Maybe because he knew she had dressed to be invisible and had failed miserably.

The muted color of the dress made her eyes an even deeper green. She'd pulled her long red hair back into a sleek ponytail that he would guess was easy and wedding-appropriate yet gave her a sexy-librarian air. Even her low-heeled shoes were oddly appealing and he had no idea why.

But while he was having all kinds of inappropriate thoughts, she barely acknowledged him, instead focusing on Silver.

"Catering is good to go. The cake is delayed. They're claiming traffic, but I have my doubts. The baker is in Orange County. Once they clear Palm Desert, there's nothing between them and Happily Inc but a few jackrabbits. I think they got a late start."

Silver winced. "How late?"

"We're hoping they arrive during the ceremony." Renee pointed to the waiting table with small plates, a large carving knife and no cake. "The design is supposed to be simple so they say setup will be less than thirty minutes, but that still means they're setting up during the reception."

Renee drew in a breath. "The alternative is to have them work in a private room, then carry the completed cake out during the reception."

"That could go very badly," Jasper said, picturing a towering wedding cake falling to the ground.

"Tell me about it," she said. "I explained to Stacey that a Friday delivery was preferable but she was afraid something would happen to it in the night. As if we haven't kept hundreds of wedding cakes safe before."

"If the cake people need help carrying anything, I'm available," he told her.

She flashed him a quick smile. "Thanks." She looked back at Silver. "Please tell me you're in good shape."

"I'm in great shape. I'm about to start mixing up the appletinis. The kegs are set up and ready to go. My staff will arrive in the next fifteen minutes and I have extra help from Jasper. Go back to your wedding."

"Thanks. I can always count on you." She looked at the empty cake table. "Stacey is going to have to decide what she wants to do about the tardy cake."

With that, she turned and went into the building. Jasper watched her go.

"Does that happen a lot?" he asked. "Things being late?"

"There is always a disaster somewhere," Silver said cheerfully. "The key is good planning so whatever it is, it's mitigated. A few years back we were all robbed at gunpoint." She chuckled. "Turned out it was only a flare gun, but still. Scary in the moment. Oh, and another time there were zebras that got loose."

They reached her trailer.

"Want to learn how to make great appletinis?" she asked.

"Sure."

"Good answer. Some people go straight for the apple-flavored vodka, but I think that's cheating. Mine use regular vodka, lemon juice, apple liqueur, apple juice and simple syrup. More work for me but a better product for the client. And as you know, it's all about the bride and groom."

Nearly three hours later Jasper stood holding a surprisingly heavy tray, waiting for guests to walk out of the ceremony.

Across the reception area, the cake people were frantically setting up a three-tiered cake frosted in pale green and decorated with flowers and small crab apples. He only knew they were crab apples because Silver had told him. Otherwise, he wouldn't have had a clue.

The doors to the main building opened and people flowed out—most of them heading for him. He held his tray steady and murmured, "Appletini?" as they grabbed glasses.

"Got anything else?" a tall older man asked, glaring at the green drink.

"Beer over by the bar."

"Thank God." The man looked at the woman next to him. "Can you believe it?"

"It was a little upsetting," she said, taking an appletini and finishing nearly half of it in a single swallow.

Seconds later, Jasper's tray was empty. He set it down but before he could pick up the second one he had ready, the guests swarmed around and emptied it, as well.

Sixty drinks in less than a minute, he thought, a little stunned by the realization that Silver hadn't been kidding about the post-ceremony rush.

Fortunately she and her team already had two more trays ready. Jasper stepped in to help at the second keg and quickly filled glasses, all the while listening to murmurs of outrage. Obviously something had happened, but he had no idea what.

When the initial drink rush was over, Silver set him to work mixing more drinks. Renee hurried over to check on them.

"We're good," Silver told her. "No problems here. What happened during the ceremony? Everyone's talking about something."

Renee winced. "The officiant was a friend of the family, from the groom's side. He called the bride by the ex-girlfriend's name twice during the vows. The best man forgot the rings back at his hotel and he's not staying in town, so there wasn't time for him to rush back and get them."

Jasper might not know anything about weddings, but even he could guess that using the wrong name was not a good sign. Before he could say anything, the bride and groom appeared and everyone applauded.

For the next hour, he circulated with appletinis while the guests mingled and snacked on appetizers. The best man appeared with the rings and there was an impromptu second ceremony where the bride and groom slipped them on, then kissed.

He returned to the trailer only to have Silver whisper, "Are you listening to the music?"

"I haven't been." He'd been too busy trying to take in all the activity while still doing his job.

"The DJ is only playing breakup songs. Someone told me his girlfriend dumped him last night. This wedding is turning into a disaster. Poor Renee."

He searched the crowd and saw Renee heading purposefully toward the DJ. She looked plenty determined and if Jasper were a betting man he would put his money on the fiery redhead. As far as she was concerned, this was her couple's special day and no one, not even a heartbroken DJ, was going to get in the way of that.

Renee didn't bother drying her hair after her shower. She combed it out and then quickly braided it to get it out of the way. She pulled on yoga pants and a T-shirt before walking barefoot to the kitchen. After getting out plates and napkins, she poured herself a big glass of water and then slumped into a chair.

Her feet hurt, her back hurt, her head hurt, but the apple

wedding and reception were behind her. She didn't have to think about anything for the next forty-eight hours and she planned to take full advantage of that. And lucky for her, after the wedding, Jasper had offered to stop by with dinner—which made him fifteen kinds of hero in her book.

She heard a knock on the door.

"It's open," she called, then watched Jasper walk in with a big pizza box and a six-pack of beer. Whatever misgivings she might have still harbored disappeared when she saw him. Right now, she would forgive nearly anything if someone fed her and got her a little liquored up.

He opened a beer and passed it to her, then slid a slice of pizza onto her plate.

"Eat," he told her. "You've got to be starving."

"I am. This is great. Usually I have to forage around for leftovers. I keep telling myself to plan ahead and have a simple meal waiting, but so far that hasn't happened."

She took a bite of the hot pizza and tried not to moan at the deliciousness of it. They ate in silence for the first slice, then took a second to catch their breath before diving in again.

"What did you think?" she asked.

"It was overwhelming. There are so many moving parts. I know you have that program and all, but I still don't know how you do this every single weekend. The cake disaster, the DJ, the guy who choked on a piece of apple. There was something happening all the time."

"We don't usually have guests choking," she said, reaching for more pizza. "Thank goodness we had people there who knew what to do. I can perform the Heimlich maneuver, but that guy was huge. I wasn't sure I could get enough leverage. But he was fine and the party went on."

"What about the parents fighting? They got loud."

"Parents fight all the time. It's a way to release tension

after months of dealing with their baby getting married. At least the DJ's song selections got more upbeat." She grinned as she spoke.

He studied her. "What did you do to make that happen?"

She raised a shoulder. "I might have mentioned his predicament to one of the bridesmaids who thought he was really cute. They started talking and I'm pretty sure they stole away for a quickie."

Jasper's mouth dropped open. "You're kidding."

"I'm guessing, but I'd put money on it. They were both holding hands and smiling a lot after his break."

"I had no idea."

"Now you do." She reached for her beer. "No more wedding mysteries for you. Now you've seen one up close and personal. Well, not the ceremony, but the rest of it."

As she spoke she realized she probably should have told him he could watch the ceremony from the back. The next one, she told herself.

"It was a learning experience for sure," he said. "Silver hustles with the drinks. She said there would be a rush, but I had no idea what she meant until it happened. I enjoyed being thrown in the deep end. I really do learn by doing." His gaze locked with hers. "I want to apologize again, for going behind your back. I am sorry."

"Stop apologizing. I believe you. Of course if it happens again, I'm going to hire someone to beat you up."

"I'm sure you have the name of someone in your contact list."

She smiled. "I just might."

"I wouldn't be surprised. So was this a typical wedding?"

"There is no such thing. They're all different. Not just the themes but the people involved. The families generally set the emotional tone and that makes a difference. I've had bitchy brides like you wouldn't believe but if everyone else is normal, then it's not so bad. Weddings are highly stressful so we often see the best and worst of people. Every now and then either the bride or groom surprises me on their wedding day, but usually not. I generally know who's going to be easy to work with and who is going to make me earn my paycheck."

They'd finished the pizza and beers. Jasper opened a second bottle, then stood and pulled her to her feet.

"I learned a lot today," he said, drawing her close.

Renee slipped into his embrace and let a sense of anticipation wash over her. Yes, she was tired, but Jasper was exactly what she needed to end her night.

The thought of him touching her, arousing her, bringing her to climax had her on her toes and pressing her mouth against his. He kissed her slowly, deeply, as if they had all the time in the world. His hands moved up and down her back even as his tongue claimed her. She was just about to suggest they take this party into the bedroom when he stepped back.

He handed her the open beer and pointed to the sofa. "You need to relax and then get some sleep. I'll talk to you tomorrow."

He was leaving? He was *leaving*?

"What are you doing?"

He gave her a slow, sexy smile. "You said you wanted foreplay. That was foreplay."

Before she could say anything, he kissed her again, then left. Renee stared at the closed door, then shook her head. And people said women were complicated.

CHAPTER NINE

Monday night Renee sat across from Jasper at The Board-room. While they'd texted a few times yesterday and this morning, she hadn't seen him since the "foreplay" kiss at her place, Saturday night.

She still wasn't sure what she made of what had happened. While she respected his willingness to go along with her requests, she had kind of been interested in a little more. Maybe later tonight, she thought happily as Nick and Pallas joined them.

"Does anyone know what the game is tonight?" Pallas asked, concealing a yawn behind her hand.

"Rough night with Ryan?" Renee asked sympathetically. "Is he teething?"

"He was pretty good, but that wedding on Sunday about did me in."

Renee tried not to react as a jab of guilt pierced her. "I should have been there, Pallas. I'm sorry."

"No, you shouldn't have. You've been working six days a week for months now. It was a small wedding party of thirty people and it was a brunch. Everyone was gone by three in the afternoon. I'm not complaining, I'm just saying I'm out of practice."

"Weddings are a lot of work," Jasper said. "It's no wonder you're tired."

Pallas smiled at him. "That's right. You went to the apple wedding. I heard there was some excitement. So what did you think? Did you find out who your serial killer is?"

"He's going to crash the weddings he goes to. That allows me to set them up however I want. I think he's righting wrongs—killing a cheater, or a child abuser. Doing the wrong thing for the right reason."

"I'm not sure there is a crime that deserves someone being killed by a serial killer," Renee said.

"That's because you're a good person," Jasper told her. "I look forward to being around more weddings to get a real feel for them. The level of drama means everyone is on emotional high alert. That's good for me."

He glanced at Renee as if expecting her to say something. She supposed she should mention his serial killer cooties messing up her couples' happy day, but she really didn't have it in her. He'd been great at the apple wedding. Stacey and Felix hadn't known he wasn't one of Silver's regular servers. He'd done his job and had observed in such a way that no one had guessed. Given that, she supposed there wasn't really a reason to object.

Pallas yawned again. "Sorry. I'll rally."

Nick looked at her. "You're being ridiculous."

"You don't think I'll rally? I really will."

He squeezed her hand. "Not that. You're working too hard. Ryan is still a baby and while I understand you want to be back at work, you also want to be with him. You're running yourself ragged doing both."

"But I need to be in the office. Renee has been doing both our jobs for too long already."

"Agreed." Nick smiled at her. "There's an easy solution. Make Renee a partner so she can manage things, then hire staff to take care of the day-to-day wedding business. You two can't keep doing it all yourself. The business is getting too big. You need help."

Pallas nodded slowly. "You have a point. I need to think about it."

She smiled at Renee, who was doing her best to sit there calmly, as if they weren't discussing her future. She had no idea what to say or do other than look normal and wait for the game of the night to be announced.

Take her on as a partner? Would Pallas want to do that? Would she want it for herself?

She knew the answer even as she mentally asked the question. Of course she did. She wanted to be a part of something. She wanted to have a place in Weddings Out of the Box and the town. Not just an "I work here" place but one that said she totally and completely belonged.

Hope blossomed. She told herself it was early days yet and a lot of things could change, but still, a partner!

The Boardroom servers began passing out the game of the night. Renee glanced at the familiar cover of Risk and tried to remember how to play. She was too excited to think.

She felt Jasper reach under the table and lightly squeeze her hand. She looked at him and he winked, as if he got what she was thinking and he was there for her. Which was a lot to read into a hand squeeze/wink, but she was going to go with it, regardless.

Jasper sat in the Weddings Out of the Box conference room and had no idea what to expect. Renee had texted him that she had a meeting with Hanna and Graham and that he was welcome to attend. But when he arrived, she'd told him it was a video conference meeting, which was how a lot of her prep meetings were handled.

"Not everyone can get to Happily Inc a dozen or so times before the wedding," she said, setting up her computer and tablet. "Hanna and Graham live relatively close, so we'll see them more than we see most of our clients, but even they don't want to drive in every time."

She had him sit across from her at the large table, then passed him an agenda. "We're hoping to cover all this today. Not every decision will be made, but we'll make a run at them. I have a few samples to show them but the most important issue is the timetable. They've booked the venue for an entire weekend. I want to work out the hours to make sure the contract doesn't need to be amended and that we're charging them the right amount."

She smiled. "Too much information?"

"Not yet but I'm sure we'll get there."

He'd never helped plan a wedding so he had no idea what to expect beyond what he'd read in the bridal magazines. He'd ripped out to-do lists to bring with him. Hanna and Graham's wedding had been fast-tracked so they wouldn't have the usual year or so to plan.

Renee set file folders on the table, then typed on her computer. The large screen on the wall lit up. He saw that Hanna and Graham would be on the left, while whatever material they were sharing with each other would appear on the right. Exactly at 10:00 a.m. Renee initiated the phone call that would conference them together.

Hanna appeared first, waving at them. Graham followed.

"Hi, everyone," Hanna called, waving. "Hi, sweetie. How's New York?"

"Busy," Graham said. "I miss you."

"I miss you, too." Hanna laughed. "We'll be done now with the lovey-dovey stuff and we can start the meeting."

"The lovey-dovey stuff is my favorite," Renee assured her. "You know Jasper's here for the meeting, as well, right?"

"Hi, Jasper," Hanna said. "We're so excited about the book. Thanks for the notes you sent. I love being involved in the process."

"Thanks for letting me sit in on this," he said. "Pretend I'm not here."

Renee picked up the first folder. "Let's confirm the events," she said. "Friday night is the rehearsal dinner. We'll have the actual rehearsal at five and the dinner will follow at six. Things will wrap up by nine."

She paused, as if waiting for them to respond.

"I want to go later," Graham said with a shrug, "but you and Hanna are right. The big event is the next night and we don't want to be tired or hungover."

"Exactly." Renee flipped to another page. "The ceremony will start Saturday at five, with the reception at five thirty and running until eleven. Then you're back here at ten the next morning for a goodbye brunch."

Hanna glanced down at several pieces of paper. "That's what I have, too. Jasper, does that work for you?"

Jasper thought of how Renee had warned him just being around the couple would change things. "I'm good with whatever you decide."

Hanna nodded. "Okay, then the times work. What's next?"

Graham sighed. "My mom really wants the bagpipes to play 'Amazing Grace.' I know it's usually played at funerals, but this is important to her."

Jasper was more caught up in the fact that they were going

to have bagpipes at the wedding. He wasn't sure he'd ever heard live bagpipes before.

Hanna smiled. "Honey, it's fine. I already told you it was."

"But you really didn't want that song at the wedding."

"It's not what I would have picked but she's your mom and you're her only son and it's important to you. I want you to be happy and I want her to feel good about the day, too. It's one song. I can live with it, I swear." She looked at Renee. "'Amazing Grace' at the wedding."

"Why don't we have him play one or two songs while everyone is being seated," Renee said, making notes. "That way it's not just a single song that everyone focuses on. We can have 'Amazing Grace' be the last song performed on bagpipes, right before you walk down the aisle. You'll still be in the bride's room, so you can hear it, but it's less, um, in your face."

Hanna laughed. "An excellent compromise."

"Perfect." Renee pulled several lengths of fabric out of a bag. "I have the table runner samples to show you. We have a simple blue that matches the color in the tartan we're using or we can just go for it and use the tartan itself. Keep in mind the fabric is the same weight regardless. We'd use a computer generated design to print the tartan on the runners so while there's a cost difference, we're not talking about a heavy wool fabric."

She held each sample up in front of the camera at the head of the table.

"What do you think?" Hanna asked.

"Tartan," Graham said.

"Oh, good. That's the one I like, too."

The meeting went on for nearly two hours. After a while, Jasper stopped taking notes and instead just listened. Renee kept things moving along, but also gave the couple as much time as they needed to make decisions.

They all agreed they would have the caterer at the next meeting, along with Silver, so they could nail down the food and bar menus. Hanna had already picked a local florist who would work directly with Renee as the decoration decisions were made. By the time everyone logged off, they were further along than they had been but there was still work to be done.

When the screen went blank and Renee closed her computer, Jasper handed her back the agenda.

"I don't know how you do this, week after week."

"It's a lot of work but then a wedding is often the biggest party a couple will ever throw together. Details matter, so does making sure it all comes together."

"Which is where you come in." He thought about what they'd discussed and what he'd observed at the apple wedding. "I see the similarities."

"Some elements remain the same. The dress, the flowers, walking down the aisle, the food." She smiled. "Some kind of drama. But every wedding has its own personality. This is going to be a fun one."

"I'm looking forward to it."

"Me, too." She glanced at him. "There are people who say getting married doesn't change anything for a committed couple. That a piece of paper doesn't matter. But I don't believe that. It's a rite of passage in our society and the choice to participate in that, or not, makes a statement."

He wouldn't have thought of a wedding that way, but knew that she was right. So what did it say that his serial killer wanted to destroy that moment in someone's life? Did he care he was ruining the memories forever? Did he not think of it that way? Was the killing for the greater good?

"And I've lost you."

He looked at Renee. "Sorry. I was—"

"Working on the book. Yes, I'm starting to recognize the glazed look. Go home and be brilliant."

"No. You let me be a part of this. I should at least..." What? Buy her lunch? Take her to bed? The latter was the most appealing, he admitted. But would it be tacky to ask?

She laughed as she stood. "Go," she repeated. "I will see you later. You're in the zone. Take advantage of it."

He grabbed his notes, circled the table, kissed her briefly, then headed for his truck.

Maybe the serial killer wasn't thinking about the damage he was doing. Maybe that was something he figured out along the way and it bothered him. That would give him some interesting angst as he plotted his next murder.

So many possibilities, Jasper thought happily as he drove home. Inspiration was everywhere.

"I've been thinking about what Nick mentioned the other night," Pallas said at their weekly update meeting.

Renee kept her expression neutral, waiting for Pallas to come down on one side of the issue or the other. She didn't want to assume good news.

"I don't know why I didn't think of it myself." Pallas smiled at her. "I'd love to have you as a partner, if you're interested."

"I am. I have a lot of ideas about how we could divide the labor—especially with you having Ryan. And I've been thinking about hiring people. Would we want one or two full-time employees who can do everything or more part-time employees who are specialized?"

"Oh, you mean like wedding specialists to help on the day? I think that would be great. Another pair of eyes and hands to help with whatever happens."

"Exactly." Renee leaned toward her. "I think you should stop handling wedding days completely. At least for the next few months. Why not manage more of the meetings and let me deal with the weddings?"

"Until we hire some people," Pallas said.

"Until then."

"You are exactly who this business needed. You're so reliable and creative and easy to get along with. I'd be lost without you." Pallas paused. "I really want to move forward with this. Let me think about the best way to bring you on board. In the meantime, I'd like you to be thinking about what you would like the partnership to be. We'll discuss it all in a couple of weeks. Does that work?"

"Absolutely."

Renee floated back to her office. On her next day off, she would take the morning to put together her thoughts. She'd been given an exciting opportunity and she really wanted to make it happen.

When she slipped into her chair, she had the brief thought that if Pallas knew *everything* about her, she might not be so willing to take her on as a partner. Not that she ever needed to find out. Renee was getting good at keeping that part of her life separate.

She finished up her paperwork and was about to head home when she got a call from Jasper.

"How's it going?" he asked when she picked up the phone.

"Good. Today was actually light and I was just about to go home." She hoped she sounded more casual than she felt. To be honest, she was hoping he was asking for a booty call because she was so over the whole foreplay thing. What had she been thinking when she even suggested that?

"I was wondering if I could get your help with something," he said. "Want to come by? I'll provide dinner."

"Sure. What do you need help with?"

He hesitated a second before admitting, "Kissing."

Renee started to laugh. "I can say from personal experience, that's not really true."

"Thanks for the endorsement, but I'm talking about in the book rather than in life. I don't know what to write or how to describe it. Writing 'he kissed her' seems like cheating, but if I go much further than that, it's too much detail."

"Porn?" she asked helpfully.

"So I've been told." His tone was a little defensive. "How do other writers do it? I could never write romance. Give me an action scene anytime. Shooting is fun or I can always do a nice scene where someone's throat gets slit. I'm good at that."

"Poor Jasper. Brought to his knees by touchy-feely emotions and a few kisses."

"I wouldn't say brought to my knees," he grumbled.

"I know and that's what makes it so fun. I'll wrap things up here and drive to your place."

Before she hung up, she got his address, then quickly finished her work for the day. She thought about stopping by her place to change clothes, but didn't want to take the time. She felt all fluttery with anticipation. She and Jasper hadn't really had much of a chance to hang out for a while now. Okay, they'd recently had dinner and before that they'd been working on wedding stuff, but it wasn't the same as just spending an evening together. Plus, there was the promise of kissing, at the very least. He was always saying he learned by doing and she was up for a fair amount of doing, wherever that might lead.

She put his address into her car nav system, then followed the directions out of town and up the mountain. She knew that Ronan and Natalie also lived well above the town, but thought their place was in a different direction. Despite having lived in Happily Inc well over a year, she hadn't done much exploring. Work kept her busy and it wasn't that fun on her own.

She went up the side of the mountain, occasionally glancing at her outside temperature gauge. In Happily Inc, the sunny afternoon had been ninety-seven degrees. Up in the mountains, the temperature had dropped to seventy-eight, which was a big difference. She would bet at night it got even cooler. Jasper could sleep with his windows open, if he wanted.

She was still fantasizing about cool breezes on bare skin when she spotted his house number on a mailbox and pulled onto the long, paved driveway. There were trees on either side and a sense of being a long way from Happily Inc.

She saw the house up ahead. It was plenty big, but in a hodgepodge kind of way, as if it had been added on to every generation or so, with no thought of symmetry or style. There was a big porch and what looked like the original cabin, then additions jutting out in all directions.

She parked and got out of her car. Jasper walked out to greet her, looking all tall and manly and sexy enough to make her whimper. Kissing was not going to cut it, she told herself. She was going to have to insist they go all the way or she was going to be really cranky.

He smiled and drew her into his arms, then pressed his mouth to hers. He tasted of mint and promise and just hanging on to his lean, strong body was enough to get her ready.

"Hi," he said when he drew back. "Thanks for coming over."

"Thanks for inviting me," she said, staring into his eyes. "Is this really about research or did you lure me up here?"

One corner of his mouth turned up. "A little of both."

"I like the honesty." She briefly rested her head on his chest, then turned to the house. "So this is great."

"It's a mess but it works for me. Come on inside and I'll give you the tour."

They walked up the front steps and moved into the house.

It took a second for her eyes to adjust to the less bright interior. She had a brief impression of hardwood floors and big windows and really ugly furniture. She was about to tease him about it when something moved. Something large and dark and alive.

She jumped back and pressed a hand to her chest. "You have a dog!"

She knew she sounded horrified, which was pretty okay because that was how she felt. She swung to face him, hoping he would say she was wrong and it was just a big, hairy rocking chair or something.

Jasper looked surprised. "That's Koda. You knew I had a dog."

"No, I didn't. When did this happen? You never said you had a dog. You can't. You really can't. I don't do well with pets." Dogs especially, because they seemed so knowing and aware and what had he been thinking?

She risked a quick glance at the massive creature stalking her. "Okay, I have to go."

"Renee, what's going on? Are you afraid of dogs? He's just an old guy who's very gentle. You don't have to be scared."

Scared of a dog? If only it were that simple, she thought, all thoughts of kissing and sex and good times vanishing as she stared at the creature who would be her undoing.

It wasn't fair—not in the least—yet here she was, facing her worst fear and knowing the second she admitted the truth, nothing was ever going to be the same.

CHAPTER TEN

Jasper had no idea what was going on. If he were to line up ten people he knew, he would assume Renee would be the last one to have an irrational fear of dogs. And while he still thought of Koda as *the dog* rather than *my dog*, he found himself feeling protective of his new family member.

He dropped to a crouch and called Koda to his side. When the dog sat next to him, Jasper looked at Renee.

"See, it's fine."

Her expression had faded from panicked to wary—an improvement, he supposed.

"He's a good guy," Jasper said, careful to keep his voice low and gentle. "I got him when I was on my book tour. Someone dumped him at an RV park and he was starving to death, so I took him in. He's very gentle. He likes it when I throw the ball or sticks and he has a stuffed toy rabbit he carries around in his mouth. He likes apples and cookies and sleeping by the fire. There's nothing to be frightened of."

Renee didn't look quite as worried, but she also wasn't getting any closer to Koda.

"I'm sure he's the perfect animal, I'm just not a dog person."

"But you're so softhearted."

"It's not anything I can explain. When I was little..." She pressed her lips together. "I always thought maybe one day I could get a cat, but so far I haven't been able to. It's more about my mother."

"Was she attacked by a dog?"

"No. It's— You wouldn't understand." She kept her gaze on Koda as she backed toward the kitchen. "If you can accept my fear isn't rational, then you should stop trying to explain it away."

She had a point, he thought, giving Koda another pat before rising to his feet. "Do you want to go home?"

She shook her head. "I'll still help. Why don't you leave him here and we can work in your office? You do have an office where you write, don't you?"

"Out the back of the kitchen."

She glanced over her shoulder, as if judging the distance, then began inching in that direction. Jasper told Koda to stay until she'd escaped to the hallway leading to his office, then released him.

"I'm sorry about this," he told the dog.

Koda seemed more resigned than upset. Jasper gave the dog a doggie cookie, then left him in the house and made his way to his office. He wasn't sure what to make of what had just happened. Renee being scared of dogs bothered him. No— not her being scared. It was how she'd reacted. He was disappointed that she hadn't made more of an effort. He didn't want to think she was the kind of person who didn't even try.

He pushed his questions and concerns aside and joined her in his office. She stood in the center of the room, looking at his desk and the pictures and plotting cards he'd pinned to the giant corkboard against the far wall.

"I didn't read anything," she said when she spotted him. "I don't want to intrude."

"You're not and I invited you. You can look at anything you like."

She stayed where she was and gave him a tight smile. "So do you have pages you want me to look at or are we going to talk about where you are in the book or what?"

What he'd wanted was for her to help him figure out how to describe a kiss only right now that didn't seem likely. Neither of them appeared to be in the mood. Pages might be safer.

He'd already printed out the scene he'd been working on. He grabbed the sheets from the printer.

"There have been three murders at different weddings around town," he said, handing over the sheets. "Vidar can't figure out the connection. In the first wedding, the victim is the bride's mother. At the second, it's a guest and with the third, it's one of the musicians. He's worried about Mandy's safety because with nothing tying the victims together, he can't find the pattern. They've been arguing about it and then he kisses her."

Renee listened, then glanced at the pages. "You want me to tell you what I think?"

He nodded even as he realized he didn't want to know she thought they were crap. Not that he wanted her to lie about them. Honest to God, when this was over, he was never writing a woman again. It was just too difficult.

Renee set down her small handbag and took the pages, then quickly scanned the four pages before starting over and reading them more slowly. When she was done, she said, "Mandy isn't mad."

"Why would she be mad?"

"Maybe *mad* isn't the right word. I'm not a writer, so I don't know how to describe it, but there should be something more going on. Vidar's really worried. He's telling Mandy the problem and that he wants her to be careful. She listens to him, smiles and says 'Yes, I will.'" Renee walked to the window, then looked back at him. "I can't explain what I'm feeling, I'm sorry."

"You're saying there's no energy between them. He's trying to save her life and she's buying apple juice."

"I'm not sure I would have put it that way, but sure."

She was right, he thought grimly. Vidar was upset and Mandy didn't share his feelings.

"She's not in danger," he said more to himself than to her. "She could be but we don't know if the serial killer is going to be at one of her weddings and regardless, she wouldn't be a victim. She's not a bad person. She'll never be in danger."

He swore under his breath. "This book is a disaster. I need Mandy in danger and I'm keeping her as far away from the bad stuff as possible, which is what Vidar wants but if she's not involved then there's no tension and what happened to my talent?"

"What if the bad person is someone she cares about?" Renee asked. "Like her sister or her boss? So the killer will be close and she's in danger but without being icky?" She shrugged. "Unless that's dumb, in which case forget I said it."

Jasper stared at her. "That would do it. Her business partner. Not her kid but someone else. Having it be her sister would work. What if her sister *is* her business partner?" He stalked toward her and grabbed her by her upper arms. "What if they're twins?"

"Twins is good."

"Twins is perfect. And just now—" He jogged back to where he'd been and retraced his steps, trying to maintain the right amount of energy as he looked at her.

"Vidar is trying to get her to understand she could be at

risk and she's not buying it. He's frustrated. He cares about her as a potential victim, of course, but it's more than that. He cares about her and she won't listen."

He looked at Renee, trying to feel what his character would feel. He grabbed her and held on, letting the emotions flow through him. He was focused on where his hands gripped her and how hard he held her and, when he kissed her, what her mouth felt like against his.

"That," he said eagerly, racing around to his laptop. "Just let me make a few notes. The kiss, the twin thing, all of it. Fifteen minutes tops."

He struggled to type fast enough to get it all down. His mind was flying as he made notes on various possibilities. He wrote until it was too dark to see his keyboard and suddenly realized that it had been a whole lot more than fifteen minutes and it was very unlikely that Renee had waited for him.

He got up and hurried to the house. After letting Koda out, he checked for her car, but it was gone. She'd left a note on the counter saying she was going to let him work and that she hoped it went well.

"Way to screw up," he muttered as he texted her an apology. Some days it seemed as if he couldn't get anything right. Worse, he'd really wanted to spend the evening with her. He'd missed them hanging out.

Koda walked back into the house and looked at him as if asking the state of meal service that evening. Jasper petted his dog as he headed to the pantry.

"I'll get right on that."

As for Renee and her reticence about animals, there was something there. Something she didn't want to tell him. He was going to have figure out a way to get her to trust him enough tell him the truth.

★ ★ ★

Renee berated herself the entire drive home. She shouldn't have reacted the way she did. She should have been more accepting of Jasper's dog. It was just…did it have to be a dog? Couldn't he have gotten a fish? She was pretty sure she could survive a fish. After all, what could it possibly have to say?

She got back to her apartment in time to realize not only wasn't she getting that booty call she'd been hoping for, she also didn't have anything for dinner. She debated the sensible decision of the grocery store where she could get a nice lean protein and some salad, but decided today was not the day to be sensible. Instead she ordered takeout Chinese, getting enough for three so she would have plenty left over for lunches for the rest of the week.

After loading her plate with a scoop from each of the containers, she went into the alcove/study where she had a small desk. She opened her personal laptop and checked to see if she had email (she did not) then went on Facebook to check out the happenings.

She smiled at the requisite postings of toddlers discovering something they hadn't encountered before, be it grass, a puddle or snow, then read up on her friends' lives. Her friend Nell had posted a link to a video of a party. Renee clicked on it, then found herself watching yet another video and another until she unexpectedly came across a gender reveal party.

A pretty brunette with an obvious baby bump motioned for two sets of parents to pull a cord. When they did, pink balloons floated down from the ceiling. There was lots of hugging and happy crying and plenty of laughter. The proud parents-to-be stood arm in arm, obviously thrilled with the news. The camera panned across the excited guests to a sign someone was putting up on the wall. *It's a Girl!*

Renee set down her plate and told herself it didn't matter.

So Turner and his wife were having a baby. It was bound to happen. Turner had always wanted kids. He loved children and couldn't wait to be a dad. He'd always said he wanted a girl first because he'd read a study in one of his psych classes that fathers bonded easily with the firstborn, regardless of gender, but if a daughter was born second, he might not make as much effort to connect with her.

Renee remembered how she'd pointed out that wasn't going to be a problem for him. He loved kids, wanted kids and he was going to bond regardless. Besides, unless he was going to have to stern talk with his sperm and get them to cooperate, there was no way to determine the outcome of any particular pregnancy until after the fact.

He'd called her Miss Smarty-Pants, as he had whenever he'd been teasing, then he'd pulled her into his arms and had kissed her.

"I want us to get married now," he'd whispered intently, as he'd undressed her. "I want us to get started on our lives."

His intensity had thrilled her and she'd nearly agreed. Only they both still had a year of college left and he hadn't yet met her mother. Renee knew however much she wanted to keep the two of them apart, she couldn't. Before she and Turner made things permanent, he was going to have to know the truth.

Now, in her small apartment, she brushed away tears. Not that she still loved Turner—she didn't. The pain was more about what could have been than anything specific, but that didn't make it any easier to deal with.

Renee had a difficult night of tossing and turning. The next morning she was exhausted and wished, just once, she could call in sick. But she had two weddings this coming weekend and a thousand details to deal with. She would suck it up and get through the day. And in a very few minutes, there would be coffee.

One shower and some leftover Chinese food for break- fast later, she was feeling a little more perky. The sadness had slipped below the surface where, she hoped, it would fade in time. If it didn't, she was going to have to get a few of her friends together to go out drinking one night. And wasn't it nice she had friends she could call to go out for an emotional emergency?

She hung on to that happy thought all the way to her of- fice. After booting her computer, she threw herself into her work. Staying busy was the best distraction and it had the added benefit of getting things done.

By eleven, she'd made a serious dent in her weekly list and was feeling much better about everything. She was just ar- ranging doggie day care when Jasper walked in.

He winked when he saw she was on the phone and qui- etly took a seat while she made arrangements for Buster to be kept company for six hours, including a long walk and dinner.

"Interesting," Jasper said when she hung up. "Given your reaction to Koda, I wouldn't have thought you'd have a dog care service on the side."

She briefly thought about trying to explain about Koda, then told herself she simply wasn't up to it today. She was feel- ing too emotionally frail. Later, she would come clean and deal with the consequences, but not just yet.

"The Halloween-themed wedding has the bride's dog as the best man. It was the groom's idea, so Buster wouldn't feel like he was being replaced. It's all charming and wonderful, but then there's a huge golden retriever to deal with. I was ar- ranging for him to be picked up here after the ceremony. He'll have company for the evening. Once the reception is over, the bride's parents are taking him through the honeymoon."

"You are a full service wedding planner."

"I try to be."

He studied her for a second before saying, "Thanks again for your help yesterday. I'm sorry I got caught up in my work."

"It's your process. I'm kind of getting used to it. And it's fun to be the source of inspiration."

"You were that and I appreciate it." He set several pages on her desk. "At the risk of being needy, would you mind letting me know what you think about those? No rush. Whenever you get a chance."

He looked hopeful, desperate and worried. Renee hid a smile. It was good to know someone as successful and impressive as Jasper had his own insecurities. It kept them on a semi-level playing field.

"I have a few minutes right now," she said.

He stood up. "That would be great. I'll just step outside so you don't feel pressure. It's okay if you hate them. It's been tough getting Mandy right. I'm not sure I have her all the way, but I think it's closer."

He ducked out before she could say anything, leaving her alone with the pages. She picked them up and saw he'd added a few notes, setting up the scene.

Vidar wanted Mandy to be careful. He had a gut feeling one of her weddings would be targeted. She didn't believe him.

"You're not going to come in here and mess with one of my weddings," Mandy said, glaring at him. "This is their special day. They'll remember it for the rest of their lives and I want those to be happy memories—not tainted by some detective lurking in the background."

"They wouldn't know I was here."

"You say that now, but what happens if you see someone

suspicious in the crowd? Are you going to attack Grandmother Patricia because you have a nervous stomach?"

Vidar told himself yelling at Mandy would accomplish nothing and it wouldn't help his case. He had to win her with logic, not bully her with brute force. But damn, she was bugging him.

"I need you to see that my concern is for the wedding party and the bride and groom. I don't want to ruin anything, I want to protect them."

"I'd be more likely to believe you if your teeth weren't clenched."

"You are the most frustrating woman in the world."

She surprised him by smiling. "You can't actually know that, can you? At most you've met one or two thousand women, so how can I possibly take you seriously?"

Without thinking, he grabbed her by her upper arms, drew her close and pressed his mouth to hers. He didn't know how she felt about the kiss, but it shocked the shit out of him. Then it made him want to push her onto her desk and—

Renee flipped the pages, looking for more, but that was where the scene ended.

"What?" she shrieked. "You're kidding."

Jasper appeared in the doorway. "What? You hate it?" His mouth turned down. "It's okay. I can fix it. What didn't you like?"

"Where you cut me off." She flung the pages at him. "You are such a guy, leaving a woman hanging right as things get good."

"What are you talking about?"

He grabbed the pages and flipped through them, then started laughing. "Sorry. I didn't mean to end things there.

I wanted you to read through the scene. I must have entered the wrong page numbers when I printed everything out."

"I'm not sure if I believe you," she fake grumbled, then grinned at him. "They were great. I like him and I like her. Probably because she sounds a lot like me."

"She's based on you. Sort of. Parts of you. How you protect your clients. I like that part, how you're always there for them. So it reads okay?"

"It's way better than okay. You've always known Vidar but now it feels like you know her, too."

"Thanks. That's a relief." He sank back into the chair. "You've been great, Renee. I couldn't have gotten this far without you."

"I'm happy to help. It's interesting watching your process. I have learned that there is no way I could write a book. It's too intense. When you get into a scene, that's all that exists for you. I like my life a little more balanced."

"I do what I have to do. Which you said last night. Again, I'm sorry I got lost in what I was doing."

"It wasn't a problem. I had a quiet evening at home."

Which was absolutely the wrong thing to say, she thought, as she remembered the shock of finding out about Turner becoming a father.

Maybe it was exhaustion or hormones or just bad luck, but whatever the reason, Renee was horrified to realize her eyes were filling with tears. One second she was fine and the next she was sniffing and blinking and reaching for a tissue.

"Hey," Jasper said, coming to his feet. "What's wrong? If you're mad about yesterday, you have every right to be."

"It's not that," she said, struggling for control. But the more she tried not to cry, the more she actually did cry, which was embarrassing and so not her.

She half expected Jasper to bolt, but instead he circled around her desk, drew her to her feet and held her.

"Whatever it is, we can fix it together."

A wonderful sentiment, but not at all true. In fact the thought of her explaining and him *helping* had her laughing through her tears.

"What?" he asked, stepping back enough to stare into her eyes. "I'm lost here."

"Yes, you are." She sniffed. "It's okay. You didn't do anything wrong. In fact, no one did."

He took the tissue from her and gently dried her cheeks. "Then tell me what has you so sad."

"I'm not sad—not really." She drew in a breath. "I used to go out with this guy. Turner. Back in college."

"So not the married guy?"

"No. Turner and I were engaged. We were happy and planning our lives together and—" She hesitated, not sure what to say about how things had ended. No, not ended. How Turner had dumped her, breaking her heart into a thousand pieces.

"He ended things and it was hard. I'm not still in love with him or anything, but it took me a while to get over him and last night I accidentally stumbled on a video." She squared her shoulders because she was strong and capable and she would be fine. "He and his wife had a gender reveal party. They're having a girl." The tears returned. "Turner wanted a girl first. He talked about it a lot. I'm glad he's getting that now. I really don't care. It's not like I want him back or anything, it was just unexpected."

"Sure it was." Jasper pulled her close again, then kissed her before brushing away her tears with his thumbs. "Turner was always a jerk, but you're the kind of woman who overlooks that."

She managed a slight laugh. "Thank you."

"He's got to be sorry he let you go."

"I doubt that."

"You're wrong. I'm a guy and I know about these things. He wonders about you."

She knew he was mistaken, but the words were nice to hear. "Thank you."

"You're welcome." He kissed her again, lingering this time. "So, I was thinking, we need a do-over. Why don't you come up to the house after work? Koda will be on his best behavior and I'll cook and maybe you could spend the night."

She had no idea if he'd had those plans in mind when he'd first arrived or if they were in reaction to her story. She told herself it really didn't matter—either way, Jasper was a good guy and she wanted to be with him.

"Is there going to be sex?" she asked teasingly. "Because I'm really only in it for the sex."

He laughed, then leaned close to whisper in her ear. "You get more amazing by the day. There will be dinner and wine and sex."

"Then I'll be there."

"And you'll spend the night?"

She thought about the large dog who would be lurking and how much she wished Jasper had taken him somewhere safe that wasn't his house. But she knew she couldn't say that— there was no way he would understand and she really didn't want him thinking less of her. Koda seemed like a very nice dog—seriously, what was the worst that could happen? A question she knew she shouldn't tempt fate by asking.

"I'll spend the night," she said. "Oh, I went shopping a few days ago. I probably should have asked first, but where do you stand on the issue of sexy lingerie?"

His eyes immediately dilated and his eyebrows rose. "I'm in favor of it."

"Oh, good. Then I'll bring what I bought."

He kissed her again, the pressure a little more intense. "You are an amazing woman. I'll see you after work."

"Yes, you will."

CHAPTER ELEVEN

Renee arrived at Jasper's place a little before five. Her morning productivity had meant she could leave early. She'd gone home, showered, packed a bag and had driven up the mountain. Whenever her thoughts had threatened to slide in the direction of Turner or Koda, she'd reminded herself that she was about to have hot sex with a guy who knew where all her buttons were and exactly how to push them. Thinking about that was just the distraction she needed.

She parked and got out her overnight tote. She'd left her work dress on a hanger. Before she could even close her car door, Jasper was heading toward her.

"You're here," he said, sounding happy. "I'm glad." He took the tote from her. "I'm going to barbecue ribs."

"You know how to do that?"

"As a matter of fact, I do. I marinate them in big batches and freeze them, then pull out what I want for the evening and cook them on the barbecue."

"Impressive."

"Tell me about it. Now a lot of people would consider ribs

man food, so I made a pasta salad in deference to your fair gender."

"Because women like pasta?"

"Yes. I say that with great authority."

She laughed as they walked into the house. "I'm not going to argue. Sounds delicious. I brought a bottle of merlot, which should complement the menu very nicely."

He closed the door behind them and motioned for her to lead the way down the hall.

As she walked, she was aware of a clicking sound following them. Koda, she thought grimly, telling herself she would simply ignore the dog. It wasn't as if she were afraid he was going to attack her. Nothing that simple. She would just pretend he wasn't there. Hopefully, with time, he would sort of blend into the background of the house.

She'd been so busy with her dog thoughts, she hadn't paid attention to the house and unexpectedly found herself in a huge master bedroom. The space was one of the new additions, she thought, taking in the large windows and big fireplace on the far wall. There was a king-size bed, several rugs scattered on the hardwood floors and a massive dog bed in the far corner.

"You can put your stuff in here," Jasper said, motioning to an open door that led to an apartment-sized master bath with his and hers closets. There were double sinks, a steam shower, jetted tub and one of those fancy toilets with lights and a remote control.

In the "hers" closet, Renee found built-in drawers, glass doors protecting shelves and a floor-to-ceiling shoe rack, along with what seemed to be miles of hanging space.

"I'm in love," she breathed, turning in a slow circle. "Who knew I could be bought for the price of an amazing closet, but apparently I can be and I don't even have that many clothes."

"Really? It's just a few shelves and hanging space."

"Silly man. It's so much more. It's the stuff of dreams."

She sighed happily, then quickly unpacked. Jasper only used one side of the long vanity, so she set her makeup case on the other and glanced longingly at the tub. For a second she allowed herself to wonder what it would be like to live here permanently—not just to enjoy the magical closet, but to be a part of all of it.

That wasn't happening, she reminded herself. She wasn't willing to go there ever again. She was going to be smart and sensible and that was going to be more than enough for her.

While he made them cocktails, she peeked in the refrigerator and saw that yes, indeed, there were ribs and pasta salad and some kind of chocolate cake thing that looked delicious.

"You know how to show a girl a good time," she said, closing the refrigerator door. "I'm going to have to up my exercise program to make up for tonight's dinner."

He pushed a button on a wall panel and soft music immediately filled the space. "Or we can work it off another way," he said, pulling her into his arms and moving to the beat of the slow song.

She relaxed in his embrace. "You know how to dance."

"A little. My dad made me take lessons one summer. I was maybe fourteen and at that gangly stage guys go through. I kept tripping over my own feet or stepping on my partner or giggling uncontrollably or getting an erection. It was horrible."

She smiled. "You were charming."

"I was a teenager, so no. Not charming."

She wondered what he'd been like before he'd gone into the army and served so many tours in a war zone. How had he been different? What traits did young Jasper share with the man in front of her?

She relaxed against him, resting her head on his chest. "This is nice."

"I'm glad. I might not be able to give you babies, but I can seduce you."

Renee knew exactly what he meant and appreciated the sentiment behind the words, but had a feeling he would immediately freak out. Or the manly-Jasper version of freaking out.

She didn't have to wait long. There were maybe two beats of silence, then he slowly, carefully, drew back. His eyes were wide and filled what she would guess was panic. His mouth twitched, no doubt from him trying to figure out which words would get him out of the trouble he found himself in.

He cleared his throat. "What I meant was..."

She watched him, thinking she would let him flounder for a couple of minutes before saving him. "Yes?"

"I'm not saying I can't have children."

"Good to know."

"Just that we're not going there and this is about..." He half turned away and muttered something she was fairly sure was at least R rated. "The thing is... It's not like we're looking to fall madly in love and I know—"

"Wow." She kept her voice soft. "You really are just using me for sex. I don't know what to say to that."

Jasper stayed upright on the outside, but she had a feeling he was crumbling on the inside. "Renee, no! What I meant was—"

"No babies for me." She sighed dramatically. "No love, no anything. Just whatever the night brings."

She'd been teasing him right up until she realized she was telling herself the truth and it wasn't pretty. She knew love wasn't in the cards—she'd tried and failed too many times.

She didn't have another heartbreak in her. But did being sensible have to hurt so much?

None of this was Jasper's fault. She'd wanted to keep things light between them. She'd chosen him because she knew that was what he wanted, too, and it avoided anything messy. So why, at this moment, did that feel like a bad idea?

She was sure the answer was all wrapped up in Turner and his on-the-way baby and the reason he'd broken things off and that sometimes she felt life really wasn't fair, but again, none of that was Jasper's fault. He was playing by the rules they'd mutually established. The rules she still totally supported. She was just having a bad day.

"Renee." Jasper sounded worried, probably because he thought he'd hurt her.

He hadn't, not really. In fact he was a really sweet guy who looked out for her. Her feelings were her responsibility and so was the remedy.

"You are the most ridiculous man," she said softly, then raised herself up on tiptoe and kissed him. "Take me to bed and have your way with me, then feed me ribs and chocolate cake."

"Done!"

He shocked her by sweeping her up in his arms and carrying her to the bedroom. She hung on to him, not liking the sense of being so out of control.

"We should have talked about this before," she gasped. "You need to put me down."

"Probably, but I won't."

He bypassed the bedroom and walked directly into the bathroom. She had no idea what he was thinking. Steamy shower? Tub time? Either way, sign her up. But his final destination was the vanity, which she found confusing.

He slowly, carefully, lowered her to her feet, then patted the smooth countertop.

"I've been thinking," he began, his tone suggestive.

"Interesting." She glanced from the counter to him and saw the heights were perfect. "How much have you been thinking?"

"A lot."

She laughed and kicked off her shoes, then tugged her T-shirt over her head. She pushed her jeans to the floor and shimmied out of her panties. Seconds later, her bra went flying.

Jasper took care of his own clothes, all the while glancing at her, as if enjoying the show. When they were both naked, he opened a drawer and set a box of condoms next to the sink, then he pulled her close.

She went into his embrace, but instead of just feeling the heat and strength of his body, this time she got to enjoy the way his bare legs felt against hers and how her breasts flattened against his chest. Even as he claimed her mouth with his and slipped his tongue inside, she reached between them so she could take his erection in her hand and stroke him.

He was unbelievably hard—the silky skin of his penis contrasting with the tension just below the surface. She explored the length of him before sliding her hand between his thighs and gently stroking his testicles.

In retaliation, he drew back just enough to lightly nip on her lower lip before kissing his way along her jaw. At the same time he cupped her breasts in his hands and rubbed her hard nipples.

As she had before with him, she found herself going from "this is nice" to "take me *now*" in about eight seconds. Wanting grew until it was unbearable. She was wet and swollen and hungry for him and there was absolutely no way to get

friction. She was just too short to ride his erection and rubbing against his leg seemed sad.

"Condom," she said, thinking that should get the message across.

"Yeah, no."

Before she could fully absorb what he'd said, he grabbed her
around the waist and set her on the counter. The cold surface
shocked her into gasping. The second gasp happened when he
placed an openmouthed kiss on her very center, then sucked
her clit, all the while filling her with at least two fingers.

It was the most perfect combination of sensations. She
couldn't think, could barely breathe as all her attention focused on the feel of his tongue and lips and fingers moving
in tandem, teasing her, testing her, going slow then fast, then
faster still until she lost control and screamed as she came.

The shock waves crashed into her, causing her to arch her
back and push toward him. He continued to love her until
the last shudder faded and she could breathe again.

He gave her clit one last flick of his tongue before he stood
and reached for the condom. After putting it on, he pushed
into her, filling her, stretching her and making her nerve
endings sigh happily.

He grabbed her hips, locked eyes with her and began
pumping.

"This is not going to be long," he said between gritted
teeth. "Doing that was incredible."

She drew back her knees and braced herself as he pumped
in and out. "Yes, it was."

She was just settling in for part two when he called out
her name and stiffened. Caught off guard, she couldn't help
laughing.

He groaned. "I know. Unimpressive."

She ran her hands up and down his arms. "I think I would have liked you at sixteen," she teased.

"Thanks. It's your fault."

"Then I'll take the compliment."

He touched her cheek. "Do-over after dinner?"

"Absolutely."

The next morning, Jasper paused at the entrance to the "hers" closet and studied the single black dress hanging there. On the hanger it was kind of shapeless—at least to him—but he recognized the simple style and could imagine it on Renee's petite frame. The sleeves would come to her elbows, the scoop neckline was modest and the skirt part would end at her knee.

It was just one dress, hanging in the large closet. There was a pair of plain pumps on a shoe shelf and her tote bag tucked in a corner. Whatever else she'd brought, she'd put away in one of the drawers. Still, he liked seeing her things there. Wynn was the only other woman he'd had over to the house and her visits had been about having sex and then getting back to their lives. Sometimes she'd stayed long enough to have a quick meal, but they'd never lingered over anything and she'd never spent the night.

He found he enjoyed having a relationship that demanded a little more from him. He liked rolling over in bed and finding Renee next to him. He liked her using the other sink and how they worked together to cook dinner and then clean up after. He appreciated that she understood how he worked and wasn't mad when he disappeared for a few hours to work on his book. If he had to explain the combination of attraction and familiarity, he would say they fit together.

Funny how when he'd first moved to Happily Inc he'd barely been able to nod at people when he went to town and now he was enjoying having a woman spend the night. The mind's ability to heal was an amazing thing.

He went into his closet and pulled on sweatpants and a T-shirt, then made his way to the kitchen. Renee was hovering over the coffee maker, as if willing it to brew more quickly.

"Rough night?" he asked, his voice teasing.

She glanced at him over her shoulder and smiled. "A good night, but not a lot of sleep."

She looked well-loved. Her hair was mussed, her skin glowing. She had on some short robe thing and a pair of slipper socks that looked like bright green mice.

When the coffee maker's steady stream of brew turned into a hissing, gurgling splutter, she gave a sigh of satisfaction, then turned to reach for a mug.

At that exact moment, Koda crossed her path. She spun, nearly ran into him and then jumped back as if any kind of contact with the gentle dog would be fatal. Jasper felt his happy mood evaporate.

What was up with her and the dog? She wasn't a mean person. She was caring and kind and thoughtful so why was she so apprehensive when it came to Koda?

He waited until they both had their coffee and were seated at the kitchen island.

"Tell me what happened with the dog."

He spoke softly and deliberately made his tone coaxing. He wanted information, not a fight. There was something she wasn't sharing with him and he wanted to know what it was.

Renee cradled her mug in both hands. "Nothing. I'm fine. He just, ah, startled me."

"Were you bitten as a kid? Did someone you know get attacked? There aren't any scars, so I don't think a dog came after you. What was it?"

"You don't want to know."

So there was something. "I do. Renee, please. You can trust me."

"Oh, I doubt that." She set down her coffee and shook her head, as if she were arguing with herself. "It's not that I don't like animals. It's all animals, by the way, not just your dog, and personally I've always wanted a cat. There's just something about their fur and the way they purr. But I can't and I really don't want to tell you the reason. It will change everything."

She looked at him as she spoke and he saw the truth in her eyes. At least the truth she believed. He touched her arm. "Nothing will change. You have my word."

Her mouth twisted. "You say that now." She drew in a breath. "Fine. You want to know what my problem is? It's my mother."

Jasper hadn't been expecting that and had no idea how to respond. "Okay," he said slowly. "What did she do?"

"It's not what she did, it's who she is. My mother is… She's kind of…" She squeezed her eyes shut, then opened them and groaned. "My mother has a psychic ability to communicate with animals. No, that's wrong. It's not a two-way communication. She looks at them and knows what they're thinking, which wouldn't be horrible. The part that makes everything complicated is once she gets whatever information they want to share, she's compelled to blurt it out."

Jasper stared at her and waited for the punch line. The "No, really, here's what it is," only Renee stopped talking and stared at him—as if that were it. She was done talking.

He wasn't sure how to react. Annoyance flared—he was trying to be serious, trying to help her or at least understand. Her response was dismissive and…

She looked at him. "I'm not kidding."

"Your mother talks to animals?"

"No. She can hear what they're thinking. It's a thing. It was cute when I was a kid but then it became a problem, as you can imagine. As I got older, I started to worry that I had it, too, and it's not anything I want in my life."

She glanced at Koda and then away. "So far there hasn't been an indication and my mom swears she had her talent or whatever you want to call it from the time she was born, so I should be safe, but I worry. I don't want to hear some squeaky voice in my head."

It was like being back in group therapy at the VA, he thought grimly, listening to the really bad ones try to explain what was happening to them. Or talk to someone who wasn't there. Only with those wounded in war, he'd been understanding and patient. With Renee he leaned a whole lot more toward pissed and disappointed.

"You are afraid you're going to start talking to animals, too?" He tried to sound like he was listening instead of fighting anger and he was pretty sure he failed miserably. "Dammit, Renee, I'm serious."

"So am I." She slid off the stool and glared at him. "I didn't want to tell you and you insisted it would be fine, yet here we are. You think I'm lying. Or if you do believe me, you're now worried that I'm taking a train to Crazytown." Frustration sharpened her tone. "I'm serious, too, Jasper. This is real."

She turned and ran for the bedroom. He wasn't sure what to do, so he gave her a few minutes to get herself together. By the time he followed her, she was already dressed and was throwing her things into her tote bag.

"We have to talk," he said, wondering when it had all gone wrong. He liked her. He liked being with her, and now this?

"What are we going to talk about?" she asked, her voice thick with emotion. "I shouldn't have said anything. I knew better and I did it anyway. Well, fine. Now you know. You can believe me or not." She faced him. "If you have any feelings for me at all, do me one favor. Don't say anything. I don't want my life here messed up like it's been messed up everywhere else, okay? Just keep your mouth shut and everything will be fine."

He wanted to point out it wasn't fine now and that they still had to talk and he honest to God had no idea what to say.

Part of him wanted to demand she take it back and explain why she would play such a stupid joke on him, but the rest of him knew it was worse than that. The rest of him knew she believed what she was saying. And if that was true, where did it leave them?

"I'm going to go," she said.

She grabbed her things and walked out. Jasper told himself to go after her, but he couldn't. Or he didn't want to, and in the end, weren't those the same?

As she drove down the mountain, Renee chastised herself. She'd been stupid. No, she'd been what was stupid times a zillion to the millionth squared. She'd made a fool of herself in front a man she really liked and now she had nothing. No guy, no sex and the very real possibility that her life was about to blow up in her face.

She let herself into her apartment and dumped her clothes, then got undressed and stepped into the shower. When the water was flowing over her, she gave in to tears as she worried that she'd screwed up everything.

What had she been thinking when she told him? That he would be fine with it? That he would laugh and say "Hey, that's cool. What do you want for breakfast?" It didn't work like that—it never had. What if Jasper told people? What if she lost her job? What if once again she had to pick up the pieces and start over? Because it had happened again and again and again.

At six, her friends had loved that her mom knew what their pets were thinking but in high school it had meant being a freak. Later... Well, she didn't want to think about that.

She washed her hair and rinsed the tears from her face, then stepped out to start her day. Her stomach was in knots and her heart was heavy to the point of weighing her down.

The potential for disaster was going to follow her for weeks. She would never know if or when Jasper was going to repeat what she'd told him and then what? She loved Happily Inc. Pallas was talking about making her a partner. Everything could be lost if word of the crazy got out.

She got ready for work then drove to Weddings Out of the Box. At least there she could distract herself with various tasks. The weddings this weekend were low-key affairs that wouldn't require much more than the usual attention, so she would get ahead on the upcoming weddings. There was always plenty to do.

She spent her morning doing her best to get lost in her job. It was impossible to do, but she made the effort and went entire minutes without worrying. She didn't hear from Jasper, but then why would she? No doubt the man was changing his cell number and considering getting a security system at his house.

A little before eleven, just when she was thinking she should stop drinking so much coffee and eat something, she heard footsteps in the hallway followed by a shockingly familiar voice calling, "Renee? Are you here? Do I have the right place?"

Her mouth went dry, her heart physically stopped beating and her life flashed before her eyes. No. No! But there was no denying the identity of the visitor when her door was pushed open and her mother stepped into her office.

"There you are," Verity Grothen said with a smile. "Hello, sweetie, and surprise!"

CHAPTER TWELVE

"Mom!" Renee came to her feet and circled the desk. "What are you doing here?"

They hugged. Verity was exactly Renee's height with slightly darker red hair and blue eyes. She'd always been an attractive woman but after Renee's father had left, she'd never allowed another man in her life.

"I thought I was coming to San Diego in a few weeks."

"You were, but I needed to talk to you so I thought I'd pop by and surprise you."

Renee did her best not to panic. Her mother was in town. *Her mother was in town!* No and no! This was bad and it was going to get worse and there was literally nothing she could do to make things better. Even more upsetting, mentally screaming about it wouldn't accomplish anything because now she had to deal with the reality of it.

For months, there had been nothing, but in the space of a few hours, she'd told Jasper about her mother and now Verity was here—as if conjured.

"Is this your office?" her mother asked, looking around. "It's very nice."

The space was maybe ten by ten, with a desk, a file cabinet and two chairs. Hardly anything luxurious, but then Renee always had her client meetings in one of the two conference rooms and she and Pallas spoke wherever they happened to be and this was a mess!

"Thanks," she said, trying to focus. "Sorry, Mom. You threw me with your unexpected arrival. Let's go to the break room. It's more comfortable. On the way, I'll give you a tour."

"That would be so nice." Verity linked arms with her. "I want to see everything."

Renee let go of the fear and worry and told herself to simply enjoy being with her mom. Whatever else had happened, she knew her mother loved her and would always be there for her. The other stuff wasn't anyone's fault.

"As I've told you, we have theme weddings here. This weekend is a *Star Trek* wedding, complete with costumes." They walked downstairs.

Renee took her by the bride's room and then down the hallway into where the ceremony would take place. Instead of an arch, or an altar or anything signifying a church of some kind, there was a replica of the bridge of the Starship Enterprise.

"Oh, my. Is that where they're getting married?"

"It is. Both families worked on it, then had it delivered here. It's mobile so when the ceremony is over, we'll wheel it out to the reception area. We bring in another captain's chair and a small table and that will be where the bride and groom eat. They have some really fun things planned."

"It's quite elaborate."

"It is. Not every wedding is this complicated. Some are

easier. We'll be having a Halloween wedding soon. That requires more props but less custom furniture."

Verity smiled. "It's lovely and you're doing such good work here."

"You can't know that."

"Of course I can. I know you."

Renee showed her how they could hang different panels to simulate different places. "We have gorgeous wood panels, but we don't use them much. They're too valuable. Plus printed paper is easier to deal with and a whole lot cheaper to customize."

They walked through the open courtyard where most of the receptions took place, then went back inside and headed for the break room. Renee poured her mother a cup of coffee and got herself some water. There had already been too much caffeine in her morning. After sitting at one of the small tables, Renee braced herself for whatever her mother had to tell her.

"So, you came a long way just to talk," she said brightly.

"I know." Verity worried her lower lip. "I needed to see you, and speaking over the phone just isn't the same. I thought I'd stay a few days, if that's all right."

So not a quick visit, Renee thought, hoping her disappointment didn't show. She wanted to suggest they both head back to San Diego, only there was no way she could simply take off, and making the suggestion would hurt her mother's feelings.

"That sounds great," she lied. "You'll love my apartment. It's small, but I can sleep on the sofa."

"Oh, no. I wouldn't want to get in the way. I've already booked a room at the Sweet Dreams Inn." She smiled. "I have the Harry Potter room. I think it's going to be very fun." Her smile faded. "A hotel is better, sweetie. I don't want to be a bother."

And there it was—the sense of being a terrible daughter

and horrible human being. "Mom, you're not a bother. I want to spend time with you. Stay with me."

"Thank you, but I'll be at the hotel." Verity looked at her and then away. She shifted in her seat.

Renee suddenly remembered there was a reason for the visit and from the looks of things, it wasn't happy. She went cold all over. What if her mother was sick? What if it was something bad?

"Mom, tell me."

Verity smiled. "It's actually good news. Very exciting. I've been in talks for a while now and I didn't want to say anything until I was sure…"

She picked up her coffee, then put it down. "It's not that I haven't loved being a hairdresser. You know my clients mean the world to me. But I'm not twenty-five anymore and the long days on my feet are getting to me so when I had this opportunity—"

"You're not sick?"

"What? Of course not. Oh, darling, is that what you thought?" Her mother grabbed her hand and squeezed. "I'm perfectly fine. And I'm getting a show on Animal Planet."

The world spun twice to the right, once to the left, then settled back in place. Renee told herself to keep breathing, that if she didn't she would pass out, possibly hit her head and then who knew what might happen.

"I'm sorry, what did you say?" she asked, her voice faint.

"I'm getting a show on Animal Planet."

What? "Talking to animals?"

"You know that's not what happens."

"Yes, I do, but you know what I mean. Is that what you're going to be doing? Listening to animals then blurting out their every thought?"

She tried to sound curious rather than horrified. A show?

Animal Planet was a big deal. If Verity had a show then her ability wouldn't be a secret anymore. It would be out there for all to see.

"It won't be like a talk show or anything," Verity told her. "I'll be visiting families to help them with their pets. I'm also going to do some shelter work. If I can let prospective pet parents know what they're dealing with, the adoptions will go more smoothly."

Which totally made sense, for those who believed in the whole I-can-talk-to-animals thing.

"I'm very excited," Verity continued. "This is a wonderful opportunity."

"It is. You're going to be a big success, Mom. I just know it."

Because why not?

On the one hand, she was thrilled for her mother. Verity had always worked hard to provide for her only child. She deserved something wonderful in her life. On the other hand, why?

"You can see why I wanted to tell you in person," her mother said. "Plus spend a little time with you. Once we start filming, I'm going to be so busy, we might not see each other for a while."

"You were right to come here," Renee told her, confident that at some point, she would even mean what she said.

Everyone was going to know. There was no hiding the truth now. It would come out and when it did, well, things would go badly because they always did. But Verity was her mother and she loved her and if only her stomach would stop writhing and she could have a moment to think...

"Renee? Who are you—" Pallas walked into the break room. "Oh, hi. Sorry. I heard voices, which was odd, but now I see you're visiting with someone." She paused, as if not sure what to do.

Renee smiled at her. "Pallas, this is my mom. Verity, Pallas is my boss."

"So nice to meet you," Verity said, shaking hands with her. "Renee has told me all about you. She does love working here."

"Good to know," Pallas said with a smile. "Because I want her to stay forever."

They both laughed. Renee wondered if she should try fainting. Maybe a head injury wouldn't be so bad.

"My mom's in town for bit," Renee said.

"That's so nice. Take the day off and get her settled. I can deal with whatever needs taking care of."

"Actually the weddings for this weekend are pretty much on track," Renee admitted. "Mom, why don't I help you get checked in to the hotel and show you around town?"

"Nonsense. I can handle that myself. You need to work and I need to make a few phone calls. But I would like to have dinner later, if that's all right."

Renee wasn't sure if her mother was really busy or if she was giving her kid an out. The former was acceptable and the latter made her feel crappy.

"Dinner is required," Renee said lightly. "Then I'll show you around. You'll love the town. It has a great history and the people are so friendly."

"We are," Pallas assured her.

"Then it's a date," Verity said.

They rose and Renee walked her out to her car. She hugged her mother, promised to call her later, then watched her drive away. As she retraced her steps, she told herself to be happy for her mother. The show was such a wonderful opportunity. Maybe no one she knew would watch it or put together the fact that Verity and she not only looked alike, they shared a last name. Uh-huh. That was likely.

Pallas was waiting just inside the main doors. "Your mom seems nice. I'm jealous."

Renee had met Pallas's mother. Libby was a stern, difficult woman who obviously preferred her son to her daughter. It was not an easy relationship.

"She's great," Renee said, thinking that except for the whole animal thing, Verity was fantastic. "After my dad took off, it was just the two of us. She's always been there for me."

"That's nice. I'm glad she's going to be around for a while. I look forward to getting to know her."

As Renee had no idea what to say to that, she simply nodded. "Uh-huh. So I'm going to get to work."

"Sure, but if you want to go hang with your mom, you should."

"And that makes you the best boss ever."

Pallas laughed.

Renee retreated to her office where she paced and mentally screamed and paced some more. The truth was her mother was in town and nothing was going to change that. Nor was the show going away, so Renee would simply have to deal.

Maybe it wouldn't be so bad, although if Jasper's reaction was anything to go by, she wasn't holding her breath on that one.

"Renee?"

She jumped and spun only to find Jasper standing in the doorway to her office. What was going on? Did she suddenly have the ability to make anything she thought of appear?

"I'm thinking of a million dollars," she murmured under her breath. "I'm thinking of a million dollars."

Jasper's look of concern deepened. "Are you okay?"

"No. I'm not. I'm really not." She glared at him. "Let me

guess. You want to talk about it. You want me to admit I was lying about all of it, which you think is a really crappy thing to do. You don't believe me at all. Which is fine because you know what? She's here. My mother just showed up. Poof. One second she wasn't here and the next—"

"You're saying she transported in or something?"

"What? No! She drove, you idiot. I'm saying—" She shook her head. "Never mind. That's not the point. She's here because she wanted to tell me about getting a show on Animal Planet. That means everyone is going to know. Everyone. So telling you was just a practice session and we all know how that went, but who cares because you think I have a screw loose and..."

A thought formed. Of course. Why not?

She looked at him. "I will meet you at your place in an hour. I'll bring my mom and then we'll see who doesn't know what they're talking about."

He frowned. "Renee, I'm really worried about you."

"I'm sure you are. That's nice. An hour. Then if you're not convinced, we'll make an appointment with the doctor of your choice. Fair enough?"

"Sure."

She ignored his patronizing tone and the fact that he still didn't believe her. It didn't matter now. She would convince him the only way she knew how. At the very least, she was about to have the satisfaction of watching Jasper eat his words. Metaphorically, of course.

Renee kept her attention on her driving as they headed up the mountain. Beside her, Verity looked out the window and admired the scenery.

"I can't believe how different the topography is up here," her mother said. "We're only a few miles from town, but it's totally different. How wonderful to live so close to the mountains."

"It is nice. I don't get up here often, but I really should make more of an effort."

She could start camping, she thought, holding in a laugh. Or hiking. Maybe she could commune with the wild animals. They could tell her about buried treasure or an abandoned gold mine. Only they didn't talk to her, they spoke with her mother and now everyone was going to know.

Renee had yet to find her zen center on the topic—obviously—but she was going to have to get there eventually. After years of ducking and weaving, of hiding, pretending and twisting the truth, the family secret was going to be exposed and then...well, she didn't know what was going to happen.

"So who is Jasper?" her mother asked. "Dare I hope you've met someone?"

Renee wanted to bang her head against the steering wheel. She'd been so intent on showing Jasper she wasn't a loon that she'd acted without thinking and now she had to tell her mother that she and Jasper were...were...

"We're friends," she said cautiously. "He has a dog, Koda."

"Friends? What kind of friends?"

"The kind who don't fall in love and get married. I'm sorry, Mom."

"Renee, you have to get yourself out there. You have to be willing to risk your heart again."

"No, I don't. You haven't. You haven't been with anybody since Dad left." She paused, realizing she actually didn't know all that much about her mother's love life. "Not anyone special enough to tell me about."

"That's different. I'm fine. You're the one I'm worried about."

"I'm fine, too."

Her mother looked at her. "Not everyone is going to be frightened of me," she said gently. "You need to give people a chance to surprise you."

Renee held in a sigh. "That's the problem, Mom. They rarely do."

Jasper had no idea what was going on. He didn't want to believe Renee was unhinged, but she'd been acting strangely ever since telling him she believed her mother could talk to animals.

Nothing about the past few hours made sense. They'd had a great time together the previous night. The sex, the conversation, all of it. They'd laughed, they'd gotten to know each other better. Was she reacting to that? Was she so scared of getting involved that she was putting up barriers to keep them apart?

He didn't think that was possible or even likely and if she didn't want to see him anymore, why not just say so instead of inventing such a weird story? It wasn't like her at all and that was what troubled him the most.

He glanced at his watch. She should be here any minute, he thought, admitting he was unexpectedly nervous about seeing her. He didn't want there to be something wrong with her. He wanted them to go back to what they had been. He liked her and liked what they had—he didn't want to lose that. But in the end, it might not be up to him.

He heard a car pull up and hurried to the front door. Renee got out, along with an older woman who looked enough like her for Jasper to believe it was her mother. Verity Grothen was about her daughter's height, with a similar build. Her hair was darker, her eyes blue, but they definitely came from the same gene pool. While Verity was casually dressed in jeans and a flowy blouse thing, Renee still had on her work clothes.

"You made it," he said, moving toward them. He held out his hand to Renee's mother. "I'm Jasper."

"Verity." She smiled. "It's very nice to meet you."

They shook hands, then she glanced past him and raised her eyebrows. "Who is that handsome boy?"

"That's Koda," Renee said, leading the way inside. She hesitated just before reaching Koda, then seemed to steel herself before petting him.

So she wasn't afraid of dogs in the traditional sense, Jasper thought, not sure if the news was good or bad.

He and Verity went inside and followed Renee into the family room. Koda eased in behind Jasper, as if not sure what to expect.

"Renee tells me you're an author," Verity said easily. "While I'm sure I've heard of you, I have to admit, I don't read suspense novels. I prefer a little less violence and death."

"Makes sense." He wasn't sure what to do. Stay standing? Sit down? Bolt?

He motioned to the sofa, then said, "Can I get you something?"

Renee ignored him. "Mom, could you talk to Koda, please?"

Her mother's looked sharpened, but she nodded and sank to the floor, then called Koda over. The dog crossed to her before sitting in front of her. Their eyes met.

Jasper didn't know what was about to happen. Renee wouldn't look at him and from the tension he saw in her body, he knew she was on the edge.

He returned his attention back to Verity and Koda. They just stared at each other for a few seconds, then Koda whined and lay down while Verity stroked him. She nodded, as if she were getting information and wanted the dog to know she understood. Which wasn't happening, he reminded himself. Whatever was going on, it wasn't—

"He's a sweet boy," Verity said, looking at Jasper. "He belonged to an older woman who got very sick. Koda says she went away. I don't know if that means they had to move her into a nursing home or if she died. She made her son promise to look after Koda, but instead he dumped him somewhere that frightened Koda. He was lonely and scared and starving when you found him."

"Everyone knows how I found Koda," Jasper said, trying not to sound disappointed in the badly done show. "The touch about the old lady is nice but—"

Renee glared at him. "Just listen," she snapped.

Verity looked between them before continuing. "He still misses her, but thinks she would approve of you, Jasper. He wasn't sure, at first. You almost didn't keep him, but he's glad you did. He likes living here. He likes the forest and the house and how you whistle for him when he's gone too long exploring. You have nightmares and at first they frightened him. He would get on the bed to calm you. Now he knows you're going to be okay. Sometimes he wakes you up so you stop screaming, but most of the time he only has to bump your arm to settle you. If he does wake you, he pretends he has to go out so you don't know it's really to help you."

She paused and looked at Koda. "He says you work too much and should take more breaks and you need more people in your life." She smiled at Renee. "He likes you and wishes you weren't so scared of him. He would never hurt you."

Jasper sank into a chair, unable to grasp what she'd told him. While she could make up a bunch of crap about Koda's former owner, there was no way she could know about the nightmares or the fact that Jasper had almost not taken Koda or how much he worked or any of the rest of it. No one knew. No one except Koda himself.

No, he thought, shaking his head. It was a trick. It had to be. Only it wasn't and with a certainty he couldn't explain and that sure as hell didn't make sense, he believed her. He *believed* her!

Holy crap—Verity could talk to animals.

He looked at Renee. "Why didn't you tell me?"

She rolled her eyes. "Really? Because I did tell you and you said I was lying. You thought I was insane."

She was right. He'd gotten angry because he'd been disappointed. He'd thought she was playing him. But she hadn't been. She'd been telling the truth and based on what he'd just heard, he had no choice but to believe her.

"I didn't get it," he admitted. "I mean I know you said the words, but this is incredible."

He glanced at his dog, not sure what to say to him. "Is he happy?"

"He seems to be."

All this time Koda'd been thinking those deep thoughts and Jasper hadn't known. He returned his attention to Verity. "How does it work? Do you hear words or get impressions or what?"

"There are some words. The ones the animal knows. Koda knows his name. It was Buddy before, by the way, but he likes Koda. The rest of it is feelings or images. I see what they see, feel what they feel. It's a one-way communication. I can't ask questions. They tell me what's most on their mind at the moment."

"Is it all animals or just some?"

"So far, it's been all animals. Domesticated animals are easiest. I've tried to communicate with wild animals, but everything is a jumble. We need a joint frame of reference." She rubbed Koda's ears. "He's a very good boy. You were lucky to find him."

"I was."

And now being a pet owner suddenly seemed like a much bigger responsibility.

Renee watched him cautiously. "So you believe me?"

"Sure. You heard what she said. How could I not believe you both?" He thought about how he'd acted before. "Man, I was a jerk. I'm sorry. It was just too incredible. But it's real." He grinned. "Damn."

She didn't seem convinced. "You seem okay with it. Are you sure?"

He thought about the question, wanting to let it all sink in. Was it unexpected? Of course. But the world was filled with things he had to take on faith—things that were real but that he couldn't see. Like gravity and quarks.

"Your mom can communicate with animals. That's fantastic."

She didn't look convinced. "I don't think it's sunk in yet."

"Renee, I'm not going to get upset. I think it's a great gift." He looked at Verity. "You're really lucky."

"That's what I think, too."

CHAPTER THIRTEEN

Renee wasn't sure what to make of everything that was happening. Jasper had invited them to stay for dinner and Verity had agreed. Not that Renee minded—she enjoyed Jasper's company and was relieved he seemed to be accepting of what he referred to as "Verity's gift," but she wasn't quite ready to let go of her concerns. There had been too many consequences of the truth coming out for her to believe everything was going to work out so easily.

Jasper defrosted some hamburger patties. There were buns in the pantry and plenty of pasta salad left over from the night before. Verity helped with the prep work while Renee set the table.

Koda watched her and she had to fight the urge to ask her mom what he was thinking. If she had to guess, she would say he wanted to know if she finally accepted him. Not that she had a clue. So far she was blissfully unaware of animal thoughts, which should have allowed her to relax. Only she kept waiting for that to change and it wasn't a comfortable thought.

When they were seated at the table, Jasper continue to pepper Verity with questions about her "gift."

"Can you turn it off?"

"Not really. I still hear thoughts, as if someone is standing next to me, having a conversation." She smiled. "It can get tiring after a while, which is why I've never had a pet at home. I need to be able to get away."

Renee added mustard to her bun. "Why are you so accepting? A lot of people have trouble believing in what my mom can do."

"Because of what she said. I was wrong before. I should have believed you, Renee. I'm sorry I didn't. What you said sounds far-fetched, but it's real."

He added pasta salad to his plate, then glanced at Verity. "I don't know how much Renee told you but after I got out of the army, I had pretty bad PTSD. I had different kinds of treatment. For some of it, I was in a hospital setting. Some of the guys there saw things. The doctors said they were hallucinations, but now I wonder if all of them were. Maybe they had a gift, too, because of their injuries or something."

"That's very open-minded of you," Verity said. "Not everyone can see it that way. There have been problems, especially for Renee."

"Mom, don't."

"It's all right, darling. Jasper should know."

"No, he shouldn't."

Verity ignored her. "Renee always wanted to study fashion. She was interested in the business end of things, working with the designers. While she was in college she got an internship with a famous fashion designer."

Renee sighed. "I was his assistant for the summer and I was perfectly happy to change directions. Marketing was a better fit for me."

"What happened?" Jasper asked, looking between them.

"I came to visit her," Verity said. "I was so excited. I'd never been to New York before. She took me to her office and gave me a tour." She paused as tears filled her eyes.

"Mom, it's okay."

"It's not. I'm so sorry." She sighed. "I met her boss, who was a hideous little man with a Pekinese dog who was wonderful. She told me he was having an affair with three of the other interns and wanted me to warn Renee that she was next."

Renee turned to Jasper. "When my mom gets information, she can't help blurting it out. She not only told him she knew about the affairs, she told him off for taking advantage of college-age students and threatened to tell his wife."

"I couldn't help myself," Verity admitted. "I was so angry. Unfortunately, my temper cost Renee her internship."

"I wouldn't have stayed after learning that."

Verity picked up her wine. "It wasn't that she quit, it was that he ruined her reputation, telling lies about her so no one would hire her. And it's all my fault."

"You told the truth." Jasper looked furious. "He was the scumbag. I hope you told his wife."

Verity shook her head. "I didn't, but I heard later they split up so maybe she found out."

"It turned out for the best," Renee said lightly. "I'm where I belong. I love my job and my clients." And her new hometown, she thought, wondering how her mother's show was going to change things.

"But you would have loved working in fashion."

"Mom, let it go. I'm happy. That's what matters."

Jasper met her gaze. She wondered what he was thinking, but didn't feel this was the best time to ask.

"Tell Mom about the book you're writing," she said instead.

"Jasper writes about a grumpy detective and now he has to write in a love interest. It's been a challenge."

Jasper chuckled. "He's not grumpy, but he does have an edge. I've learned that I don't write women well. It's very humbling."

"Men and women think different," Verity told him. "Men are very good at compartmentalizing. For women, it's everything at once. When a man has a bad day at work, he can decide to not think about it that night, but a woman has more trouble letting go."

Jasper stared at her. "You're right. I knew that but I never put it so concisely."

Renee smiled knowing that if her mother weren't having dinner with them, Jasper would have excused himself to go make some notes. He would promise to be back in five minutes and wouldn't resurface for hours.

"Renee mentioned you're getting a show on Animal Planet. What's that about?"

Verity waved her glass of wine. "I just had a wonderful conversation with my producer. They're very excited. They already have several families with pets lined up. I'll go into their home and observe the situation, then listen to what the pet has to say. After that, the whole family gets together and we try to work on whatever the problem is. We'll have animal behaviorists there, along with family psychologists. Our goal is to help the entire family unit, not just the pet."

She glanced at Renee. "I just hope it's not too difficult for you."

"It won't be," Renee assured her. "Mom, you deserve this. The show is going to be a big success and I want that for you."

"But everyone is going to know who I am. We have the same last name and you have a life here."

"I'll be fine."

"No one is going to mind," Jasper said. "If any of your friends figure out the connection, they'll be good with it."

Renee was less convinced, but she hoped he was right. Either way, they were here and there was no going back.

"We'll have miles of silver tulle," Renee promised from her seat at the conference table.

"And fourteen Christmas trees?" Katya asked anxiously.

"As requested." And life-size nutcrackers and centerpieces of wrapped presents and blown glass ornaments and all things seasonal, Renee thought. "Katya, your wedding is going to be a magical day. We're all excited to see it come together."

The slightly overweight blonde relaxed. "Thank you. It's just I want everything to be perfect."

"That's what I want, too," Renee told her. "So you'll get me your decisions by the middle of next week?"

Katya nodded. "I promise. Thanks, Renee. Bye."

Renee disconnected the call, then looked at Pallas. "That went better than I thought."

"Uh-huh. You handled her well but she is going to be trouble. I like how you didn't promise things would be perfect."

"Not a promise I can keep, but I can work in that direction."

Pallas gathered up her notes. "You don't like them."

"Who?"

"Katya and Jeremy. You think they're far more interested in the wedding than the marriage."

"There's no way you could know that without thinking it yourself."

Pallas laughed. "Fine. I feel it, too. It's the weirdest thing, how we get a sense about our couples. There must be subtle signals they're putting out. So far I've been right on every couple I thought wasn't going to make it."

"Me, too."

"So we're psychic. That makes us special. How's your mom?"

The change in subject, not to mention the recent mention of being psychic freaked out Renee just a little bit.

"She's fine."

"I saw her jogging through town on my way to work," Pallas admitted. "I so need to get back into exercising. What does she do?"

"My mom?"

Pallas tilted her head. "I asked the question casually, but now I'm really curious. Is everything okay?"

"It's fine. Completely. She's great. As for what she does…" Renee held in a groan. She wasn't handling the situation well at all. "She, ah, used to be hairdresser."

"She seems young to have retired. Did she hit the lotto? Because that would be so fun."

"No, not the lotto." Renee knew there was no point in not telling her boss the truth. "She's going to get her own show on Animal Planet."

"What? Really? Her own TV show? That is so cool! What's it about?"

"My mom knows what animals are thinking. So she can figure out if something's wrong."

She spoke as casually as she could, all the while bracing herself for derisive laughter or shrieking and pointing.

"She talks to animals?" Pallas asked.

"No, they talk. She just listens. It's not a two-way thing."

"I've never heard of that. It could be a really useful skill. Remember when we had the zebras at the black-and-white wedding? We could have used someone to intercede with them for sure."

"I wasn't here then," Renee murmured. "But I heard about it." The zebras had escaped and had to be rounded up.

"It would have been nice for someone to give them a stern talking-to." She rose. "A show on Animal Planet. Your mom's going to be a celebrity and I can say I knew her before it all happened. Cool."

With that she walked out, as if nothing had happened. They were just talking—sharing idle conversation. First Jasper and now Pallas. While the acceptance was nice, it was very unexpected. In the past, people finding out the truth had been a disaster. She'd lost so much, including her own father. But maybe things were different this time. Or maybe the disaster was lurking right around the corner.

As always, when the writing started to be a lot more work than usual, Jasper headed for town. Now that the summer heat had eased into slightly more reasonable fall temperatures, the tourists were back, so there was always something interesting going on. Maybe when it got closer to dinner, he would text Renee and see if she was available. With her mom in town, they might have plans. Still, she could invite him along.

He parked in one of the big public lots and headed for the river. Walkways lined both sides of Rio de los Suenos, as did stores and restaurants. The Boardroom was on the southeast side of the river, along with Chapel on the Green—competition for Renee's Weddings Out of the Box. On the northwest side were lots of shops, including the Willow Gallery.

He paused to watch a stretch limo cross the river, no doubt taking a wedding party to their hotel before the festivities began in a couple of days.

He paused outside Starbucks, not sure he wanted coffee this late, then headed down the block to get a slice of pie. He'd just taken a couple of steps when he heard someone calling his name. He turned and saw Verity walking toward him.

"I thought that was you," she said, waving at him. "You're in town."

"I am. Taking a break from the writing."

"I'm exploring. Happily Inc is a wonderful little town. So charming. Did you see that huge limo that just went by?"

"It's nearly the weekend. We're all about weddings here. It's big business."

"Renee has mentioned that but I had no idea it was so all encompassing."

He motioned to the 1950s-style soda shop up ahead. "I was going to get a piece of pie. Want to join me?"

Verity smiled at him. "I'm not much into pie but I would love a milkshake."

"You're on. Any flavor you want."

She laughed and let him guide her into the brightly lit café.

"Brace yourself," he said as they entered. "They take their time warp very seriously."

There was a long counter at one end and big, red vinyl booths in front of the window. A working jukebox sat against the far wall and "Rock Around the Clock" played on overhead speakers.

"I love it!" Verity told him.

A waitress waved toward the booths. "Take whatever's open," she said. "I'll be right with you."

They sat across from each other. Verity looked over the menu, her lips curving up as she read. "Now I'm sorry I already had lunch. I'll have to come back tomorrow for sure and have a burger. In the meantime I'll indulge myself with an Oreo cookie milkshake."

"Just avoid the place on the weekends," Jasper told her. "The wedding crowds pretty much take over. It's easier to hunker down and wait them out."

"Is it really that bad?"

"You'll see for yourself. My friend Garrick is a cop in town and he spends his weekends chasing down people who've had too much to drink and want to pick a fight because of something that happened at a wedding or one of fifty-seven other crimes that aren't much on their own but do tend to add up in volume. Come Monday, we return to our sleepy selves."

"How fascinating. Does everyone in town work in the wedding industry?"

"Most. There are all the service providers, that sort of thing. Three brothers I know are artists, and Cade and his wife have a horse ranch just outside of town."

Their server appeared. She wore a red apron over a frilly white dress. "What looks good?" she asked cheerfully.

"I'll have the Oreo cookie milkshake," Verity told her.

Jasper glanced at the specials written on a blackboard. The pie selections were blueberry and apple.

"Blueberry pie with a scoop of vanilla."

"You got it. Want the pie warmed?"

"Sure. Thanks."

Their server left.

"Did you grow up here?" Verity asked.

"No. Montana. I got here via the army and my writing career. I was on a book tour, driving myself because I couldn't deal with flying." He paused. "Did Renee tell you about that?"

"No." Verity's expression turned sad. "She's learned to be very good at keeping secrets. She would never tell me yours."

"It's not a secret. I was in the army for about ten years. Military police. I saw a lot of crap you shouldn't have to see and when I got out, I was messed up in the head, big-time. I went through a lot of treatments. One day our assignment was to write. No subject, just try to get something on paper."

He smiled. "I started writing and writing. A few weeks

later, someone gave me an old laptop. About a year in, I realized I might have something close to a story."

"The mind's ability to heal is a miraculous thing," Verity told him.

"I agree. I managed to sell my first book and they sent me on tour, but I was still too shaky to get on a plane." He shuddered at the memory. "Way too many people too close together, so I drove. My car broke down right here in Happily Inc."

He paused, wondering if Renee had told her Happily Inc's origin story. "You don't know how the town got its name, do you?"

Sadness flashed in Verity's eyes. It was quickly replaced by interest, but not fast enough. Jasper saw the emotion and wondered how much of her life Renee kept from her mother and why. Was it all about fear or was there something else going on?

The server returned with glasses of water and their orders. Verity unwrapped her straw.

"I don't know anything about the town. Not really. Tell me."

"Back in the 1950s, the town was going under. There was no industry, no tourists and no hope. Frank Dineen owned the local bank and he refused to lose everything, so he invented a history for the town. He talked about how a stagecoach taking brides to the gold fields back during the gold rush had a breakdown. Back then it took a long time to get parts and by the time the coach was ready to go again, all the brides had fallen in love and the stagecoach left empty."

"That's a nice story, but it's not true?"

"Not a word of it. Frank got the town to officially change its name to Happily Inc, then sold the whole thing in Hollywood. A few big stars came out here to get married and the wedding destination idea was born. The town's been growing ever since."

Verity smiled. "That's wonderful. Not the lie, of course, but the rest of it. So when your car broke down, you were experiencing your version of the origin story."

"I didn't know it at the time, but yes. I was stuck for a couple of days. The mechanic loaned me an old clunker car to get around. I went up the mountain and found a house for sale." He took a bite of pie. "I had my advance money burning a hole in my pocket. Between that and my savings, it was enough to buy the house. I bought the place, drove back to LA, packed up and returned here."

"You sound happy."

The statement surprised him. Jasper didn't think of himself as *happy*. He was broken or damaged goods or whatever variation of that made sense in the moment. But happy?

"I wouldn't say that."

"I would." Her tone was firm. "Have you been married before?"

"What?" He put down his fork. "No. I'm not the marrying kind."

"You don't like children?"

"What? No. Of course I like kids. Why would you ask that?"

"Just curious. It's a reason not to get married."

"You never remarried," he pointed out.

"That's different."

"How?"

Verity sipped her milkshake for a minute. "At first I didn't want to hurt Renee more than she had been already. You're very accepting of my..."

"Gift," he said firmly.

"Fine. My gift, but not everyone is. Renee's father left because of it. I'm not so sure he wouldn't have left anyway, but my abilities gave him something to blame." Verity looked away, as if trying to keep him from seeing what she was feeling. "It was hard on her. Renee loved her dad."

"They didn't keep in touch?"

Verity returned her attention to him. "No. He was simply gone. I suppose I could have forced him to visit her through the courts, but to what end? It wouldn't have been better for her. My point is, getting involved with a man seemed to invite more heartbreak into her life and I didn't want that. I suppose by the time she grew up, I was out of the habit of dating."

"You could start now."

Verity laughed. "I see. Because you're writing about a relationship, we all have to be in one?"

"Maybe."

"Do you expect us to be serial killers, too?" She shook her finger at him. "I've been reading up on you and I know what you write." Her humor faded. "There's darkness in those stories."

"There is, but to quote Shrek, 'Better out than in.'"

Verity laughed. "That's an excellent point. How do you know about Shrek?"

"I'm friends with a kid in town. His mother and I used to be involved. Hunter always claimed to be too old for animated movies but he would bring them up to the house for us to watch together." Jasper thought about Hunter's most recent visit and grimaced. "I miss the movies. He's growing up too fast. He's thirteen and the last time we hung out he mentioned a girl in his class. I'm not ready for him to be interested in girls."

"You can't stop time."

"I can try."

"Good luck with that."

He finished his pie. "Why didn't you ever go into animal consulting?" he asked. "You could have done well with something like horse racing. Or maybe helping with the big dog shows."

"I never thought about it," she admitted. "I suppose I could have...after Renee left for college, of course."

Because Renee didn't like that her mother was so different. No, he mentally amended. She didn't like the impact it had on her life. He wondered what other pain Renee had inadvertently suffered.

"I'm happy with the show," Verity said. "I want to help and I think it will be fun."

"You're going to be a big success."

She ducked her head. "I don't really care about that. I'm just ready for a change. I'm not getting any younger." She took another sip of her milkshake. "Are you in love with my daughter?"

Jasper nearly bolted. He felt his muscles tense as fight-or-flight kicked in. As there was no way he was going to fight Verity, and running was stupid and cowardly, he was left with an uncomfortable adrenaline rush and nowhere to put it.

Love? No and no. He didn't love Renee and they weren't going there. That was the point. Sex with a few laughs and nothing more. Not that he could say that to her mother.

"That's a pretty personal question."

"Is it?" She studied him. "You care about her a lot."

"She's, ah, great and we have fun together but I haven't known her very long. Besides, it's not like that for us. Renee doesn't want anything permanent and I can't."

"What do you mean you can't? You said you weren't married."

"I'm not. I'm single. It's what I told you before. About

coming back broken. The therapists warned me I would get better, but I might never be normal."

"That's ridiculous. You might have had issues before, but there's nothing wrong with you now, Jasper. Anyone can see it." She sighed. "You young people today. Why are you so afraid of commitment? Loving someone is a wonderful thing. I would like to fall in love again at some point. Don't hide from one of our greatest blessings. The ability to love and be loved is what gives us our soul."

She sighed. "I'll stop lecturing you now, except for one thing. Please don't hurt my baby girl. I know she seems like nothing gets to her, but she has a heart and it can easily be shattered. Please don't do that to her."

He would rather she shot him than continue on the current topic. He didn't want to think about hurting Renee or who might have hurt her in the past or any of it.

"Yes, ma'am. I'll do my best."

"I suppose that's all any of us can ask."

She changed the topic, asking about Koda, and while Jasper answered her questions, he was still stuck on the love thing. Love? No way. Not him. He couldn't. But like Verity, he had to admit there was a part of him that wished it could be. Maybe just once.

CHAPTER FOURTEEN

By Sunday afternoon, Renee needed a break from her life. Having her mom around was much easier than it had been in the past and she was happy to spend time with her, but between the visit, her work and trying not to think about how her mother's new show would change everything, she was exhausted.

Both Friday's and Saturday's weddings had gone smoothly with only the slightest of hiccups. The Sunday morning "goodbye brunch" had ended when promised and the catering staff had cleaned up in record time, leaving Renee with a few extra hours she desperately needed.

Knowing Renee would be working pretty much 24/7, Verity had gone back to San Diego for the weekend with the promise to return on Monday, so Renee was off Mom duty until then. She had laundry to catch up on, bills to pay and an empty refrigerator, but she didn't want to complete any of her chores. She felt restless and uncomfortable and neither state had an explanation.

She went home and changed into crop pants and a T-shirt,

then told herself she really had to tackle the growing pile of laundry. She'd nearly convinced herself to start sorting when she heard her phone chime, notifying her of a text.

How's it going? Want some company?

Hearing from Jasper immediately made her feel better. I'd love some. She looked at the mess that was her apartment then added, Why don't I come there?

Perfect. See you in a few.

She stepped over the laundry, grabbed her keys and was out the door in less than a minute.

When she arrived at Jasper's place, he was waiting for her out front. He walked over and pulled her into his arms. She sank into him, savoring the strength of him, the way he enveloped her entire body.

"You give good hugs," she said.

"Thank you. I've been practicing."

"On who?"

"I believe the correct question is 'on whom' and I meant that more as a feeling than a declaration."

She smiled. "Just checking."

They walked into the house. Koda was waiting. Renee glanced at the dog, told herself it was going to be fine, then reached out and petted him. He gave her a tail wag and a quick lick on the hand and that was it. There was no voice screaming in her head, no hint of his thoughts at all. She was pushing thirty—maybe she could let the whole "I can talk to animals" thing go. Maybe the gift skipped a generation, which meant she could never have children, but that was a different problem.

"You okay?" Jasper asked.

"Just tired. It was a busy weekend at work, plus my mom's visit. She's great and I'm happy to spend time with her, but I beg you, do not bring up her name while I'm here."

She expected Jasper to laugh and agree or nod or anything but shift his gaze and look guilty. Seriously? She couldn't even get past his foyer without there being something?

"What?" she demanded. "She said she was going home for the weekend. Is she secretly hanging out here?"

"What? No. That would be uncomfortable for all of us. I'm fine not talking about your mother." He pointed to the kitchen. "Why don't I make you a margarita?"

"You know how?"

"I can look it up. It needs limes, right? I have limes and tequila. We can fake the rest."

"What about my mother?"

He shifted his weight from foot to foot. "I hung out with her for a bit."

"What? When? What does—" she made air quotes "—'hung out with' mean?"

"I came into town because the writing wasn't going well and I ran into her. We walked around for a bit then got pie. Well, I got pie. She had a milkshake."

Which all sounded fine but there was only one thing they could have been doing the entire time. Talking.

"Yes to the margarita." She waved him toward the kitchen. "What did you talk about?"

"Lots of stuff. How the town got its name. How I ended up here. Whether or not I want kids."

She slid onto a stool at the island. "She asked you that?"

"It came up." He stood across from her, his hands on the counter. "She doesn't know much about your life."

Not exactly words designed to get her to like him more. "Don't judge me. You don't know anything about me."

"I know some. I know she loves you and misses you."

"You're taking her side?"

"There's no sides, Renee. I don't get it, is all. I never knew my mom. She died when I was a baby, so it was just me and my dad. He was a great guy. I know what that's like—being a team. I miss him every day. I guess I don't understand how you can cut her out of your life."

Annoyance flared. "Not that it's your business, but I don't cut her out. I stay in touch with her and I visit her."

"But you don't want her here."

"No, I don't. Or I didn't. It's not going to matter anymore. The secret's about to come out in a big way."

"Why does it matter so much? It's her thing, not yours."

Anger battled hurt. She shouldn't be surprised. It was always this way—at first everything was fine, but then it went to hell.

"It was her thing until all my friends found out. At first they were great. They would bring over their pets and ask her to tell them what they were thinking. So fun. But in high school, I was considered a freak. Even the weird kids avoided me. It was lonely. Eventually we moved so I could start over and that helped, but I was always afraid people would find out."

She could tell he didn't get it. Maybe he couldn't. Maybe it was something you had to live.

"My dad left because of her," she said.

"Maybe he would have left anyway. He didn't stay in touch with you, so he wasn't exactly a great guy."

Her eyes burned but she blinked back tears. "He was my father—you don't get to say that. You know what he told me the night he left? Do you know what he said? He told me it was just a matter of time until I was like her, too. That's why he couldn't stay and that's why he would never see me again.

I never told her. I didn't want to hurt her more than she had been, but he told me that was the reason he didn't want to see me again."

"He was an asshole."

"Regardless, he left me because of what might happen." She sucked in a breath and tried to hang on to her control. "Turner, the guy whose wife is pregnant? We were engaged. We were in love. We had our lives planned. It was everything I'd ever wanted. Then he met my mother and it was never the same. Two weeks later, he ended things. He didn't want to risk whatever it was being passed on to our children, and then he walked out."

She slid off the stool and glared at him. "It's so easy for you to judge my life. It's easy to tell me what to think and how it should be, but you don't know. You can never know."

"I get that, Renee. I'm sorry for all you've been through and I'm not trying to hurt you, but I know you're seeing this all wrong. You don't have her gift. You can't know what Koda's thinking any more than I can. So let that go. Just deal with your mom. Worrying about whether or not you will suddenly get what she has is messing up your perspective." He softened his voice. "I wish I could know what you're afraid of. Is it being different? Being rejected? Being blamed?"

She knew in her head he was probably trying to help. He was doing a sucky job of it, but intellectually she was willing to give him the benefit of the doubt. But in her heart and her gut, she wanted to lash out. She wanted to verbally and emotionally slash him until he lay on the floor bleeding and in pain. She wanted to hit him in all his soft places so he was the one exposed and vulnerable and then she wanted to judge him.

"You first," she said sharply. "You get over your past, your pain, your nightmares. You heal yourself. You come to me and tell me you figured it all out and then we'll talk. Until then, stay the hell out of my life."

Jasper stood stoically, taking it all in and not saying a word. She grabbed her bag and headed for the door. The sound of nails clicking on the floor followed her. Just before she walked outside, she turned and saw Koda right behind her. He looked anxious, as if he sensed the tension.

She paused. "It's okay. You're a good boy. Only Jasper is the asshole," she told the dog before closing the door behind her and driving away.

Tuesday morning Renee had moved from fuming to hurt. She hadn't heard from Jasper since leaving his place Sunday afternoon and she really thought she would. For all his macho guyness, he was actually kind of self-aware and she had been sure he would figure out that he'd basically dismissed her feelings, told her she was wrong about everything and that she had to get over it.

But her phone had been silent on the Jasper front, making her think getting involved with him had been a huge mistake. Her mom's return to Happily Inc on Monday had been a distraction. They'd had a nice afternoon and evening. Renee had managed to sleep a little and now she was determined to have a good week with absolutely no Jasper thoughts getting in her way.

Her plans lasted until 9:01 a.m. when she arrived at Weddings Out of the Box only to find Jasper in the parking lot, leaning against his truck, obviously waiting for her.

She stayed in her car for a second, thought briefly about running him over, only she knew it was wrong and she would have regrets later. She'd never deliberately hurt anyone in her life. It wasn't smart to change that now, even if he did deserve it.

She got out and slung her bag over her shoulder. Maybe she could pretend he wasn't there and march to her office without acknowledging him. Not as satisfying as physical violence but certainly more morally correct. But still kind of cowardly. So in the end, she walked toward him, determined not to react to anything he said.

When she stopped in front of him, he surprised her by cupping her face in his hands and kissing her.

"I was wrong," he told her as he released her. "I meant well, but I was wrong. I jumped all over you when I should have listened. You're right. I can't know what it was like and after a couple of hours with your mom, it's easy to take her side, but how does that help? There shouldn't be sides. You went through things I can't begin to understand. You're a good person and you're doing the best you can, just like she is and I am. I messed up. I'm sorry."

It wasn't a *bad* apology, she thought grudgingly. "You mess up a lot."

"I do. Especially with you."

"Why is that?"

She expected him to smile or make a joke. Instead he looked away, as if he couldn't meet her gaze.

"I haven't been in a real relationship before," he said, glancing back at her. "I had a girlfriend in high school and a few flings in the army, but since then there was only Wynn and that was more about..." He shrugged. "We didn't talk much."

Relationship? They weren't in a relationship. They were sex friends. But even as the thought formed, she thought maybe it was wrong. After all, there'd been a lot more friendship and a lot less sex than she'd imagined. A relationship. Could she? Did she want to?

She told herself this was not the time to deal with anything like that. She already had plenty going on. But a relationship? Maybe...

"I liked your mom a lot," he said, surprising her with the shift in subject. "I feel bad for her." He held up a hand. "I'm not saying you're wrong. You're not. It's a difficult situation. I got carried away. I want to tell you it won't happen again, but it probably will. I'll learn from what happened and try to do better next time. I mean that."

She felt her tension easing. "I'm sorry, too. I shouldn't have gone on that 'you first' rant. I felt attacked so I hit back. I'm explaining, not justifying."

"Relationships are hard."

Why did he have to keep saying the *R* word? "We could go back to just sex."

"No, I like this better."

She thought maybe she did, too. "Thank you for coming to apologize."

"You're welcome." He kissed her again. "Now you have to get to work and I should be writing. Do-over on you coming by for margaritas?"

"Absolutely."

"Good."

He got in his truck and she walked into her office. Her mood had lightened considerably and the knot in her stomach was gone. She might not want a relationship but she had to admit if she was going to try again, Jasper almost made it worth taking the risk.

The morning sped by quickly. At eleven thirty, she went out in the lobby to greet Tara and Owen, who were finalizing their football-themed wedding.

They arrived right on time, Tara greeting Renee with a happy hug, while Owen shook her hand.

They were a handsome couple, tall, athletic and easy to be

with. Tara was at least five-eight or -nine and Owen tow-ered above her. Next to them, Renee felt like a miniature version of the species.

"It's nearly the happy day," Renee said, leading them to the conference room. "I think you're going to be very pleased to see how everything is coming together."

"I found this really great meditation app," Tara said, smil-ing at Owen. "To keep myself centered."

"Someone was getting a little snappy." His tone was more teasing than annoyed.

"I was, but I'm better now. It's a lot to think about."

Renee motioned for them to take seats. She settled behind the computer and activated the connection with the screen. "I'm hoping that today's wrap-up meeting will calm your nerves and allow you to simply enjoy the experience."

Owen grabbed Tara's hand and kissed her knuckles. "It's nearly here, baby. We're going to get married."

"We are."

Renee sighed happily. Her gut told her this couple was going to make it and that made her feel good about their wedding.

She pulled up the file and they went through the entire day from arrival to the final dance. The football theme—with a heavy emphasis on the Dallas Cowboys—had turned out per-fectly. The silver-and-blue color scheme worked well for the reception. The food had been ordered, the drinks decided on.

Renee opened a box of jerseys that had been delivered for the wedding party and showed them to Tara and Owen.

Tara fingered the fabric. "It's really nice quality, just like you said. I like that they're not too thin."

"We'll have them all steamed and hanging by the time of the wedding," Renee assured her. "They'll be perfect. Do you want the steamer heated for your reception dress?"

Tara was wearing her great grandmother's wedding gown for the ceremony, then changing into a more contemporary party dress for the reception.

"I shouldn't need it."

Renee made a note on her tablet. "I'm going to make sure it's ready for you, just in case."

They went over the rest of the details. The groom's cake was in the shape of a jersey and instead of throwing the garter, Owen would be throwing a football signed by Dak Prescott. As he did every time the signed football was mentioned, he grumbled about giving something away that he would rather keep. Renee was careful not to look at Tara, afraid her amusement would give away the secret. What Owen didn't know was that Tara had two signed footballs and Owen would receive the other one after the reception.

The meeting took less than ninety minutes. Tara and Owen left reassured that their big day would go smoothly. Renee added a few things to her master calendar, then shut down the conference room and returned to her office. She'd barely started to think she should eat the lunch she'd brought from home when her friend Carol walked into her office.

Renee didn't bother hiding her surprise. "What's going on?" she asked. "You never just pop in. Is everything all right?"

Carol nodded even as she twisted her fingers together in obvious distress.

"What's wrong?" Renee asked. "Just blurt it out. We'll both feel better."

Carol hesitated a second before saying, "Pallas told me. I don't know if she was supposed to or not, but she did and now I can't stop thinking about it and is it really true? Can your mother talk to animals?"

Renee held in a groan. "She doesn't talk. She listens while

they tell her what's on their mind." She braced herself for laughter and possibly derision, because really? Communicating with animals?

"Thank God." Carol moved closer to her desk. "I need her help. I'm desperate. There's something wrong with the giraffes. I don't know what, but they feel off to me and I'm responsible for them and I worry I'm not giving them enough attention with Devon and everything, and I could really use her help." She paused to breathe. "If that's not asking too much."

"You want my mother to communicate with your giraffes?"

Carol nodded vigorously. "Please. I know something's wrong, but I can't figure out what and I'm scared."

Renee had no idea what to say. It was not the reaction she'd been expecting, or had ever gotten before. "Um, sure. Let me call her right now." She pulled out her cell phone and dialed. When her mother answered, she explained the situation, listened for a second, then hung up.

"She says she will absolutely do her best. I'm going to get her right now and we'll meet you at the animal preserve."

"Thank you." Carol raced out, turned. "Really. Thank you so much. I can't wait to meet your mom."

"Give us twenty minutes."

Renee was still contemplating the unexpected turn of events as she parked in front of the Sweet Dreams Inn. Verity was waiting by the main doors and quickly hurried to the car.

"I hope I can help," her mother said as she fastened her seat belt. "I've never been able to understand wild animals because we don't share a language. Domestic animals are different, of course. I'm hoping your friend's giraffes have been around people enough that they can share their thoughts with me." She smiled at Renee. "This is very exciting."

"It's not how I spend my day—that's for sure."

Renee drove out past the dump and recycling center and entered the animal preserve. Carol was there, along with Ed, her father. Renee made the introductions.

"I put the female giraffes in their barn," Carol said, leading the way. "I've kept them separate so they won't distract each other."

"I have to warn you that while I'll do my best, I can't make any promises," Verity said before explaining how she couldn't communicate with wild animals. "We don't have a shared frame of reference."

"Makes sense," Ed told her. "What about birds and fish? Or is it just mammals?"

"I've never been able to tell what a fish is thinking. I can get through to some birds. Doves are silent but swans don't shut up and they have opinions about everything. I've always wanted to try communicating with a dolphin, but I haven't had the chance."

"Fascinating," Ed murmured, holding open a large door. "Let's go see what the ladies think of you and vice versa."

Renee felt incredibly out of place in a dress and pumps. Her mother was in jeans and Carol and Ed wore what she would describe as safari gear—khakis and polo shirts. Given their work at the preserve, their wardrobe made sense.

The barn wasn't a barn at all, but a huge open building with big cages or stalls with wood and chain-link walls. The ceiling had to be at least twenty-five feet high, which made sense when one was housing giraffes.

There were tall windows, plenty of light and lots of ventilation. Renee inhaled the scent of hay and fresh air. Three beautiful giraffes watched them curiously. They were leggy and powerful with stunning faces and incredibly long lashes.

"The giraffes are usually kept outside during the day," Carol told them. "We bring them in at night to keep them safe. They're not exactly domesticated but they were all born in captivity and have a 'will work for food' mentality. I'm hoping you can tell me what they're thinking."

"Wonderful," Verity said. "They are simply wonderful. What a joy to work with them every day." She glanced at Ed. "You started the preserve?"

"My brother and I did. We'd had plans for a while and just needed the right location and an influx of cash." He shrugged. "We found this place right as a distant relative passed away, leaving us the heirs. It all worked out."

They smiled at each other. Renee couldn't help thinking this was the strangest afternoon she'd had in maybe forever.

Carol led them to the first giraffe. "This is Mrs. Santora. She's the one I'm worried about the most. She's just not herself lately."

Verity nodded and looked into Mrs. Santora's brown eyes. "You are a beauty, aren't you?"

The giraffe stared back, then took a step forward. The barn went silent. Anticipation crackled in the air. Renee desperately hoped her mother would be able to—

"Oh! That was very clear." Verity smiled at Carol. "Who is Dave?"

"Our male giraffe. I left him outside. He can be a little bit of an attention hog."

"Mrs. Santora doesn't like him at all. She wishes you'd stop putting them out together. She finds him annoying and just wants to be with her friends."

Carol's mouth dropped open. "No way! I was thinking of taking her off birth control so she and Dave could mate but first I wanted to see how they got along. That's why she's been acting so weird." She looked at Mrs. Santora. "Is that what it is? I'm sorry. I won't make you hang out with him if you don't want to."

"Well, I'll be," Ed muttered. "That's amazing."

"It is," Carol said, leading Verity to the second giraffe. "This is Ida. She and Mrs. Santora came together. They're Millie's girlfriends, her herd. I just want them to be happy."

Verity nodded, then stared at Ida. Once again the barn went silent. Renee watched her mother and saw her lips twitch, as if she were trying to hold in laughter. Verity listened for nearly a minute before looking at Carol.

"Ida doesn't have many concerns, except she would like you and the man I'm assuming is your husband to stop having sex in the savanna. She finds it upsetting and not anything she wants to see. You should stay in your own barn for that sort of thing."

Carol flushed. "Oh. I didn't know they could— Um, well, that's interesting. Let's go meet Millie. She was our original giraffe. We did some fund-raising to get her a herd so she could have friends."

As Carol approached Millie, the giraffe lowered her head over the gate. Carol rubbed her face while Millie nibbled her fingers.

"You're a beautiful girl, aren't you," Verity said, smiling at Millie. The giraffe looked at her.

This time there was no laughter. Verity's expression was intense and their conversation went on for a long time. Finally Verity looked at Carol.

"Millie is very worried that you're going to get distracted by your husband and baby and won't have time for her anymore."

"Oh, that would never happen." Carol looked at Millie. "You'll always be my girl. You have to know that."

"There's more," Verity told her. "Millie's pregnant."

Carol stared at the giraffe. Ed walked over and hugged his daughter.

"Did you hear that?" he asked. "Millie's pregnant." He looked at Verity. "We were hoping, but with a giraffe, it's difficult to tell. Plus the gestation is so long." He grinned. "We're going to have a baby."

"That's wonderful."

Renee felt as if she couldn't keep up. There was too much information coming at them too fast. Not liking Dave, Millie worrying about being abandoned, a new giraffe baby.

She squeezed her mother's hand. "You're doing great, Mom."

"Yes, it's fantastic." Carol hugged her. "Thank you so much. This means the world to me. I've been so worried and now I know what to do."

"You're welcome. I'm happy to help. Shall we go see what Dave has to say?"

"Let's."

Carol paused to give Millie one last pat before taking them outside where Dave stood in a large pen, dining on leaves. Several massive branches had been hoisted up and hooked onto a pole that was just the right height for him. As they approached his pen, he glanced at them before strolling over.

"He's quite the handsome man," Verity said.

Carol laughed. "Dave has some attitude, that's for sure. I'm curious as to what he's concerned about. He doesn't seem to have any problems in his life."

"Men are simple creatures," Ed said with a laugh. "I'll be the first to admit it."

Verity and Dave established eye contact. It was only for a couple of seconds, then Dave turned and walked away.

Carol glanced at Verity. "Anything?"

"He would like more of something called a leafeater treat. That was it. He was fairly insistent."

Carol laughed. "They're like giraffe cookies and Dave loves

them. I'm not surprised he wants more." She spun in a circle. "I'm so relieved. Thank you, thank you, thank you."

"You were incredible," Ed said. "This has been a big help. If I promise not to make you talk to any other residents, would you like to take a tour of the grounds?"

The question surprised Renee, as did her mother's response, "I'd like that a lot, but I'm afraid I came with my daughter and I would guess she has to get back to work."

"I can take you where you need to go when we're done," Ed said, as he smiled at Renee. "If that's all right with you."

"Of course." Renee hugged her mother. "Have fun on the tour. It's a wonderful place."

"I can see that."

"I'll walk you out," Carol said.

They returned along the same path they'd taken on the way in.

"Thank you for loaning me your mom. I'm relieved and happy and excited to know what my giraffes are thinking. I can't believe Millie's pregnant. I hate that she's been worried about me not being there for her. I'll take extra time with her. Maybe I should bring Devon out to meet her. Do you think that would comfort her or make her jealous?"

"I have no idea. Sorry."

Carol grinned. "That's okay. Giraffes aren't your thing the way they're mine. I wonder if there's any research on the topic. I'll have to go online and see."

Renee was more caught up in the total acceptance of her mom's ability and the fact that Carol believed everything she said. It hadn't ever been like this before. Not that she'd had many friends who'd needed help with their giraffes.

"I'm glad she could help," she murmured as they approached her car.

"More than helped. I can't wait to see her show. It's going

to be amazing." Carol hugged her. "Thank you again. You're the best."

"I didn't do anything, but sure, thank me all you want."

They both laughed. Renee headed back to work, happy about what had happened and just a little confused about how easily her mother was fitting in. Maybe she'd been worried for nothing. Maybe it was all going to be just fine.

CHAPTER FIFTEEN

"Are you sure?" Verity asked for the third time as she set a stack of plates on the long table next to a cafeteria-size take-out container of enchiladas. "You're sweet to invite me, but this is your life. I don't want to interfere."

Not that long ago, Renee would rather have had root canal than invite her mother to hang out with her friends, but ever since the "giraffe incident" as she thought of it, Renee had found herself much more relaxed when it came to her mother. Maybe she'd just needed a few positive experiences to put things in perspective.

"You're only in town a few weeks," she said. "Once the show starts, you're going to be wildly busy and I'll never get to see you. The girlfriend lunches are a big part of my life. Of course I want you here."

"Thank you, sweetie. I appreciate that. So how often do you have these lunches?"

"Mostly every week. We rotate through the locations." Renee smiled. "When it's Carol's turn and the weather is nice, we eat out with the animals."

"Did that bother you?"

"At first. They got a little close but I never heard their thoughts." Something for which she would always be grateful. "When it's my turn or Pallas's turn, we eat here, at Weddings Out of the Box. Whoever is hosting provides an entrée. Everyone else brings what they want."

Renee and Pallas had already set up a long table with enough chairs in the shade. There were pitchers of iced tea, along with lemonade.

Pallas walked in a few minutes before noon. She set down a nine-by-thirteen casserole dish and waved a large bag of tortilla chips.

"To complement your enchiladas," she said. "Seven-layer bean dip. We are going to party today." Pallas smiled at Verity. "I'm so excited you're going to join us. This is fun."

"Thank you for letting me participate."

Wynn and Bethany walked in together. Renee made introductions all around, then poured drinks for everyone.

"I heard what happened with Carol," Bethany said. "It's so great how you were able to help her." She paused. "Cade and I have some horses we're concerned about. We have a horse ranch. Do you think you could come talk to them or am I asking too much?"

"I'd be happy to help if I can," Verity said easily. "I get along well with horses."

"Me, too, and I can usually guess what's going on, but a little direct communication would be helpful."

"You should open a satellite office here in Happily Inc," Pallas teased. "Verity's Animal Communication Network— East."

They were all laughing when the rest of the women arrived.

Everyone met Verity and got drinks, then they put food on their plates and settled at the big table. Renee quickly realized she didn't have to worry about her mother. Wynn sat on one side and Silver sat on the other and she had both of them laughing.

Carol was next to Renee. She leaned over and lowered her voice. "I hope you're okay with us stealing your mom like we did."

"Of course. She was thrilled to help."

"Are you upset—I guess you wouldn't be anymore—but when you were little, were you upset that you couldn't do what she does?"

"What?"

"Her gift or whatever you call it. You don't have it. That must have made you sad."

Something Renee had never considered. She hadn't wanted what her mother had, she hadn't wanted her mother to have it. But Carol's perspective was totally different. Not just because she hadn't lived through what Renee had, but because she had a practical application for the information.

"I wasn't sad," Renee told her, not sure what else to say.

"So Hunter's getting interested in girls," Wynn announced, drawing everyone's attention. "I can't believe it. He's only thirteen. I thought I had a couple of years left until I had to deal with that."

"Thirteen." Pallas looked shocked. "Don't tell me that. I don't want to have to deal with Ryan and girls for a while yet."

"He's barely six months old," Silver reminded her. "You have a ways to go."

"But still." Pallas sighed. "My baby."

"What did you do?" Renee asked. "Talk about it with him or lock him in his room?"

"I wish I could lock him in his room, but they frown on that now." Wynn grinned. "I told him to talk to Jasper."

Everyone burst out laughing. Renee chuckled as she

thought of what she would guess was a serious case of panic on Jasper's part.

"I have an announcement," Bethany said. "I told my parents I'm pregnant."

"Good for you."

"Yikes, how did it go?"

"Oh, no. Poor you."

Verity glanced around the table. "I'm confused. Why wouldn't you tell your parents? Don't they want grandchildren?"

"Oh, they want them. There was shrieking and tears and a thousand questions about my health, and that's just from my dad."

"Bethany comes from an unusual family," Pallas told Verity. "How should I put this…"

"Oh, you're the royal one," Verity said. "Did I get that right?"

Bethany sighed. "You did. My dad is the king of El Bahar. Technically he's my stepfather, but he adopted me and I'm the only daughter and my brothers are much younger, so it's a lot of pressure. I wanted to tell them because they're my parents and I didn't want to tell them because he's going to be overprotective and make my life a nightmare."

"Ah, I see. He loves his little girl." Verity nodded. "That's lovely."

"You say that now, but you're not the one who's going to have fifteen bodyguards and a cadre of servants making sure I don't fall, trip or otherwise injure my delicate self and his very first grandchild."

"It's tough being royal," Silver said. "Bethany, be brave and endure the pain."

"Bite me."

They all laughed again. Conversation shifted to different

topics. Renee enjoyed the time with her friends and appreciated how easily her mother fit in. She couldn't help wondering how everything would have been different if her mother wasn't...special. In some ways, a lot of ways, life would have been easier. But Verity's ability made her who she was and Renee knew that whatever happened, she wouldn't want her mother to change for anyone. Not even for Renee herself.

Jasper had no idea what Verity wanted, but she'd sounded upset on the phone. He drove to town and met her in the lobby of the Sweet Dreams Inn.

She was pacing anxiously when he walked in and immediately hurried over to him.

"Thank you for coming. Something's happened and I just don't know what to do."

Jasper had just texted with Renee a couple of hours before so he knew she was fine. He led Verity to a quiet area of the lobby and pulled a chair close to hers.

"Tell me what's going on."

She bit her lower lip. "Odele, my producer, called. They've been brainstorming fun prelaunch ideas for my show. Something that would get the public's attention and get them interested. Odele wants it a little gimmicky, but not off-putting. I was fine with all that and said she could reach me here if she wanted to talk."

Jasper really wanted to hurry her along, but knew it was better to let Verity tell her story in her own way. Eventually she would get to the point.

"Odele called me this morning," Verity admitted. "They've come up with what they think is a wonderful idea."

He waited.

"A giant dog wedding."

Her voice was thick with emotion and he had the horow many dogs would there be in a giant dog wedding? Twenty? Fifty? And why did it matter?

Her lower lip trembled. "Odele knows where I am and she must have done research on the town because she wants to have the ceremony or whatever it is at Weddings Out of the Box!"

Ah, so there was the problem.

"You're concerned Renee is going to be upset."

"Yes. I just got my baby girl back. We're getting along and she's letting me into her life and now this! She's going to hate the idea. What a nightmare. Dogs running everywhere, me talking to them, the TV cameras." Tears filled her eyes. "I tried to tell Odele we couldn't, but she was insistent and then she had to go. She's very determined and I don't want to jeopardize my show, but if I have to choose, of course I want Renee to be happy."

Jasper knew the situation was more complicated than that. He also knew Verity really wanted to make her show a success and that Renee wanted that for her mother.

"Has Odele booked the, ah, event?"

"Not yet. She's finalizing details before she calls. She said it would be a day to set up and a day to film. They're talking midweek."

"Then that's a good thing. Pallas gets more business without a lot of work and none of the scheduled weddings get impacted."

"You're right. I hadn't thought of that. I'm sure the production company is paying very well." She brightened. "That will help. So all that's left is for you to tell Renee what's happening."

"Me?"

"Please, Jasper. She won't get mad at you."

He knew that Renee was more than capable of getting plenty angry at him, but that wasn't Verity's point. She didn't want to have to fight with her daughter now, when things were going well between them.

Damn, he thought grimly, seeing no way out of the situation. If he refused, he would upset Renee's mother. If he said yes, he would upset Renee. Either way, he was screwed, because Renee wouldn't like him upsetting her mother or herself so hey, no win for him.

"I'll do it."

"You will? Oh, thank you, Jasper."

"Uh-huh. In return, you're going to tell her how great I am until she's done wanting to back the car over me."

"I promise."

Pallas and Renee met weekly to discuss the upcoming weddings and share leads they had about future clients. While Renee generally enjoyed the breakneck pace of their days, she found herself looking forward to the last three weeks of January, when Weddings Out of the Box would shut down for vacation. She didn't have any plans at the moment, but she was thinking somewhere quiet and peaceful with absolutely no brides or wedding parties or drama.

As Pallas reviewed the schedule, Renee took a second to wonder if Jasper would be interested in joining her for some of that time—just the two of them with no distractions except the ones they came up with together.

She had no idea if they were in a place where that was a question she could even ask. While he'd used the *R* word, she was less sure of their status. A relationship? But going away with him would be nice.

"You have it all under control," Pallas said, closing the calendar program. "We're also getting more and more busy. I used to have one wedding a weekend and I had the occasional weekend with nothing. Now we have at least two weddings or we have a wedding party booking us Friday through Sunday. I need to get serious about hiring help."

"The work is very steady," Renee said. "I would really like a couple of assistants on the days we have weddings. Someone to run and get things when we need extra thread or spot remover. I feel as if I'm forever racing back and forth across the property."

"Of course." Pallas nodded. "That would be easy enough. Most of our weddings are on Saturdays, so I could look at hiring high school kids who want a job on weekends. Of course they would have to be willing to give up their Saturday nights." She smiled. "Let me write up a job description. Once you agree I've captured what you're looking for, we'll post it and start interviews."

"That would be great." Renee knew she could always rely on her vendors to pitch in, but she needed more help than that.

"I think we need another wedding coordinator," Pallas said. "There are just too many weddings, and business doesn't seem to be slowing down seasonally anymore. I've been keeping track of your workdays and there are weeks you're here sixty and seventy hours. You should have said something."

"It's been a challenge, but you've been dealing with Ryan. I didn't want to get in the way of that."

"I'll admit taking on another full-time employee scares me, but it's necessary. If things keep going the way they have been, you're going to burn out. Worse, I could lose you."

Lose her? Renee wanted to blurt out that she had no plans to leave, but knew better than to say that. She loved working for Pallas, but she had to maintain a little bit of decorum. At least on the surface.

"I would like to work a bit less," she murmured. "But I know hiring someone is a big step."

"It is." Pallas's expression turned mischievous. "Which is why sharing the worry and pain is such a good idea. I've been thinking a lot about inviting you to be a partner in the business and I'd like to move ahead with that, if you're still interested."

Renee's heart thundered in her chest. "With everything happening, I'd completely forgotten about that possibility. But I'm interested. Very interested."

"Good. I've been talking with my lawyer." Pallas wrinkled her nose. "I can't believe I even have a business lawyer but I do. Anyway, she has come up with several ways to bring you into the business. First I'll have a professional business evaluation done so we both know what the business is worth. Then we'll discuss options. You can buy in outright or over time with a percentage of your salary going to the purchase. We'd detail the division of duties, so there are no misunderstandings."

She paused, drumming her fingers on the table. "What else? Oh, the profits. Right now they would be shared based on a percentage of ownership, but also a division of labor. That means if you buy in 50 percent, then obviously you'd get 50 percent of the profits. But if you have to buy in over time, then you'd get your percentage and an added amount because you're working more than me."

She frowned. "I hope that makes sense. The legal stuff and the accounting rules do not come easily to me. Oh, and if we move forward with this, I'm granting you 5 percent ownership as soon as we sign the paperwork, so you'd own that right away, regardless of how we move forward." She leaned toward Renee. "What do you think?"

Renee's head was spinning. Not only was there was lot of

information to take in, she also couldn't believe this was really happening.

Pallas trusted her with her business. Pallas wanted them to be fifty-fifty partners! The concept was so impossibly wonderful that she couldn't take it in.

"I'm excited," she managed to say. "Yes, of course I'm interested. It's a wonderful opportunity."

"I'm glad you think so. You'll need to get a lawyer to look over everything. Nick says I can't recommend one because it would be a conflict of interest." She sighed. "He's such a guy. I'd say ask Wynn for a name. I'm sure she uses someone and I don't think she and I use the same person, so that would work."

"I'll text her today," Renee promised.

"And I'll get going on both job descriptions. For the part-time person and the full-time wedding coordinator. I really liked the hiring service I used when I found you, so I want to go with them again."

As they weren't yet partners, Renee was fairly sure Pallas was sharing rather than asking her opinion.

"What do you think about opening the place up to midweek events?" Pallas asked unexpectedly. "Not more weddings. I'm not sure any of us could handle that, but other types of gatherings might be interesting."

"Like corporate events," Renee said eagerly. "That's what I've been thinking about. Meetings or seminars. We have the space. If all we had to do was set up tables and chairs, that would be easy. Almost no work for us but some income."

Pallas nodded. "That's what I was thinking, too. We'd only need a couple of caterers to work with. They provide their own servers, they do the cleanup afterward, so we're left with logistics and putting away whatever supplies we had to get out. I know our janitorial service would like more hours. We could find out if they would do the setup and takedown."

"We'd have to get a cut of the catering," Renee told her. "Because that's where all the money is. I suppose we could set up different menus so everything flows through us. Oh, what about themed events? We have the decorations from all the weddings. Depending on the type of business, we could offer different packages. It would add an interesting element to the event."

"A *Star Trek*–themed corporate getaway?" Pallas asked with a laugh. "I like it. You know, I was playing with this idea right around the time Nick and I got together. Then we fell in love and got married and I got pregnant and what is it they say? Life happens. I'm so glad you want to be a part of this."

"Me, too."

"Anybody home?"

Renee turned toward the open doorway. "That sounds like Jasper."

She got up and called his name. Seconds later, he came into view.

"You're not in your office," he said. "But your car is in the parking lot. I was starting to think you'd been abducted by aliens." He lightly kissed her, then waved at Pallas. "Am I interrupting?"

"We were just finishing up," Pallas told him. "Are you here to steal her away for a few hours?" Her voice was teasing.

Renee immediately thought that why yes, she could make the time, but before she could say that, Jasper looked at her. The second she saw the combination of regret and concern in his eyes, she knew he hadn't shown up to ask for a little naked time.

"What? I can see it's something, so just spit it out." She wanted to ask what her mother had done now, only she knew whatever it was Verity couldn't be involved. Since arriving in Happily Inc, her mother had been sweet and helpful and just plain—

"It's about your mom."

"Is she okay?"

"She's fine." Jasper looked past her to Pallas. "This is kind of about you, too. Her producer has come up with a really fun idea to promote the show."

Renee couldn't imagine what that had to do with her or Pallas. Unless...

"Did she find out about the giraffes?"

"What? No. It's a giant dog wedding."

Renee turned to Pallas who looked as confused as she felt.

"I don't know what that is," Pallas admitted. "How many dogs does it take to be a giant dog wedding?"

"That was my question," he admitted. "I guess we'll find out when they get here. Odele, that's her producer, thinks it will be entertaining and visual and give them something to promote that will get attention on social media."

"Because 'we have a woman who talks to animals' isn't enough of a grabber?" Renee shook her head. "Sorry. I don't know the business and if my mom's excited then it's great that they're—" The pieces came together.

"Oh, no," she breathed. "They want to have the giant dog wedding here, don't they?"

"That's kind of the point of me stopping by. Your mom said things were good between the two of you and she didn't want to mess that up, so she sent me instead." He flashed her a smile. "This would be a good time to say don't kill the messenger."

Renee wanted to scream. This was so unfair. She and Pallas were in the middle of negotiating her joining the business. Talk about an off-putting twist in their relationship.

"It would be midweek," he added. "Odele said the show will cover all the expenses and make sure the property is back to normal by close of business on Thursday. Apparently they're willing to pay a premium for the use of the space."

Pallas looked at Renee. "Premiums are always nice."

"You're saying you can be bought?"

Pallas grinned. "When it comes to the business, money nearly always talks." She turned to Jasper. "I guess I need to speak with Verity's producer."

He pulled a business card out of his shirt pocket. "I happen to have her number right here."

CHAPTER SIXTEEN

Renee and Jasper left Pallas to call Odele and work out the details of the giant dog wedding.

When they reached her office, Jasper stepped in front of her to keep her from going inside.

"You need a break," he told her. "Let's go walk around for a half hour or so to clear your head."

She thought of all she had to do and all that had happened in the past hour. "I'd like that. I'm kind of reeling from too much input."

She collected her handbag, then led the way outside. She expected him to turn toward the Riverwalk but he went in the opposite direction. As she didn't have a particular destination in mind, she went along without saying anything.

"How are things with you?" she asked.

"Good. The book is progressing. Today was all about murder and gross bodies."

She laughed. "So an easy day."

"Yeah. None of that hard emotional stuff or dealing with

Mandy's life. Give me a good dismemberment scene and I'm a happy guy."

"You're a weird guy."

"Maybe, but I'm okay with that."

He surprised her by taking her hand in his. She couldn't remember the last time she'd walked down a street, holding a guy's hand. Probably when she was with Turner, she thought wistfully. So many years ago. She didn't miss him at all, but sometimes the what-ifs of the situation were difficult to handle.

"Pallas wants to talk about me becoming a partner in the business," she said.

"That's great. Do you want to be a partner?"

"Very much. I like the business and I have some ideas about how we could grow things. It's a lot of responsibility and I'd have to buy in with a lump sum or over time. I have some savings, but I doubt it's close to enough, so I guess it will be over time."

"I have money."

She rolled her eyes. "I'm sure you have more than all of us, but that isn't relevant to the conversation."

"I could—"

"No."

"But I don't need it for—"

She glared at him. "No. Jasper, stop. There's no way you can just give me money to buy into Pallas's business without making things weird between us. Not only would it change things, it would completely freak me out. So just no."

He studied her for several seconds. "Fine. I will respect your wishes on this topic."

"Thank you."

"Even though you're wrong."

She made a low noise in her throat. "Boys are stupid."

"Liar. You can't get enough of me. Now no more talk of business." He pointed across the street. "See that building there? We're going inside. It's a magical place, so there will be no fighting."

Across the street was a very unassuming structure. It was plain with big windows and large glass doors. The sign out front read Happily Inc Public Library.

"I don't understand. It's just the library."

"Not just the library," he told her. "When I was a kid, my dad worked a lot of hours. Our house got lonely so I would spend afternoons in the library, reading everything I could. The librarians watched out for me, made recommendations." He smiled. "Brought me cookies. Come on."

He tugged her along as he crossed the street. They went inside.

She looked around and saw thousands of books in rows of shelves. There were posters on the wall and signs pointing to various sections. It was, well, a library. But when she turned to Jasper, she realized he saw something completely different. His gaze was slightly unfocused as if instead of books, he saw journeys and possibilities.

He winked at her. "Let's go explore. I want to start in travel. It's over here."

He went directly to the travel section. This was not his first time here, she thought, wondering if the seeds of his writing career had been sown long before he'd realized.

He showed her an old book on Egypt, pointing out the sketched pictures and the original binding. There were coffee table-sized books of maps and books with shiny new photographs of different parts of the world.

At the end of the aisle, they went in different directions. She found herself in front of cookbooks from around the world. One published in the 1950s showed a sketch of a woman wearing high heels, pearls and an apron, as if that was the expectation.

"I would so fail at that," she murmured softly, flipping through the pages and finding an entire section of gelatin mold recipes.

Someone tapped her on the shoulder. She turned and saw Jasper standing very close. He leaned in and kissed her on the lips—a sweet kiss that unexpectedly made her eyes burn.

"Score!" he whispered. "I always wanted to kiss a girl in the library. It's been a fantasy of mine since I was fifteen and had a thing for a girl named Bambi."

"Seriously? Bambi?"

"I swear. She was so hot and she never noticed me."

"That's her loss."

"I like to think so."

Then he was gone, continuing his library exploration. Renee hugged the cookbook to her chest. Jasper was surprising in so many ways. She'd thought he would be brooding and quiet and a little scary, albeit good in bed. Except for that last one, he was nothing she'd imagined. Not that she was complaining. She really liked the funny, slightly quirky, affectionate man she'd come to know. He was a down-to-his-bones good guy and someone she was lucky to have in her life.

She'd been so frightened for so long, she thought as she shelved the cookbook. Afraid of getting hurt, afraid of being like her mother. She was nearly thirty and as Jasper had pointed out more than once, she had no hint of her mother's gift. There was no reason to think it would suddenly show up now. If she wanted to get on with things, she needed to let that fear go. Hanging on to it wasn't helping her at all.

As for not wanting to risk her heart, well, that was harder to deal with. She'd lost her father, friends, the career she'd wanted, Turner and maybe a piece of herself because of what had happened. The losses weren't her fault, but how she dealt with them was completely on her. She could be a victim and wallow in a lifetime of "poor me" or she could put on her big girl panties and figure out a way to move forward. The choice was hers. It always had been. It seemed like it was time to start acting like it.

She walked along the main aisle until she spotted Jasper poring over some car manual. She stopped in front of him.

"I would very much like us to go back to my place and make love for a couple of hours. What do you think?"

He shelved the book, grabbed her hand and practically ran out of the building.

"I knew the library would make you hot," he said as they headed back to where their cars were parked. "I love it when a plan comes together."

Ninety minutes and two orgasms later, Renee felt a little melty and a whole lot more like herself. While she would have loved to spend the rest of the afternoon in bed with Jasper, he had to get home and do some writing and she needed to head back to the office. She still had some work to do before she could call it a day. But she would be smiling the whole time.

"Thank you," he said, kissing her as they picked up their items of clothing and put them back on. "Want to come over and spend the night?"

"Let me check with my mom. I don't know if she has plans or not. She's been pretty busy the last couple of days. If she's available, I really should spend time with her."

"If she's not, I'm happy to be your second choice."

She laughed and wrapped her arms around his neck. "You're not my second choice."

"I know."

He kissed her and she had a brief thought that being ir-

responsible had definite benefits. Then her better angels reminded her about her career goals and she reluctantly drew
back.

When they were both dressed, they walked to his truck
and he drove the short distance to Weddings Out of the
Box, where she'd left her car. He'd just stopped at a light on
the west side of the river when a helicopter flew overhead.
A helicopter that was getting lower and lower, as if it were
going to—

"The pilot is going to land in The Promenade," Jasper said
over the noise, as he drove through the intersection and then
pulled over.

They both got out of the truck and walked the few feet
to The Promenade—an open area in front of stores by the
Riverwalk.

Sure enough the helicopter was sitting on the concrete, its
rotors slowing as the engine wound down. There were no
markings indicating it was part of a law enforcement task force
or even from a news station. Renee was fairly sure the Happily Inc police department didn't need or own a helicopter,
so who could it be and why were they landing there?

More people spilled into the area. Renee saw several of her
friends. Her mother came up, Ed, Carol's father, with her.

"Renee, this is so exciting. What do you think is going
on?"

"I have no idea. We don't get things like this happening
in town very much."

"Maybe it's a celebrity," Ed said.

Someone pushed through the crowd. "Oh my God!"

Renee saw Bethany running toward the helicopter.

"What are you doing?" Bethany shouted. "You can't act
like this. You're disrupting people's lives!"

The engines were turned off. The sudden silence was nearly

as shocking as the noise had been. Bethany stood with her hands on her hips as the doors to the helicopter opened.

"Oh, no," Renee breathed. "It's her parents."

"The king and queen of El Bahar?" Verity asked. "That's so thrilling. I've never seen anyone royal before. Well, I have, but only on television or in magazines. They look normal."

Renee recognized the older couple from the previous year's prewedding party for Bethany and Cade. The king was very handsome and just a little imposing. Liana, Bethany's mother, was a slightly older version of her daughter, with blond hair and blue eyes.

"Darling!" Her mother held out her arms. "There you are. We went to the ranch first, but they told us you'd come to town so we decided to surprise you."

"You couldn't drive?" Bethany asked.

"The helicopter was faster." Her father kissed both her cheeks.

"Where did you even get a helicopter?" Bethany asked.

"I bought it," her father told her. "It will be wherever you are, from now until you have your baby. There are pilots on call, 24/7. If you need to get to a hospital, they'll get you there in a few minutes."

Bethany looked horrified. "Please tell me you're kidding."

"Not at all. Now come. We'll fly back to the ranch together."

Bethany cast a helpless glance over her shoulder. "But my car is here."

The king waved and a man jumped out of the helicopter. "Give him the keys. He'll meet us there."

Bethany dug in her handbag and pulled out a set of keys, then sighed heavily and got in the helicopter. The engine started right up and then they all flew away.

Renee watched them go.

"That was quite the show," Verity said. "What an amazing town you have here."

"It's not usually like this, Mom." Renee said automatically, all the while thinking Bethany's worst fears about her parents were being realized. A helicopter standing by until she had the baby? What else was her father going to do to "help"?

The crowd began dispersing. Ed whispered something in Verity's ear. Verity nodded, then looked at Renee.

"Did you have plans for us this evening? Because I can keep myself busy."

"Not really. Did you want to have dinner?"

Verity hesitated. "Rain check."

"Sure. No problem."

They hugged, then Verity and Ed walked away. Renee was just thinking how nicely that worked out when she suddenly got what had happened. She came to a stop on The Promenade.

"No," she said, shaking her head. "No. It wasn't that." She looked at Jasper. "My mother wasn't with Ed, was she?"

"You mean like dating or something? I don't think so. Didn't you tell me they met when she talked to the giraffes? He would be interested in her gift. I'm sure they're just friends."

He was right, she thought. That made sense.

Jasper put his arm around her. "So dinner and a sleepover?"

"I'll be there."

Hanna reached up and touched her hair. She'd had her hair done at a local salon earlier that morning and the complicated updo suited her face.

"It feels weird to have my hair up on my head like this," she admitted with a laugh. "But I wanted to see if I liked it."

Renee grinned. "You look great, but you have to be comfortable with whatever style you decide on. Live with it for the day, take some pictures, then decide."

"You're right. Okay, so champagne."

For once Hanna was the only one attending the planning meeting. Graham was out of town and Jasper had a conference call with his publisher's marketing team. Not that Jasper was an actual decision maker but he did want to be as involved as possible. Or at least in the loop.

Thinking of Jasper made her happy inside. Things were good between them—which, while interesting, was not anything she wanted to have on her mind during an important meeting.

"Champagne," Renee echoed, then waited.

Hanna raised her shoulders up and down several times. "I can argue both sides."

"Then let me offer an opinion. No one is expecting a drink before the wedding. You have to pay for bar service along with the champagne and you're starting your guests on the road to getting drunk even earlier than usual. I'm not sure it's the best use of your money. Just as important, I don't think it adds to the experience of the ceremony."

"It seems so elegant," Hanna hedged. "Plus, not everyone likes bagpipe music so we thought it might help."

"Not everyone likes 'Ave Maria' yet you hear it all the time at weddings. This is *your* day, Hanna. My job is to help you and Graham have the most amazing wedding possible, so if you want champagne available to your guests ahead of time, then that is what you'll get. I'm just saying to think about it before you spend the money."

"You're right," Hanna told her. "What is it called? Gilding the lily? I just want everything to be perfect. I think I'm getting nervous because it's such a big deal." She wrinkled her nose. "Don't take this wrong, but I wish Graham and I hadn't started down this path. The whole big wedding, theme thing. I'm super excited about everything we have planned and we love that Jasper's using our wedding for his book, it's just we're kind of quiet, stay-at-home people, so this is a lot out of our comfort zone. We want our wedding to be significant to us and not just a big party."

"I totally get that. What you need to tell me is if you're just talking or if you really want to cut back on some of the things you have planned. We're about to reach the point of no return on a lot of things, so now is the time to decide."

Hanna briefly covered her face with her hands, then sighed. "I'm sorry. I'm being neurotic."

"You're not. You're spending a lot of money on a single day and while it's traditional, it's not exactly your style. Of course you're second-guessing yourself."

"Thank you for understanding. I don't mean to be difficult."

Renee smiled. "This is not the least bit difficult. Trust me. A three-hour conversation on the different shades of ecru and which one works the best for table linens is difficult."

"Thank you for saying that, even if it's not true."

"I wish it weren't, but I was there for every second of it."

"Okay. Then I'll accept my nerves as normal." She looked at the papers spread out on the table. They were printouts of the various elements that would be at the wedding. "I love it all. I don't want to get rid of anything."

Renee was used to brides having varying levels of freak-outs along the journey from proposal to ceremony. Hanna's was nowhere near noteworthy.

"Think about it. You still have a few days to change your mind on nearly everything."

"Thanks. I appreciate how calm you are." Hanna picked up her glass of water. "How did you and Jasper meet?"

The question was unexpected. Renee thought for a second. "We both live in town. Technically he lives on a mountain, but close enough. Happily Inc is small so eventually you run into everyone. We have mutual friends. It wasn't an actual meeting so much as at some point I knew who he was."

"How long have you been going out?"

Ack! Renee knew she couldn't say they weren't really going out in the conventional sense. They were, um, what? He would say they were in a relationship and she was still comfortable with not defining anything although she had to admit the man got to her in ways she wouldn't have anticipated.

"I didn't mean it to be a hard question," Hanna teased.

"It's been a couple of months now."

"The beginning is always fun. I remember when Graham and I were first together. We were crazy about each other from the start."

"How did you meet?"

Hanna laughed. "We were waiting in line for a movie. *Black Panther* actually. We each went with a group of friends who left us to hold their places in line while they got Starbucks. They were gone forever and we started talking." She sighed happily. "It was just one of those things. We sat together at the movie, we went out to dinner after and by the end of the weekend, we were in love."

She looked at Renee. "I'd never felt like that before. Not really. I was so sure he was the one and he felt the same about me. We really fit, if that makes sense. When my family makes me crazy, which is a lot of the time, he talks me down. When his twin sister expects too much from him, I'm a buffer. It works."

"That sounds lovely. You're going to have a wonderful wedding and a long, happy marriage."

Hanna's expression turned troubled. "I hope so. I worry

about that. Graham comes from a long line of people who stayed together forever, but not me. My parents have each been married and divorced four times. I can't tell you how many stepbrothers and sisters I have. My older sister has already been divorced once. She's engaged again and we can all see it's not going to last. I don't want to be like them."

Renee knew better than to offer a pat "you're not." That wouldn't help at all. "Do you know why any of the marriages failed?"

"Let's see. My sister married someone she barely knew, so they didn't have much of a chance. This guy is throwing up red flags, which she ignores. He's been unfaithful a bunch of times, he lies and he's kind of a jerk, but because he's really good-looking and has a great job, she's all about excuses. My mom keeps choosing the same type of guy over and over. It didn't work the first four times, but she can't seem to learn to avoid that type. My dad is more of a mixed bag. He married his second wife because she got pregnant. I'm not sure about the other two."

She paused. "Sorry. That was probably more information than you wanted."

"I can handle it," Renee said lightly. "But you've made my point. Hanna, you know exactly why nearly all those marriages didn't work out. You can see the flaws and you're not making the same mistakes. You know Graham and he knows you. You're clear on what each of you wants from your relationship. Isn't he a good guy?"

"He's the best."

"If you're just worried about repeating your family's pattern, that's one thing, but if you're genuinely concerned about your relationship with Graham, then you should see a therapist and get some counseling."

"That's good advice. Thank you. You're always so calming

to be around." Hanna drew in a breath. "Okay, I'm ready to make some decisions. No champagne at the ceremony. Everyone can wait until we're married."

"Good choice."

"I'm pretty sure I like my hair up and I will work really hard to keep my family from making me doubt what a fantastic man I have in my life."

"Sounds like you have a plan."

"I do and it's wonderful."

CHAPTER SEVENTEEN

The planning meeting for the "wedding of many dogs," as Jasper thought of it, took place in the same conference room as every other planning meeting he'd attended. What was different was the lack of bride and groom or any of their family members. Instead Renee was there, looking sexy and business-appropriate in a simple black dress, with Pallas, Wynn and Natalie also in attendance. Verity rushed in five minutes late, looking flushed and rattled.

"Sorry," she said, taking a seat across from her daughter. "I had a last-minute call from Odele, finalizing everything." She turned to Pallas. "Odele said she sent you the specs and a budget. Did you get them?"

"I have them right here." Pallas tapped a folder in front of her. "I have to say, for the record, I love TV weddings."

"Me, too." Renee grinned. "Their budget is very generous."

Which would mean lots of profits for the business, Jasper thought. Something Renee would appreciate now that she was going to be an owner.

"Good news for all of us," Wynn said. "Order lots of signage. I could use the business."

"We will." Pallas waved at Renee. "Take it away."

Renee flipped open a folder. "All right. First, the giant wedding is turning into a medium-sized wedding. Instead of sixteen pairs of dogs, we're having eight pairs. A more manageable number. Odele's team has arranged for the care and feeding of the dogs. Each dog will have a handler, so we're only responsible for the ceremony and reception and the humans who will be there."

"Who are the humans attending?" he asked.

"The dog handlers, Odele and her team, the filming crew and I guess us." Renee flipped through her notes. "Oh, we have ten extras to be seated during the ceremony." She scribbled on a pad of paper. "I'm getting about fifty people. Does everyone agree?"

"That's my number, too, but let's plan on sixty to be safe," Pallas told her.

Renee entered the information on her tablet. "All right. So the dogs will come, have a little playtime to burn off energy, then get married. It's a group ceremony, so that should be quick. Again, assuming here, they'll need to do it a couple of times to get good footage. So say an hour?"

Pallas handed over a minute-by-minute accounting of the day. "That's what they say. An hour. Then a reception for another hour." She looked at Verity. "You're doing a one-on-one with each of the dogs. That's going to take a while."

Renee's mother shrugged. "It should be all right. They know there's no second take on that part of it. Odele's going to set up an area inside for me. A quiet room where the dogs can be comfortable."

"The groom's room," Renee and Pallas said at the same time.

"Not the bride's room?" Wynn asked. "It's so much bigger."

"We can't risk it," Renee told her. "We need it by midday on Friday and if there's any kind of accident, we can't be sure the smell will be gone or the carpet dry. The groom is just putting on a suit or a tux. The bride has the whole dress thing going on."

"I hadn't thought of that," Wynn admitted. "This is why you two are the professionals."

"You'll want to put down some kind of indoor-outdoor carpet to protect the floor," Natalie pointed out. "The filming situation could be stressful for the dogs, plus whatever food they're eating. Is there a cake or something?"

Renee typed on her tablet. "Floor protection. An excellent idea. Now, food." She read for a second. "Okay, they're providing doggie snacks. There will be a dog food cake and doggie cookies. We need to have catering for the humans. An easy lunch." She made more notes on her tablet. "I'll call the canine catering company and get information on what they're providing." She grinned. "We should either avoid cookies altogether or get sugar cookies with icing. That way we can have the bakery write 'human' on them."

Everyone laughed.

She looked back at her list. "I'm thinking we'll need to have the human catering inside. Otherwise it will be too tempting for the dogs. How about a salad and taco bar, two or three different kinds of sandwiches, water, soda and juices, plus dessert?"

Pallas nodded. "That sounds great. Odele told us we need vegetarian and vegan options."

"So no meat, no eggs, no dairy." Renee thought for a second. "Sure. We can do corn tortillas and have beans and rice at the taco bar. I'll make sure the caterer provides a vegetarian sandwich and a vegan option. Maybe we'll do some kind of a soup."

She made more notes. Jasper reminded himself to avoid the vegan dessert.

"Decorations," Renee said and activated the screen on the wall. "Time is of the essence. Anything custom has to be easy to get. So I went on Etsy."

"I love that site," Wynn murmured.

Jasper had no idea what they were talking about. "What's Etsy?"

Pallas looked pitying. "It's a website with all kinds of crafts and different creations. We bought Ryan the cutest toy box. It's just gorgeous and really well made. You should check it out."

Renee's mouth twitched. "Yes, Jasper, check it out. It's very you."

"Uh-huh. You're just messing with me."

Renee was still smiling when she pressed a button on her laptop. A picture of a floral dog collar appeared on the screen.

"I spoke to the vendor. She's doing a rush job in eight colors. They'll be here by Monday."

Renee clicked the button again. A bow tie collar appeared. "These are for the boy dogs and will coordinate with the flower collars. We went with white, pink, blue, red, green, yellow, purple and orange."

"Not black?" he asked.

Verity glanced at him. "Black might not film well. There wouldn't be definition in the flowers."

All the other women were nodding. Were they just born knowing this kind of stuff?

"So no black," he muttered.

"I'd love to do cuffs for the paws," Renee said, "but we don't have enough time. So these will have to do."

"I could do paw cuffs out of paper," Natalie offered. "It wouldn't take any time at all. I'd use peel and stick dots to hold them in place, that way they can be adjustable, depending on the size of the dog. Read me the colors again. I'll have them match."

"Are you sure?" Renee asked.

"I think it would be fun."

Renee listed the colors. Natalie wrote them down, then the meeting moved on. Renee clicked the computer again. Rows of white chairs appeared.

"Odele wants flowers at the end of each row of chairs." Renee sighed. "I've already got a call in to the florist to make sure the flowers they send over aren't poisonous to dogs. We'll have ten tables that seat six." Another picture went up on the screen, this one showing a set table.

"I'm thinking white linens with black runners, seeing as we're not using black anywhere else." She glanced at Jasper. "Black will be a good contrasting color."

"Sure. But how do you use a runner? The tables are round."

Several more pitying looks were cast his way.

"We run them north-south and east-west, so they cross. It's pretty and simple. Flowers on every table. Black chargers instead of place mats."

She glanced at her notes. "Do we want a gift table? And if we do, should it be wrapped empty boxes or should we have actual gifts inside?"

"For the dogs?" Wynn asked. "Like toys and stuff?"

"I don't know," Renee admitted, then started typing. "I'll get a list together to ask Odele."

"Is there an officiant?" Pallas asked.

Renee scanned her notes. "I don't see one mentioned. I'll put that on the Ask Odele list, as well. It could really be anyone. The weddings aren't legal."

"It would be funny to have a cat marry them," Wynn said. "Although that is probably asking for trouble."

"I got the impression the wedding was supposed to be fun and charming rather than funny." Renee glanced at Verity. "Mom, what do you think?"

"I agree. Obviously it's not serious but it's not comedy, either."

"Oh, it might be," Pallas said. "Even with a medium-sized dog wedding, it's going to be hilarious. Or a complete disaster."

"Nick would point out that is you, being a ray of sunshine," Renee murmured as she typed. "It's on the list. Anything else?"

The meeting went on for a few more minutes. Jasper listened rather than said the wrong thing—again. So he wasn't Mr. Wedding Expert. At least he was participating.

Once they'd worked through all the items on the agenda, Renee reviewed their decisions and confirmed what she had to talk to Odele about. She excused herself and left for her office.

Verity disappeared just as quickly, leaving Jasper to walk out with Wynn.

"Do not even think about putting a dog wedding in your book," she told him.

"I wouldn't do that."

"You would, in a heartbeat. You enjoy putting real life into your stories, but the tone is wrong."

He knew she was correct, but really liked the idea of writing about dogs going crazy at a wedding.

"I couldn't have a dog wedding and a murder at the same time," he said. "That would be over-the-top. Still, it would be fun."

They reached the parking lot. He saw she'd parked next to him and they headed in that direction.

"Look how far you've come," she said, her voice teasing. "I

remember when you would barely make eye contact when you showed up at The Boardroom. Now you're a social butterfly."

"That's extreme."

"Maybe but it's pretty close to the truth. You've changed."

They stopped by her SUV.

"Not that much," he said, hoping he didn't sound defensive, because he didn't feel it. Not really. Just a little apprehensive, because Wynn seemed to have something on her mind and he had a bad feeling it was more than helping Hunter with his fastball.

"Renee is really special," she said.

He held in a groan. "You and I shouldn't discuss that."

"Someone has to discuss it with you and no one else seems to be volunteering."

"We're doing just fine."

"I know and that's my point. Your relationship with her is a lot better than your relationship with me."

He had no clue what that meant, but figured the safest course was to keep his mouth shut.

"We were never going anywhere and we both knew it," she said.

"You set up the rules so we were bound to fail."

He hadn't meant to say that, but he wasn't taking it back. It was the truth.

"I did. Absolutely. I didn't want any more than we had and I was terrified you did."

"Why would you think that?" He'd been very clear on not getting involved. He couldn't.

"Because you were getting better every day. You were healing right before my eyes and I knew it wasn't going to be very long before you wanted something more." She offered him a sad smile. "I didn't realize that you would want it with someone else."

He'd gone from clueless to genuinely flummoxed. What was he supposed to say to that?

She held up a hand. "I'm not complaining. I get it. I was never going to be that important to you."

"That's not true."

"You never fought for me, Jasper." Her tone was soft, her gaze steady. "I'm not saying you should have, and I'm not complaining. I'm pointing out the fact that you never pushed back on my ridiculous rules and when I ended things, you let me go. I wasn't the one."

"I don't have a 'one.'"

"Of course you do. Don't be silly. Like I said, when you and I were together, I could see you getting better every day, but you're not anymore. You're healed. Whole. Whatever you want to call it." She touched his arm. "You're back among the normal, however you want to define that."

"I'm not," he managed through an uncomfortable combination of panic, fear and hope. "Things happened. I still have nightmares."

"You probably always will, but the band that defines normal is pretty wide and you're well within it. What I mean by this is that while you'll always have crap from your past to deal with, you're still emotionally capable of being a functioning member of society. More important, you're more than ready and completely able to be in a real relationship. One with expectation and commitment and a future. That's my point here, Jasper. Don't assume what you have with Renee is like what you had with me. It's not. It's so much better and stronger. Don't blow it by thinking you'll be able to replace it. You and Renee have something really wonderful going on."

He wanted to ask how she knew any of this. About him, about him and Renee. He wanted to make her tell him why

she would want him to think he was normal when he knew
he wasn't. He couldn't be. Even his dog thought he had issues.

"You're wrong," he said, walking to his truck. "You're
wrong."

Wynn didn't try to stop him. It was as if she knew he had to
process what she'd said. As if she knew he was running away.

Well, so what? Bolting seemed the most logical next step,
he thought as he drove out of the parking lot. Normal. No
way. Not him. He was never going to be normal. He was always going to be reclusive and solitary and distant. He was
broken—shattered—and he could never be right.

That settled, he made his way up the mountain, concen-
trating on the road and his breathing and doing his best to ignore the voice in his head that asked *What if Wynn was right?*

She wasn't. She couldn't be. Him healed? Because if he was,
if he was at a place where he could be involved with someone
in a meaningful way, didn't that change everything, including
how he defined himself? And if she was right, where did that
leave him? And assuming he could answer that question, then
he had one more to wrestle with. What on earth came next?

Renee was surprised to find herself just as nervous the
morning of the dog wedding as she was on any other day
when she had a human wedding going on. Even though the
brides and grooms wouldn't care about the decorations and
if things flowed smoothly, she wanted to get it all exactly as
it should be.

In deference to the fact that she might be called on to perform different duties at this event, she'd put on black slacks
and a black blouse, rather than a dress. She had on flats and
she'd pulled her hair back.

By eight forty-five, she'd confirmed the tables were set, the chairs were in place and the flowers had been delivered. By nine, the film crew had arrived to set up, as had the caterers.

Renee introduced herself to Odele, a tall, pretty African American woman with a take-charge attitude that Renee found comforting.

"This is exactly what I pictured," Odele told her, looking around. "I love it."

They walked the event, first going through the ceremony— to be performed by an Animal Planet celebrity dog trainer— then moving on to the reception.

"As you requested, we did only a couple of tables out here with the dogs," Renee said, pointing to the decorated tables. "The rest are inside, away from inquisitive canines."

"But there's a dog-friendly cake?"

"Yes, and cookies. There are a dozen or so water dishes around the perimeter of the reception area and I have someone who will be checking them regularly."

"Good." Odele scrolled through her tablet. "The pooper-scooper guy will arrive with the dogs."

"I'm glad you thought of that. I'm not sure I would have," Renee admitted.

Odele laughed. "I've done plenty of dog-based shows. You learn to expect that sort of thing."

They finalized all the details, then Odele went back to oversee her crew.

Close to ten, her friends started arriving. Not only would they be there to help with anything unexpected, they would also be extras at the wedding and ceremony.

Jasper had texted the previous day to say he couldn't make the wedding. Renee smiled as she thought of his excuse that he had to work on the book. She suspected he was thinking that a dog wedding could easily get out of hand and wasn't anything he wanted to be a part of. He was such a guy.

Carol, Silver and Verity all arrived at the same time. She showed them the layout and the incredible amount of food the caterers had already set up.

"I think it's called a craft table," Silver said, eyeing the Danishes. "Or maybe not."

"We're so Hollywood," Carol teased.

Verity looked around. "Renee, you've done a wonderful job."

"Thanks. Do you want to check out your room where you'll be doing the readings?"

Her mother smiled at her. "Has it changed from yesterday?"

"Odele was going to get the camera set up in it, so there's that."

"Then we should probably make sure it's as I remember."

"You think I'm overmonitoring the details."

"I think this is you doing your job, which you do very well."

"I appreciate that."

Renee told Pallas she and her mom would be right back, then they went inside to the groom's room. Sure enough, it was as it had been the day before, with all the furniture removed and cushions and a dog bed on the floor. A guy was setting up a camera. Two big lights had been placed at one end of the room and there was a chart on the wall, detailing the order in which the dogs would come in.

"You're going to be busy," Renee said. "That's a lot of dogs."

"I'll be fine. This will be good practice for me before the show starts."

They confirmed everything was in place before starting back to the main event area. Partway there, Verity came to a stop.

"I want to talk to you for a second."

Renee looked at her mother. "Is everything all right? You've been so busy working, I've hardly seen you for the past week."

Verity glanced away before returning her attention to her daughter. "Yes, well, there have been some things to deal with but it's all good. Very good, in fact. But that's not what I want to talk about. I've been thinking about what you told me about Pallas wanting you in the business."

"What? We didn't talk about that." Renee was nearly sure of it. She'd told Jasper, but that was it.

"Of course you did," her mother told her. "Anyway, I've been thinking that I would very much like to give you the money to buy in as a full partner."

"What? No. Mom, no. That's impossible."

"It's not. I have the money I made when I sold the salon, plus my payment for the show. I want to help." She smiled. "Renee, I've never been able to give you much financial support. You went to college on scholarships and before that we were always scrimping to get by. I want to do this. It would make me so happy."

Renee couldn't take it all in. "Mom, that is incredibly generous and I want to talk about it, but not right now, okay?"

"Of course. I just want you to know I love you and I'm so proud of you."

"Thank you. I love you, too."

They hugged before returning to the prewedding frenzy. Renee pushed thoughts of her mother's offer from her mind. She would deal with it later. No way would she take the full amount from her mother, but even the money for a quarter of her share would be fantastic.

They stepped outside in time to see Bethany arriving, with two tall men trailing her. She hurried over, her expression both apologetic and exasperated.

"These are my bodyguards," she explained. "They go with me everywhere and they make me insane."

"What about at the ranch?" Pallas asked. "They can't be there all the time. They'll spook the horses."

"They keep their distance, but there they are. Lurking. I hate lurkers."

"Poor you." Silver put an arm around her. "What are you going to do?"

"Endure. Be passive-aggressive with my parents. Plot my escape." She sighed. "If it's like this now, what is it going to be like when I have the baby? My parents are literally going to smother me with their concern."

"What does Cade say?" Renee asked.

"He says we should surrender to the inevitable and move to El Bahar when I'm about six months along. Then I can just be there for the birth before we come back here. But I don't know."

"Not a decision you have to make now," Pallas told her. "Although if you do go to El Bahar for three or four months, we are so going to visit."

That made Bethany smile. "Really? You'd do that for me? I'd have my dad send a plane."

Wynn put her hands on her hips. "Well, yeah. It's not as if we would go without your dad sending a plane!"

They all laughed. Renee excused herself to do one last check with Odele. They'd just finished when a couple of SUVs pulled up in the parking lot. Renee went out to meet the dogs and their handlers. As she waited, she realized she'd forgotten to ask Odele about the various breeds they were having. The collars were adjustable but if they had a pair of Yorkies, the collars might not be small enough.

The back door of the first SUV opened and two incredibly beautiful, incredibly large dogs jumped to the ground.

Odele came up next to her. "Oh, good. They're here."

"Wh-what are they?"

"Irish wolfhounds." She looked at Renee. "You know all the dogs are large, right?" She checked her list. "We have the Irish wolfhounds, mastiffs, Great Danes—"

The second SUV opened and a Saint Bernard jumped heavily to the ground. A second one followed.

"Oh, no." Renee did her best to stay focused. If she started laughing, she might never stop. "A giant dog wedding. You really meant giant dogs."

"I thought it would be appealing to viewers. We debated tiny dogs, but that's a lot of close-up shots and we had the contacts for the big dogs, so here we are."

"A giant dog wedding."

The first giggle escaped. Then a second.

"Excuse me," she managed before running back inside the grounds. She found her friends all talking together. Pallas spotted her first.

"What is it? What's wrong?"

"Nothing," Renee said, trying not to give in to laughter. "It's just..." She pointed.

Two handlers led in the Irish wolfhounds, followed by the Saint Bernards. Apparently, the Great Danes had arrived because they were next.

"Oh, no," Pallas breathed.

"A giant dog wedding," Wynn said before starting to laugh. "I am so glad I brought my video camera. This is going to be fantastic!"

CHAPTER EIGHTEEN

By midafternoon the film crew was packing up for the drive back to Los Angeles. The wedding and reception had gone reasonably well. The Saint Bernards had found a shady spot to nap and refused to be moved. The mastiffs had eaten all the flowers, then had promptly thrown them up, while the Great Danes had wanted to play and the wolfhounds looked bewildered.

Verity had done readings on all the dogs, including the Saint Bernards, both of whom had told her they just wanted to be left alone to sleep. The dogs had loved their cake, the pooper-scooper guy had kept up with, ah, production and the outdoor area seemed none too worse for wear.

Renee found herself just as tired as she was after an all-day wedding. Maybe it was because she hadn't known what to expect and maybe because she'd had so much to think about with her mother's generous offer.

"Patches. Patches! Here, boy."

Renee saw one of the handlers calling for the male Great Dane. He was close to Renee so she grabbed his leash.

He was beautiful—a black-and-white harlequin with long legs and an ever-wagging tail. Wearing flats, she was practically eye level with him, she thought humorously, leading him across the lawn.

"Did you have a good time?" she asked as he walked with her. "Did you have a good wedding?"

She reached out to pet him only to realize not only wasn't there an answer, she hadn't expected one. She'd simply reacted to being with a friendly dog. In fact, she hadn't once thought she had to worry during the entire day. She'd done her job, wrangled dogs when necessary, made kissing noises so they would look alert for pictures and that was it.

There was no gift—there never had been. Not for her. She had wasted so much time worrying about something that was never going to happen. How ridiculous.

"Thanks," the woman said, taking his leash. "He loves to explore. Okay, we're heading home. This was great. I can't wait to see the show."

Renee watched her go before returning to the reception area. She and Pallas did a quick walk-through to make sure there was no forgotten camera equipment, leashes or dog toys. Wynn had already headed back to work.

Mathias was with Carol, waiting to take her back to their place. He had Devon with him, the baby tucked in his arms.

They were a happy family, Renee thought wistfully. Like Pallas, Nick and Ryan. She doubted it would be very long before Natalie and Silver were pregnant.

Two by two, she thought. Then three by three, as they became families. She'd wanted that once, had hoped it could happen. She'd wanted to be like everyone else. Now, when she had finally realized she was totally gift-free and therefore normal, it was too late. She didn't have another heartbreak in her. She couldn't risk it.

Maybe if only Turner had hurt her. Or if she'd just fallen for the married guy. But those two combined were a massive hurdle to get over and when added to her father abandoning her...

Love meant stepping off an emotional cliff and waiting for someone to catch her so she wouldn't crash into the ground. What if no one was there? She couldn't take a chance. If her heart were shattered again, it would never be whole and she didn't want to be some sad, broken person for the rest of her life. Better to stay as she was. Lonely, yes, but functional.

Odele and her crew left, the catering staff packed up and by four, Renee was alone in the center of the courtyard knowing that the price of being safe was one she had to pay. She didn't have a choice—not when it came to her heart.

Jasper punched the air twice, right, left, followed by a quick kick at knee-level. As he moved his foot, his chair slid back about a foot. He continued to work out the fight scene in his head, shifting in his seat as he punched again.

He repeated the sequence, pausing to reassure Koda, who stared at him from the safety of his dog bed. When he had the scene clear in his head, he rolled back to his desk and began typing.

In the book, Vidar had come into contact with the serial killer. They were in an empty warehouse and it was pitch-black, so Vidar wasn't sure of his identity, but he would injure him enough that there was a limp, which was what Jasper needed for later in the book.

Thud, punch, crack. He could see the scene in his head as if it were a movie, which meant he had it all the way it was supposed to be. It was only when he couldn't figure out what to say that he knew he was screwing up with the story.

He typed as fast as he could, mentioning the grit on the

floor and the smell of something dead in the corner. He felt the impact of a blow on the side of his head. *Vidar's neck snapped to the left and he stumbled. The—*

"Hey, Jasper, you in here?"

The question, spoken just inside the office, jarred him from story world to real world. It took him a second to readjust his senses and remember where he was in space and time. He turned and saw Cade with two beers in his hand.

"You got a second or is this a bad time?"

Jasper knew if he said he had to work, Cade would understand and go away. He also knew his friend had something going on—otherwise he wouldn't have shown up with no warning in the middle of the afternoon.

"Sure. I'm at a good breaking point," he said, saving his work. He stood and called Koda, then walked toward Cade. "What's up?"

They went back into the house and sprawled on the big sofa in the family room. Koda jumped up next to Jasper and rested his head on his lap. Jasper rubbed his ears.

Cade set his beer on the coffee table, picked it up, set it back down, then stood.

"It's Bethany," he said, then shook his head. "Not her so much as her parents." He looked at Jasper. "What if I can't do it? What if can't deal with it?"

"What is *it*?"

"Royalty. Her father is the damn king of El Bahar. There are bodyguards at the ranch. They follow her everywhere she goes. If she's in the house, they stay outside, but otherwise, they're there. Her mother's called me three times already, begging me to let Bethany come home for the birth. As if I'm the one keeping her away. I'm not. I even told her we'd go back the last three months and she could have her baby there."

He paced the length of the family room, then faced Jasper.

"I don't want to be gone that long but I could fly back every couple of weeks. We have a good manager and the business would be fine. It's just not how I saw my life."

Jasper had no idea what to say. He wasn't even sure of the problem. Was Cade simply chafing at the realities of being married to a princess or was he really concerned he couldn't make the marriage work?

"I know what you're thinking," Cade told him.

"I doubt that."

"You're thinking I should suck it up and deal. I knew who Bethany was when I proposed. I'd already been to El Bahar and I'd met her father and I knew he was going to be protective of her always. She's his only daughter. The man calls her the child of his heart. He's actually a really nice guy and I respect how much he loves her."

He returned to the sofa. "Being in El Bahar isn't that bad. I work in the horse stables. You should see their horses. They are incredible. They can trace the bloodlines back a thousand years. It's something. Her mom pointed out that Bethany's friends would be able to visit, so that would help. It's just tough, you know? It's not how I grew up thinking my kid would be born."

He picked up his beer. "It's mostly the bodyguards. They hover. Still, she's safe and I like that and if it makes her parents happy, that makes her happy." He shrugged. "I love her, Jasper. There's no denying that. I'd rather deal with this times a thousand than lose her."

Cade drank from the bottle. "I guess we're going to El Bahar in a few months."

"Sounds like it."

"Thanks. I feel better. How's the book going?"

"It's moving forward."

They talked for another hour, then Cade said he should get home.

"Thanks for helping me see the situation more clearly," his friend said. "I was really confused about what to do."

"You know I didn't say anything, right? You figured it out all on your own."

"Yeah, but you listened."

Cade left.

Jasper rinsed out the bottles and dropped them into the recycling bin, then looked at Koda. "Sometimes that's how friendship works. You're just there to listen."

He supposed he'd been used to that, back when he'd been younger, but in the military, he'd lost his friends in ways no one ever should. Dealing with that and everything else he'd seen, he hadn't been able to do much more than try to keep his head together. Being with other people had been impossible.

That had changed when he'd moved to Happily Inc, he thought, returning to his office. He'd changed. Grown. Healed.

Was Wynn right? Had he inadvertently started on the road to normal? He wasn't willing to accept her declaration that he wasn't broken, but he had a feeling she was more right than wrong on the subject. Five years ago, he couldn't have imagined having a place of his own, having friends, hanging out with them, having someone like Renee in his life. Five years ago, he couldn't have gotten on a plane or gone on book tour. Five years ago, he'd assumed he had one, maybe two books in him and that would be it. Now he couldn't imagine not writing books for a living.

His cell phone rang. He didn't recognize the number but picked it up anyway.

"This is Jasper."

"Hey, Jasper, it's Graham."

It took him a second to realize Graham was the groom in the Scottish wedding.

"How's it going?"

"Great. Look, I need some advice. I wasn't sure where to take Hanna for our honeymoon so I booked like three places. I need to make a decision about which one to go with and which ones to let go. Can I email you the links and then you tell me what you think?"

"Graham, why would you care about my opinion?"

"Because you're you, man. You know things about women."

"What I know about women wouldn't cover a postage stamp, but sure, if you want my opinion, you can have it. But I think you should go with your gut. You know Hanna better than anyone. Which place do you think would make her the most happy? Does she want a lot of activities or does she just want to hang out with you? Do you need to go exploring or would you rather be on a beach? You've spent time with her, you know what the two of you enjoy. I'm just some guy. You're the man she wants to spend the rest of her life with."

"Wow—that's really deep. You're right. I do know what makes her happy. Thanks. I know what to do."

"No problem."

Jasper hung up and shook his head. People were weird. He looked at his computer and then back at Koda. "I'm not getting any writing done today. Want to take over?"

His dog looked at him as if to say, "You've completely slipped over the edge."

Jasper laughed, then turned to his phone and quickly texted Renee.

What's going on?

Her reply came in seconds.

I'm having a mini freak-out. I've decided you're right—I don't have my mom's gift and it's silly to spend the rest of my life waiting for something that is never going to happen. What a waste of time and energy.

He stared at the words. Good for you.

Thanks. So I'm going to the local animal shelter. I think I want a cat. A kitten, really, because it will be young and it won't judge me. Want to come along?

He looked at Koda. "If I say yes, it doesn't have to mean anything. It's not like I'll be bringing home a cat."

Koda didn't seem convinced.

"You like Renee. This is a big step for her. I'm going to tell her you're okay with it."

Koda sighed.

On my way now.

Renee wondered how many people actually had a panic attack in the middle of an animal shelter. She was trying to control her breathing and ignore the adrenaline rush, but neither was working especially well.

"You don't have to do this," Jasper said quietly, standing close enough to offer support but not so close that she felt overwhelmed.

"I know."

"You can just look around and see what you think about the various pets they have here. Getting a cat is a big step."

She nodded, aware of her heart pounding in her chest. "But I think it would be good for me. I'm a responsible person. With us hiring someone to help at work, I'll be home more."

What she didn't say was that her getting a cat would make her a pet person. She liked pet people. She'd always wished she could have a cat. She liked the idea of being responsible for another life-form. She wanted to be able to say, "Hey, I have to get home to my cat." And at the end of the day, there would be someone waiting for her and she liked the sound of that, too.

An older woman in a shelter T-shirt hurried up, a clipboard in her hand. "Renee?" she asked.

"That's me."

"Thanks for coming in. We have a lot of kittens right now. I want to say it's the season, but these days, it's always the season. Spay and neuter! We're trying to get the message out but until everyone is a believer, we'll have more kittens than homes." She held out her hand. "By the way, I'm Brenda. Nice to meet you."

"You, too."

Brenda explained about the kittens they had that were ready for adoption. "Have you had a kitten before?"

"No, but I'm prepared to learn. I have a nice apartment that allows pets, a small den where I can keep the litter box. There's a window that gets plenty of sun and I won't be letting my cat go outside."

Brenda nodded as she spoke. "Sounds like you've thought this through. I'm not pushing, but if you're at work a lot, you might want to consider two kittens so they can keep each other company. Kittens need a lot of play and attention."

Two? Renee felt instantly nauseous. She couldn't possibly handle two little, living creatures. It was like asking for the moon.

Before she could run shrieking into the parking lot, Jasper reached for her hand. "You don't have to decide today. Let's go look at the kittens and see what we think."

Brenda led them toward the "cat" side of the shelter. The area was large and well lit, with several kittens to a kennel.

Some were sleeping but a lot were awake and playing. Renee smiled at the big eyes and cute noses and little toes.

"Do you see one you like?" Brenda asked. "We have rooms where you can spend some time getting to know the kitten before picking the one you like."

Renee had no idea how she was supposed to decide which kitten was the one for her. Based on the color? The way it blinked at her? Weren't there personality characteristics that should be more important?

"Can you give me a minute?" she asked, hoping she didn't sound as rattled as she felt.

"Sure. Ah, I'll go help someone else and check back with you."

Jasper waited until Brenda had left to ask, "You okay? We can leave and come back another time if this is too much pressure."

"They're kittens. They aren't supposed to be pressure. They're supposed to be cute." She looked at him. "What if all my years of worry and fear mean I can never have a pet? I want to have a pet. I want to be a normal person who has a cat."

"You will be. It's going to be fine. Let's go look at the adult cats."

They walked down the hall. There were cats on either side, a glass wall between them and visitors. Larger viewing rooms had three or four adult cats, while some were in small, individual kennels. Some of the cats watched her, but a lot were sleeping. She saw an orange cat alone in a kennel, glaring at her.

He was a big guy, with dark green eyes and serious attitude. There was something about him, Renee thought. Something she couldn't explain.

A volunteer walked past.

"Excuse me," Renee said. "Who is that cat?"

The volunteer—a teenager, with her hair pulled back in a ponytail—glanced at the kennel in question. "Oh, that's Fred. He was surrendered when his owners had to move and couldn't take him with them. They weren't very nice about it and didn't tell us anything about the cats. It was kind of a dump and run. He's been here about three weeks and isn't exactly friendly. We're thinking he needs to go into foster care so he can mellow out." She smiled. "Have you looked at those calico sisters over there? They're very affectionate."

Renee dutifully glanced at the pretty calico cats, then returned her attention to Fred. He made no attempt to hide his disdain for her or his circumstances. She didn't need her mother's gift to know he was desperately unhappy, but whether or not that was because he was in a shelter or missed his family or some other reason, she had no idea.

She stayed by Fred's kennel until Brenda returned.

"What did you decide?"

Renee pointed to Fred. "Tell me about him. Another volunteer said he was surrendered because his family had to move."

Brenda looked confused, but nodded. "Fred is about eight years old. He's not really a lap cat. He's not a bad cat, just not very interested in people and he seems upset all the time. I'm not sure he would be a good match for a first-time cat owner. A kitten is going to bond with you more quickly."

Renee looked at Fred. There was something about him. Something she couldn't explain. She pointed to the sign on the wall offering a thirty-day trial on cats over five years old.

"I want to try with him," she said. "I want to see if we can be a family."

"Okay. I'll put him in a room so you two can meet. I wouldn't try to pet him or anything."

Renee and Jasper spent an hour with Fred in the meet and greet room. He stayed in the corner, hissed when either of them approached and refused to play with the feather on a stick toy. When Brenda returned, she smiled at them.

"So, a kitten?"

"I'll take him," Renee said firmly.

"You sure?" Jasper asked, sounding surprised.

"He needs me."

"He needs something, but this is a lot to take on. Don't you want a pet who likes you?"

"He will. Eventually."

Jasper looked doubtful as he said, "It's whatever you want."

It took two volunteers to stuff Fred into a carrier. Renee paid the fees and then shopped at the on-site store where she bought kitty litter, a litter box, food and dishes. She decided toys could wait until Fred was more at home in her apartment.

Jasper helped her carry everything inside.

"Want me to stay for a while?" he asked.

She smiled. "I'm good. Fred and I need to get to know each other. Thank you for coming with me today."

"You're welcome." He kissed her, then glanced at the growling, hissing cat in the carrier. "I guess I don't have to worry about him if he ever meets Koda. He'll send that dog whimpering into the corner."

She grinned and walked him to the door. Once Jasper was gone, she opened the cat carrier. Fred shot out like a bullet, raced twice around her apartment then dove under the bed. She put the litter box in place and added the litter. After setting up a feeding station in a corner of the kitchen, she put out food for him, then prepared her own dinner.

Around ten, she saw movement out of the corner of her eye. Fred had appeared. He investigated the room, careful to keep his distance. She smiled at him and he hissed back.

Right before bed, she checked and saw he'd eaten most of his food and used the litter box. She wished him good-night and got into bed. Sometime after midnight, she woke up to find him sleeping on the far corner of her bed.

"Hey, Fred."

He hissed at her, then deliberately turned his back on her. Slowly, carefully, she reached across the bed and lightly stroked his fur. He growled and promptly jumped off the bed. Renee smiled as she rolled over to her other side. She finally had a pet and while she could guess what was going on with him, she really had no idea what he was thinking. And it was wonderful.

CHAPTER NINETEEN

Renee didn't ever want to not like one of her brides, but Asia was really pushing her buttons. The tall, willowy blonde had been difficult from their very first meeting. Not mean so much as demanding in unexpected ways. She would want to start a meeting at 10:22 in the morning and she meant 10:22 a.m. Not 10:15 a.m. or 10:30 a.m. Nope, she would walk in precisely at 10:22 a.m. and things got going.

From Renee's perspective, she overmonitored her fiancé, bossed around her parents and acted like the princess she wasn't. But, Renee reminded herself as she tried to get everyone in place for the rehearsal the Thursday before their wedding, weddings were stressful and maybe Asia was a lovely person in her regular life.

"Jack is late," Asia said, glaring at her parents, the Thursday evening before the Saturday wedding. "I told you he was too irresponsible to put in the wedding, but you said I had to."

"He's your brother, Asia." Her mother's voice was pleading.

"Come on, pumpkin," her father added.

"Don't call me that." She glared at both of them before turning to Andrew, her fiancé. "Do something."

"I'm going to take Buster for a walk."

Buster was the gorgeous golden retriever who would be acting as best man. The dog belonged to Asia, but Andrew wanted him to participate in the wedding, so the dog wouldn't feel he was replaced. From what Renee had been able to observe, Andrew and Buster were great friends and the new man of the house would be accepted with a wagging tail.

But instead of going with Andrew when called, Buster whined and retreated to a stack of folding chairs and huddled next to them.

"That's the second time he's done that," Andrew said. "Is he feeling all right?"

"How would I know?" Asia snapped.

"He's your dog. Did he eat his breakfast?"

Asia rubbed her temples. "I'm sure he did."

"You can't remember?"

She glared at him. "It was hours ago. Look, you just have to show up and put on a tux. I'm the one handling all the details for our three-hundred-person wedding. It's been a lot, so forgive me if I can't remember how much the dog ate for breakfast."

Her voice rose with each word until she was shouting. Both sets of parents flinched. Out of the corner of her eye, Renee saw Jack, Asia's younger brother, walk into the room, take one look at his sister, then turn on his heel and quickly escape before anyone saw him.

At times like this, Renee really wanted to take the groom aside so he could explain what it was he saw in his bride-to-be. What was she like when they were alone, because out in public, she was a bitch. But she'd never asked the question

before and she wasn't going to start now. To almost quote
Shakespeare, that way lay madness.

"Why don't we start without Jack?" Renee said, keeping
her voice as soothing as possible. "All he has to do is seat the
mothers, then take his place next to Andrew. I'll go over everything with him later."

"No matter how many times you tell him what to do, he'll
screw it up," Asia grumbled.

"Asia!"

"You know I'm right, Mom." Asia looked at Renee. "Fine.
Let's get going. Come on, Buster. Time to stand with Andrew."

Buster whined, but didn't budge from his place by the
chairs.

"He's been upset for a while now," Andrew said.

Asia rolled her eyes. "How would you know? You see him
for like five seconds when you come over."

"That's not true. I hang out with him while I'm waiting
for you. I take him for walks every night I'm there. When
you went away for your bachelorette party, I kept him for
three days. I'm the one who took him to the vet for his last
checkup."

"Whatever."

Renee realized that both sets of parents had followed Jack's
lead and darted out of the room. Great. Twenty minutes into
the rehearsal and nearly everyone had disappeared.

"Did you want to take a break?" Renee asked quietly. "I
could—"

"Take a break? We just got here. It's a rehearsal. Let's re-
hearse and be done with it." Asia marched over to her dog.
"Dammit, Buster, act right. Go with Andrew."

The dog whimpered, crouching down. Andrew knelt next
to him.

"Something's wrong."

"Do you want me to find a local vet?" Renee asked. She knew of a nice woman with a practice nearby. Renee had taken Fred in to make sure he was all right, but except for the spitting and hissing, he seemed to be in excellent health.

"I don't think he's sick," Andrew said, stroking Buster's head. "But he's sure upset about something."

Renee thought about how they still had the rehearsal to get through, not to mention an entire wedding, and at the rate they were going, nothing was going to happen. She might not be able to fix Asia's attitude but she could help them learn what was wrong with the dog.

"Give me two minutes," she said and hurried out of the room.

"Great," Asia yelled after her. "Now you're leaving, too? What am I paying you for?"

Renee ignored her and quickly texted her mother. Verity replied immediately, saying she would be right over. Renee returned to the main room where Asia stood by herself while Andrew was still huddled by the dog.

"My mom's going to stop by," she began.

"Oh, really? Your mother?" Asia's tone was sarcastic. "Did you forget your lunch or your schoolbooks?"

"Asia, stop it."

Asia turned on him. "This is my *wedding*," she screamed. "No one is taking it seriously."

"Your wedding? Not our wedding?"

"Don't you dare start your damn semantic games with me, Andrew. This is not the time." She spun to face Renee. "What?"

Renee forced herself to relax. She might not be able to change Asia's energy, but she didn't have to feed it.

"My mom is something of an animal expert. I'm hoping she can tell us what's wrong with Buster."

"An expert? Do tell."

Renee smiled. "She has a show on Animal Planet."

"Oh." Asia looked impressed. "Okay, that would be great. Once we get the damn dog fixed, we can move on to where everyone went to."

The last few words were delivered at a shout.

Andrew shifted so he was sitting on the floor. Buster stretched across his lap and closed his eyes.

"We should never have had a dog in the wedding," Asia muttered. "Not that my stupid brother is any better."

Verity walked in. "I came as quickly as I could."

"Thanks, Mom." Renee made introductions, saving the golden retriever for last. "This handsome guy doesn't want to cooperate. I thought maybe you could help us figure out why."

"Of course." Verity started toward Buster. Her warm smile quickly faded as she stumbled to stop. The color drained from her face and she immediately turned and ran from the room.

"This is ridiculous," Asia snapped. "What is wrong with everyone tonight?"

Renee didn't answer. Instead she said, "I'll be right back," and went after her mother.

While she didn't know the details, she could guess the problem. Buster had told Verity something her mother didn't want to hear or share.

She found Verity in the hallway, leaning against the wall. Her mother was still pale and her breathing was shallow.

"I won't," her mother said, closing her eyes. "I won't ruin your life again. I love you and I want you to be happy."

"Mom, what are you talking about?"

"Those people. The wedding. I can't say it. Don't make me say it."

"Since when do you have a choice?"

Renee kept her tone gentle, but her words were true regardless. Eventually Verity would have to blurt out whatever she'd sensed. It was just a matter of time.

"I don't want to hurt you."

Renee hugged her mother. "Mom, you won't. Nothing you're going to say affects me. Even if it does, I love you."

"What's going on?" Andrew asked, hurrying up to them, Buster at his side. Asia trailed behind them.

"This is insane," she said. "You're ruining my wedding."

Renee looked into her mother's eyes. "It's okay," she said. "Just tell us what Buster told you."

Verity looked at the dog. "He's upset. He loves Andrew and knows how hurt he's going to be. He wants to tell him, but he can't, so he's trying to deal with it as best he can." She closed her eyes. "I'm sorry."

"It's okay, Mom."

Verity looked at Asia. "He knows about your affair. I don't know who the man is, but it's not your fiancé. Buster doesn't want to live with you anymore. He wants to live with Andrew."

"What are you doing?" Asia screamed, rushing toward Verity. "You bitch! How could you do this? I'll sue you. I swear to God, I'll destroy you."

Jack stepped into the hallway and grabbed his sister.

"Jesus, sis. An affair? I thought something was up but you told me I wrong. Is there anyone you won't lie to?" He held on to her as she clawed at Verity. "Stop it. Act like a human for a change. It will be good for you."

Andrew seemed more sad than stunned. He sank to the floor and held out his arms to Buster. The dog threw himself into the embrace.

"I guess I suspected," Andrew said, his voice thick with emotion. "I didn't want to believe it." He looked at Renee. "Not her first time. It's kind of her thing. I guess I was the idiot who thought he could change her."

All Renee could think was to ask why on earth he'd proposed if his girlfriend was a chronic cheater, but that wouldn't help anyone. Instead she offered a sympathetic, "I'm sorry," grabbed her mother and headed out of the hallway.

She found both sets of parents huddled in the parking lot. "You need to go inside," she told them. "There's been a development." When they'd disappeared into the building, she looked at her mother.

"Thank you."

Verity's eyes widened. "I ruined everything."

"You're not the bitch who cheated, Mom. You just told the truth."

"You're not upset?"

"No. I like Andrew. Hopefully he'll grow a pair and dump Asia. I figure the odds of there being a wedding on Saturday are slim to none, so I get a day off." She hugged her mom. "I swear, it's totally fine."

"I'm glad. I was afraid you were upset."

"Not even a little. But I do have a favor."

"Anything."

"I need you to come by my apartment. I adopted a cat and there's something going on with him. I'd like you to tell me what."

Her mother looked at her. "You're not cheating on Jasper, are you?"

Renee laughed. "I'm not. I promise."

"All right then. How about after you get this mess cleared up?"

"Perfect."

"Open, open, open," Renee chanted the next morning as she waited outside the animal shelter. She was on a mission to heal Fred's kitty heart and she didn't know if she was too late.

A volunteer unlocked the front door and smiled at her. "You're eager. How can we help?"

"I need to adopt a cat."

"Excellent. We have lots of cats."

"No. A specific cat. Her name is Lucille." Renee held in a groan. "Not that you'll know that's her name. She's gray and white and she came in with Fred nearly four weeks ago. She was surrendered by her owner. She was really sick. Skinny and throwing up."

The woman stared at her. "Was she your cat?"

"No." Renee had no idea how to explain what was going on without sounding insane. "Look, my mom has the ability to know what animals are thinking. It sounds crazy, but it's true. She has a show on Animal Planet." Credentials she was tossing around these days. Thank goodness for the network and its shows!

"I adopted Fred earlier this week. He's obviously upset about something, so I asked my mom to talk to him."

"Because she can talk to cats?" the volunteer sounded doubtful.

"Yes. Look, just hear me out. Fred and Lucille were brought in together. They're a bonded pair and he misses her and he's worried about her. She was really sick. I need to know if she's okay and if she's been adopted or not. If she's still here, I'd like to adopt her for Fred."

Another volunteer, an older woman, walked over. "I know who you're talking about. She's a sweet little thing. We're calling her Misty." The woman smiled sadly. "She had a hernia in her diaphragm. It was keeping her from eating. She had surgery and now she's healing nicely. We were going to release her to be adopted in a day or so. Would you like to see her?"

Renee nodded. She was led back into the cat area, then

through doors marked Staff and Volunteers Only where there were a dozen or so cats in various stages of recovery. Misty—aka Lucille, or so Renee hoped—was a pretty gray-and-white cat with an inquisitive expression and a soft meow.

"Hey, pretty girl," the volunteer said. "You have a visitor." She pointed to Misty. "Is this her?"

"I don't know. I think so."

Misty rolled onto her back, exposing her shaved belly and a long scar.

"That was a serious surgery," Renee said. "Is she okay?"

"She should be fine. She's eating well and putting on weight. Do you want to take her home and see if she's the cat you're looking for?"

Renee nodded and went to fill out the paperwork. Less than an hour later, she was back at her apartment, the recovering Lucille with her.

"Fred, I've got her. At least I hope I do."

She opened the carrier. Lucille took a tentative step into the living room, offering a soft meow as she walked. Fred raced in from the bedroom. He skittered to a stop and stared at her. Lucille stared back. At first there was nothing, then they hurried to each other. There was lots of sniffing and then they started to groom each other.

The movements were frantic, but loving. Fred sniffed at Lucille's healing incision, then returned his attention to grooming her face. She tucked her head into his chest. Renee could hear they were both purring.

"So now you have two cats," Jasper said.

"I do. Fred and Lucille. He had a different name before but he told my mom he likes Fred, so we're keeping that."

They were out to dinner, on a Saturday night. Something Renee couldn't remember happening for years. She was never free on Saturday night. There was always a wedding. But perhaps not shockingly, the Halloween wedding had been canceled.

"Is he any more friendly?"

Renee smiled. "He'll never be a lap cat, but he's stopped hissing at me. This morning, he let me pet him without grumbling about it. Lucille is a total lovebug. She slept curled up next to me all night. She's sweet and I adore them both."

"Are you stopping with two cats, or do you want an even dozen?"

She laughed. "I'm happy with my two."

"I heard about the wedding drama. Was the bride really taken away by the police?"

"Who said that? No. There was just a lot of screaming. She threatened to sue us for I'm not sure what. Andrew said he would make sure that didn't happen, but I'm thinking he has a lot less influence with her now. He ended things with her and he kept the dog."

"Do you think they'll get back together?"

"I hope not for his sake, but he already knew what she was like when he proposed, so I don't know."

Jasper frowned. "Why would he do that? Was she really beautiful?"

"She's lovely but she has the personality of a viper. I don't know what he saw in her. At least Buster has a good home now."

"Buster is the dog?"

"Uh-huh." She picked up her drink. "Enough about the wedding or nonwedding disaster. What's going on with you? How's the book?"

"I'm nearly done. I'm working on the ending. It's not going well. I can't figure out what is supposed to happen."

She leaned toward him and lowered her voice. "Isn't your hero supposed to stop the bad guy?"

"Is that it?" He smiled at her. "It's adding the emotional element that's more challenging. I'm still figuring it all out."

"Want me to help you block out the final action scene?"

"Could you?"

"Sure. I'm going to see my mom in the morning, but I could come by after that."

"That works. Thank you."

She smiled in anticipation. She liked helping him with his books. Not that she did any of the actual writing, but blocking out scenes was a lot of fun. Maybe Vidar and Mandy would have sex and Jasper would want to act that out, as well.

She held in a laugh. A girl could only hope!

"I can't believe it's already time for you to go back to San Diego," Renee said, folding the T-shirts her mother put on her bed.

"I know. The time has gone by so quickly. I'm just glad everything worked out for us."

"Me, too."

Renee thought about how upset she'd been when her mother had first arrived, how she'd been convinced having Verity around would ruin everything, but that wasn't true at all. If anything, having her mother around had been a positive experience. She was closer with her friends, Jasper understood Koda better, Carol knew what was going on with her giraffes and Renee had two cats. It was kind of a miracle.

"I hope you can come to the show's premiere," Verity said. "It won't be for a couple of months. They want to film the first few episodes before rolling out the big reveal." She smiled. "I'm sure they call it something different, but that's what I call it."

"I'd love to be there, Mom." Maybe she could bring Jasper. Oh! She was going to have find a cat sitter for Fred and Lucille. She smiled. Responsibility in her personal life. It felt good.

"The premiere will be in Los Angeles," Verity said. "It's not that far. You could drive out with Ed."

Renee started to ask why she would do that when she realized her mother was avoiding her gaze as she busied herself rolling socks into neat little bundles. Suddenly several pieces of information fit together. How her mother had been so busy in the past few weeks. The late arrivals, the flushed cheeks, the vague answers to "What's new?"

"You're dating Ed?" Renee's voice was a squeak. She cleared her throat. "When did this happen?"

"You were there when we met. At the animal preserve."

"Yes, he gave you a tour but I didn't think…" Renee shook her head. The meeting wasn't the point. "Is it serious?"

Her mother looked at her. "I think it might be. He's a very nice man."

Renee held up both hands in a gesture of surrender. "Mom, I'm not judging at all. I'm surprised because you've never mentioned a guy in your life. Not since Dad left and that's been decades." She smiled. "I'm happy if you're happy. I don't know him that well, but he's always seemed nice. Carol's my friend and I adore her." She wasn't sure what else to say. Her mother had a boyfriend. While it was good news, it was going to take some getting used to.

"It was unexpected," Verity admitted with a shy smile. "But I couldn't help myself. He's very—"

Renee winced. "No sex talk, Mom. Please."

"But we're both adults."

"Technically, but in my mind, I'm still the kid, so no."

Her mother laughed. "All right. I'll just say things are going very well and we're going to continue to see each other."

"I'm glad. Any other bombshells?"

"I think that's it."

Renee hugged her. "I love you, Mom."

"I love you, too, sweetie. Always."

CHAPTER TWENTY

Jasper reviewed his pages, knowing he was close to figuring out the ending, but still not there yet. If he was just dealing with Vidar and the killer, he would be fine. It was Mandy who was throwing things off. Or rather how Vidar was supposed to deal with Mandy. He just couldn't get the flow of events lining up correctly with dialogue that made sense.

Part of the problem was the book, and part of the problem was him. Or rather his definition of himself, which seemed to be changing by the minute, or at least the day.

He'd been unable to shake Wynn's statement that he wasn't broken anymore, mostly because he didn't know where that left him. Whole sounded nice, but there were expectations. If there wasn't that much wrong with him then why couldn't he fall in love, get married and have a family, just like everyone else? He kept circling back to the question, and he couldn't seem to come up with an answer.

Just as confusing, he didn't know where Renee fit in. He cared about her. He enjoyed being with her. He respected her. He wanted to spend time with her, and not just in bed.

So what did that mean? Was it like-plus? The other *L* word? He didn't have a clue and he wasn't sure how he was supposed to figure it out.

He tried to distract himself with a long walk. Koda trotted ahead of him as they made their way through the forest. They were back before eleven and just in time to get a text from Renee saying she was on her way.

"Any suggestions?" he asked Koda.

His dog rolled onto his back for a belly rub.

"I'll take that as a no."

He waited anxiously for Renee to arrive and walked out the front door when she pulled up.

"You'll never guess," she said as she got out of the car. "Seriously, it's not possible. My mother is dating Ed."

It took him a second to remember who Ed was. "Carol's dad?"

"Uh-huh. They're probably sleeping together, which I don't want to talk about, but can you believe it? I don't mind the relationship, but it's weird. My mom never dated when I was growing up. This is new territory. I tried to be all cool and sophisticated, but I think I failed. I want her with someone who makes her happy, but it's so strange to think about. Parents dating. What was God thinking?"

She sighed. "Enough about that." She raised herself on tiptoe. "How are you?"

"Good."

They walked into the house and went through to his office. Koda trailed after them, stopped at his bed and flopped down. Renee pulled the extra office chair close to his desk.

"Tell me where you are in the book."

"The serial killer has Mandy and her daughter, and Vidar is coming to rescue them. There's going to be a fight where

Vidar is injured and maybe Mandy, I haven't decided. Vidar gets the killer in the end."

She frowned. "Why do you need help with that? You do complex fight scenes all the time. You do fight scenes with sticks and all kinds of scary stuff."

She had a point. He liked the fight scenes. He could block them out like a movie, going step-by-step.

"I guess I want them to talk," he admitted. "But I don't know what they're going to say. I don't want Mandy to be completely passive, but it's not like she has any skills."

"Is she tied up?" Renee asked. "Are she and her daughter bait?"

"Maybe. I hadn't thought of that."

"If they were bait, Mandy would be really scared, but also really mad. She doesn't want to be the reason Vidar gets killed, and she doesn't want anything to happen to her daughter. The kid kind of gets in the way of the two of them dealing with each other, though, so maybe the daughter is unconscious. That would scare Mandy even more. And if Vidar's in danger, trying to save them, she's totally on the edge. She cares about him, so she won't want him to take any chances. But he cares about her, too, and her daughter. He can't not save them and he's the kind of guy who will put his life on the line."

"He would do that for anyone."

"I know, but it's different if he's in love with her. It makes the danger personal. He would take chances with her and her daughter that he wouldn't take for anyone else. He's more vulnerable."

Jasper hadn't thought about it that way, but she was right. Vidar was more vulnerable. He might push himself harder or take a different kind of risk.

He could see the scene in his mind. Having Mandy trapped worked. She would hate it and yet she wouldn't want to die.

"What would they talk about?" he asked, more to himself than Renee. "She would want to warn him."

"I don't think they'd have a regular conversation, if that's what you're asking. I'm about to die, and we need milk?"

Jasper grinned. "I was thinking more about an emotional declaration."

Renee wrinkled her nose. "Don't do that."

"Why not? What if one of them dies? Wouldn't you want to hear you were loved before a serial killer slit your throat?"

"I guess. I'm just not sure how much it's going to matter in those last few choking seconds. Plus, if they don't die, then for the rest of their lives, they're going to remember the first time they said they loved each other. The memory will be tainted."

He wanted to disagree, but he wondered if it was a guy thing versus a girl thing. Would a guy want to say it so it wasn't unsaid and would a woman…

"Would you say it, if you thought you were going to die?" he asked.

"Shout out 'I love you' right before my throat is cut?" She shrugged. "I don't know. It just seems like a tacky way to do it. Why not last night at dinner or two weeks ago when she was folding your socks? If it takes a near death experience for you to get your feelings, then maybe they're not real to begin with. Maybe they're just the adrenaline talking. Love is flashy in the movies and stuff, but in real life, love is steady. It's not the peak moments, it's the everyday grind and how love makes it better. I'm not saying it has to be wine and roses but wouldn't it be better to say it because you wanted the other person to know and not because one of you might die?"

He studied her. "When you fell in love with Turner, how did you know?"

She looked startled, as if she hadn't been expecting the question. "I don't know," she hedged, glancing away. "We were dating and spending time together. He started to matter more and more. I realized over time. It wasn't any one thing—it was a lot of little things. My feelings got bigger until they were love."

He'd never been in love. There'd been the girl he'd left behind when he'd joined the army, but he'd been a kid and she'd been just as young. When things had ended, they'd both quickly moved on. He'd had a lot of short-term relationships in the military but those were never expected to be more than a way to get through the night. After, well, he'd been too shattered to imagine ever being able to function. Love hadn't been an emotion he'd even considered.

And now?

It was a question that had no answer.

"Vidar's scared," he said quietly, turning his attention to his character. "He's been so careful to hold back, to never let anyone in. Mandy got to him in ways he didn't expect and now she's in danger and it's his fault and he's screwed." He stared at Renee. "He doesn't want to tell her he loves her, he wants to apologize. He wants to make it right and the only way to do that is to save her and her daughter, even if he dies in the process. He's always willing to save the victim, but this is different. Saving those two redeems him."

The pieces fell into place and he could see everything that needed to happen. Renee surprised him by smiling, then standing and kissing him on the mouth.

"I'll see you later," she said, already walking to the door.

"Where are you going?"

"You have that look I've come to recognize. You're going to tell me that you need just fifteen minutes to get a few thoughts down and then you'll disappear for three or four hours." She paused in the doorway. "It's okay, Jasper. It's who you are and it's kind of cute."

"Rain check?" he asked, already sliding toward his computer.

"Promise."

He pulled up his word processing program and stared at the screen. After deleting the dialogue he'd written that morning, he started typing.

Jasper finished the book about ten Sunday night. He spent two days editing it, then sent it off to both his editor and agent. Wednesday morning he woke up, took Koda on a long hike, then returned to his house to begin the ritual of cleaning out his office before he started thinking about his next project, all the while assuming Sara was going to call and tell him what he'd submitted was total crap and that not only wouldn't they publish it, they were canceling the rest of his contract and blackballing him from any future publications. Because an undisciplined imagination was a very bad thing.

He'd just finished breakfast when his phone rang. He stared at the 212 number, wondering if his editor was calling about the book, told himself she couldn't be, and that he would deal regardless, and took the call.

"Hey, Sara."

"Morning, Jasper."

"There's no way you've read the book. You've only had it since last night."

"I started it. I was only going to read the first few pages, and here I am, still at my desk. I had to cancel three meetings to keep reading! I'm eighty pages in and I can already tell it's your best one yet. I love Mandy. She's fantastic. I'll admit it—I wasn't sure you could pull off writing a woman, but you did. She's smart, she's funny, she's caring. I love her daughter. I love how competent she is at her job. The wedding planning behind the scenes is so interesting." She laughed. "So I'm just going to ask. Who is she?"

Relief eased the tightness in his chest. Maybe his career wasn't over.

"Who is who?"

"The woman who inspired Mandy. Come on. I know how you work. Real life influences your stories more than it does for most authors. Mandy is an amazing character and I'm guessing she's based on someone. So who is she?"

Jasper grinned. "Her name is Renee."

"I knew it!"

"She's a wedding planner and the big wedding at the end is based on a wedding here in town. I have the bride and groom's permission to use the details. I'll send you a copy of the releases they signed."

Sara sighed. "No way. The Scottish wedding is real? I want to see that."

"It's this weekend. Want to fly out?"

"I wish I could. So, about Renee. Tell me about her. Was it love at first sight and then you flew off to Rome?"

"What are you talking about?"

"I want the story to be romantic. That would make me happy."

"Okay," he said slowly. "Don't take this wrong, but when it comes to my personal life, your happiness isn't that important to me."

"You're no fun. But you are wildly in love with her, aren't you? You have to be. The way you write about her, what else could it be?"

In love with... In love? He went from relieved to freaked in less than a second and he had no idea what to say. He wasn't in love with anyone. He couldn't be. He was broken and damaged and all things...

"Jasper?"

"What? I'm here."

"Sorry. I crossed a line there. You don't have to tell me about Renee. I just knew one day you'd meet someone and it would be wonderful. I'm glad that's true and I really hope it works out."

"Uh, thanks."

"You're welcome. Okay, I'm going to stop reading because I have meetings I can't cancel. I'll get you notes within a couple of weeks, but I doubt they'll be much. You did great."

"Thanks. Talk to you soon."

He hung up and stared at Koda.

"She liked the book."

He was going to focus on that because thinking about anything else was just too terrifying. In love with Renee? He couldn't be. He wasn't. They weren't. It was just fun and friendship and sex.

Are you in love with my daughter? Verity's words came back to him, making him wonder what was wrong with everyone. Why did it have to be love? Why couldn't it just be what it was and everyone was happy?

Koda stretched out in his bed.

"Nothing to add?" he asked the dog. "No opinion on the matter?"

Koda closed his eyes, which Jasper took as a no.

Renee was determined that every single detail for Hanna and Graham's Scottish wedding would be perfect. Not only did she really like the couple, she was still dealing with the debacle that had been the Halloween wedding. She needed happy we'll-be-blissful-together-all-our-lives vibes resonating through the entire property.

She and Pallas had already performed their ritual cleansing with the burning of white sage smudge sticks and sprinkling salt on the floors and carpets. A good vacuum later and all the rooms seemed happier. A silly tradition to be sure, but one they followed faithfully whenever a wedding didn't happen. Better to be safe, and all that.

She reviewed her to-do list for the next few days. Friday was the rehearsal and rehearsal dinner. Saturday was the wedding itself and Sunday morning was the goodbye brunch. The Friday and Sunday events were easy. Just setup and takedown, with very little in between. The catering service was in charge of the meals. Silver was sending her smallest trailer to handle the bar service, and there were no special decorations or entertainment.

The wedding on Saturday was a big deal with three hundred guests, so a full house for Weddings Out of the Box. There was a traditional service and a dinner reception following with a live band and dancing until at least eleven. It was going to be a long day.

But a happy one, Renee thought, excited to be a part of the weekend. She and Pallas had divided the duties. Renee would take the rehearsal and the wedding while Pallas would man the Sunday brunch. They'd hired a couple of college kids to work the Saturday night reception, mostly to help out Renee and be another set of hands if needed. Renee wanted everything to be perfect.

She walked through the main building to where the wedding would be. Chairs were already in place, along with the pole where they would string the floral garland at the front by the podium. Outside, the huge white tent was up, and the tables and chairs were in place there, as well. The plates, glasses and flatware had been delivered, along with dozens of flat bowls to be used as the centerpieces. Clematis blossoms would float in the bowls with greenery scattered across the table.

Knowing she'd done all she could for today, she returned

to her office and was surprised to find Ed waiting for her. Carol's father was handsome, with dark red hair and an easy smile. Renee hadn't spent a lot of time with him, but what she knew, she liked and he made her mother happy, so that was all that mattered.

"Hi," she said, not sure if she should ask why he was here or—

"I hope it's okay I stopped by." He rubbed his hands against his jeans, looked at her, then away, then back at her. "Do you have a minute?"

"Of course." She motioned to a chair.

He started toward it then shook his head. "I should stand. It's easier."

"Is my mom okay?"

"What? She's fine. Busy getting ready for her show. It's going to be exciting for her. She'll be successful—I'm sure of it. She's a great woman. A wonderful woman."

He swallowed. "I'm in love with her. I had no idea I could fall in love again. I didn't expect to and I wasn't looking, but suddenly there she was. It was like being struck by lightning. The second I saw her, I knew. It was fate."

Renee hadn't known they'd been going out for more than a few days, so she wasn't prepared to have her friend's father declare his love for Verity. Fortunately, Ed didn't seem to expect an answer.

"I thought I had everything I wanted here, but now that I've met Verity, that's not true anymore. My brother Ted is more than capable of handling things. The recycling center practically runs itself and Carol manages the staff that looks after the animals. There's no reason I couldn't make a change."

Renee had no idea what they were talking about. "You're thinking of moving?"

"What? Yes, to San Diego. I want to marry your mother."

Renee sank down in the visitor's chair. Her mother getting married? "But you've only known each other a few weeks."

Ed nodded. "It's quick, I know, but I've never felt like this before. I'm certain I can make her happy. I want to spend the rest of her life doing that." His expression turned stricken. "It's not about the money. I'll sign a prenup. I just want her."

Renee couldn't gather her thoughts together. She managed to stand and smile at Ed. "I'm not worried that you're after her money or anything like that. It's all happening so quickly. I want her to have everything she wants. What did she say when you proposed?"

"I haven't. I wanted your permission."

"Mine?"

Everything about this moment was surreal. Why would her permission matter? Her mother was a capable woman who knew her own mind and had been making her own decisions for longer than Renee had been alive. Only Renee recognized that Ed wasn't saying Verity couldn't decide—instead he wanted Renee to be a part of things. The gesture was sweet. A little unexpected, but sweet.

"Of course," she said with a smile. "I hope you two will be very happy together."

There was a squeal from the hallway, then Carol raced in and hugged her.

"I was eavesdropping," Carol said happily. "I couldn't help myself. We're going to be sisters. I'm so excited. You can't move away. You have to promise."

Carol's sister, Violet, had moved to England a couple of years back. Carol still complained about it.

"Your mom is so great," Carol continued. "I never thought my dad would find anyone but I knew the first time I saw them together." She clapped her hands. "We're a family."

She kept talking, then Ed hugged them both and it was a happy moment, but all Renee heard was "We're a family."

While she'd always had her mom, there had never been any other relatives. Not since her dad had left. It had just been the two of them. Renee had always wanted a sister, an aunt or uncle, grandparents, and while she wasn't exactly getting anything like that, she was getting family. A place to belong.

Unexpected tears burned in her eyes. "I'm so happy," she whispered.

"Us, too," Ed told her. "I'm driving to San Diego right now. I want to propose right away. You girls take care."

He walked out. Renee stared after him. "You girls." Like they were both his daughters. She loved the sound of that.

"Do you think she'll say yes?" Carol asked, sounding anxious.

Renee thought about how blissful her mother had been and how alone she'd been for so long. Ed was a good guy and from what he'd said, it had pretty much been love at first sight for both of them.

"How could she not?" she asked with a laugh. "Come on. Let's go out and celebrate."

She was going to have a family. Later she would text Jasper and tell him the great news. Maybe he could figure out a way to put it in his next book.

Jasper hadn't slept in two days. Not because of nightmares or a book idea that wouldn't let go but because he was trying to make sense of his feelings for Renee.

He wanted to say his confusion had started with his editor's questions, but he knew the problem had begun long before that. Maybe when Wynn had pointed out he wasn't broken anymore or even back when he and Renee had first spent the night together. Or maybe the first time she'd understood that he got lost in a book and hadn't been mad about it.

There was something about her. Something that drew him in and made him want to stick around. Something that made him wonder if maybe his life was better with her in it.

God knew he'd screwed up. He still winced when he thought about how he'd horned in on the wedding, going behind her back, and later, how he'd told her to get over her fears of having her mom's gift. He wasn't perfect, but she seemed okay with that. Being with her made him a better man.

Just as important, he liked taking care of her. He liked making her laugh and helping out when he could. He liked being with her and not just for sex. He liked how she'd picked the cat who seemed right, even though Fred hadn't been easy at first. She was so competent at work. She was resourceful and brave and funny. So what was the problem?

He supposed part of the issue could be the fact that he wasn't the man he'd been three years ago. Everything was different now. He'd made a life, he'd found a new career, he'd met a girl. But did he love her?

Jasper wasn't sure what love was—not really. A feeling, yes, but wasn't it more than that? Wasn't it as much about the other person as himself? When he thought about Renee he was happy. When he was with her, he wanted to spend more time with her.

He walked around his office, Koda watching him, as if a little worried.

"I'm okay," he told the dog. At least he would be when he got his act together.

What if she was sick? What if she was dying? Would he want to deal with her then? He'd seen a lot of horrible things on his tours with the army and figured he could handle pretty much anything she had to deal with. He wasn't afraid of fighting with her, he knew she had a good heart. But was that enough?

Did he want to take care of her, no matter what? Did he want to make her happy, even if he had to sacrifice some things? What if she didn't want to live up in the mountains? What if she wanted to live in town?

He thought for a second. He could do the town thing. He would keep the house in the mountains and he might have to come up here to write for a few days at a time, but if living in Happily Inc made her happy, then he wanted to buy her the house of her dreams. He wanted to hold her and be with her and—

He turned to Koda. "I want kids. With Renee. I want kids and car trips and an IRA and a joint checking account and hell, a minivan. I love her. I'm in love with her."

Koda sighed, as if relieved he'd finally figured it out.

"You like her, too, don't you, boy?"

Koda's tail wagged.

"That's what I thought. I think you'd be good with kids. She has cats now, so that will take some getting used to for all of us. I've never had a cat."

Of course he'd never had a dog, either, and that seemed to be going well.

"I love her," he repeated, not sure what to do next. "I guess I should go see her."

They could go out to dinner to celebrate her mom and Ed's engagement and then he could casually mention his feelings. Or maybe that was better done in private. Either way, he should go to town right now and talk to her.

"I won't be late," he told Koda. "I won't stay the night. I'll be home to take care of you."

He quickly fed the dog, made sure the doggie door was operational, then drove down the mountain road leading to

Happily Inc. Along the way he tried to find the right words, but everything he came up with seemed lame, which was not a good sign. He kind of made his living with words—shouldn't he be better at this?

Still not sure what verbal direction made the most sense, he parked by her apartment building, raced across the lawn and took the stairs to her place only to hesitate in front of her door for at least three minutes. Finally he knocked.

She opened the door and smiled when she saw him.

"Jasper! Did I know you were coming by? Come on in. It's a big night here. Fred accidentally sat on my lap for about thirty seconds. Then he came to his senses, hissed at me and ran off. Lucille, on the other hand, sticks close and loves to snuggle."

She looked incredible. She was barefoot and casually dressed in capris and a T-shirt. She'd scrubbed off her makeup. There were freckles on her nose and cheeks. Her mouth beckoned. He wanted her but more than that, he loved her.

Her smile faded. "Are you okay? You have the strangest expression."

"I'm fine."

She didn't look convinced. She pulled him into the living room and sat next to him on the sofa. Once they were angled toward each other, it occurred to him that it would be so easy to slide to one knee and—

He swore under his breath, thinking he was not ready to propose. Besides, he didn't have a ring and he hadn't even told her he loved her. One step at a time, he reminded himself. He didn't want to screw this up.

"Jasper, you're scaring me."

"I don't mean to." He looked at her. "Have you talked to your mom? Is she happy?"

Renee looked slightly surprised by the question but she

nodded slowly. "She is. She said they both realize things are moving fast, so they're going to wait several months before setting a date. She sounded so excited and in love. I'm so glad for her."

"Me, too."

He continued to watch her. Renee shifted on her seat. "What is going on?"

He had to do it, he told himself. He would just put it out there and see what happened.

Lucille jumped onto the sofa and curled up next to him. He petted the cat, hoping the action would be soothing.

It wasn't. He sucked in a breath and said, "Renee, I'm in love with you. You are incredible—not just because you're beautiful, although you are, but because of everything else about you. You're smart and caring. You're funny and I want to be with you. I want to make you happy and I hope you want that, too."

Her eyes widened as she stared at him without speaking.

"You make me a better man," he continued, wondering when she was going to say something. "I think we work as a couple and—"

"No!" She sprang to her feet and hurried to the far side of the room. "Why are you doing this? We agreed we wouldn't do this. We talked about it. We have a relationship that we both like but it's not love. We're not supposed to be in love. I don't want you to love me. Love isn't safe. You have to know that."

Tears filled her eyes and her voice softened to a whisper. "Don't, Jasper. Don't make me do this. Don't ask for more than I have. I can't risk it. I just can't."

His happiness evaporated as dread took its place. She wasn't ready. Or she didn't share his feelings. Either was bad.

"What are you afraid of?" he asked, careful to keep his

voice neutral. "Your mom isn't an issue. Not with me. I'm not going to break your heart or hurt you."

"Of course you are. That's what people do. They hurt each other. You'll hurt me and then you'll leave. You're going to leave me and it will be over. I'll be shattered and damaged for the rest of my life."

He stood. "I'm not those other guys."

"It doesn't matter." Tears slipped down her cheeks. "You said you wouldn't do this. What we had was great. Don't ask me to change."

"You have to trust me."

"I can't."

"You won't."

She brushed away the tears. "Does it really matter which it is? I can't risk it. I don't have another broken heart in me."

She walked into her bedroom and closed the door behind her. Jasper stood there, alone. *But I love you.* He wanted to shout the words, only he knew they wouldn't matter. Not to her.

Hell of a thing, he thought as he let himself out and walked back to his truck. Hell of thing.

CHAPTER TWENTY-ONE

Jasper sat in his truck for several minutes, not sure what to do, think or feel. Renee's response had stunned him. He'd certainly been aware of the possibility that she might not share his feelings, but he'd never thought that she would be that upset and simply walk away from him. Funny how he'd been so worried about healing from his own past, he'd never considered that she might not be over hers.

He wanted to do something, but what? There weren't words to convince her that everything was going to be fine. How could there be? Life was always a crapshoot. If only he didn't already miss her.

His phone buzzed with a text. He grabbed it, hoping it was Renee. But instead the message was from Drew.

San Francisco is kicking the Rams's collective asses my friend. You're going to owe me $20.

At first the message made no sense. It was as if Drew were using a language Jasper didn't speak. Then the meaning sank in. The weekly football pool he was in with his friends. He and Drew always had a side bet on the Thursday night game and tonight it was San Francisco and the Rams.

He scrolled through his contacts, then pushed the call button.

"Twenty big ones," Drew said by way of greeting. "You're going to owe me, my man. Ha!"

"Can I come over?" Jasper asked.

"Sure. I'm home. What's wrong?"

"I'll tell you when I get there."

Jasper made the short drive to his friend's house. Drew had the front door open before Jasper had turned off his truck's engine.

"What's going on?"

Drew sounded concerned. That was nice, Jasper thought. Having someone who would listen, someone who would care. He hadn't had a group of friends in a long time. No matter what happened with Renee, he would get through it. He had his writing and Koda and guys like Drew. If things got really bad, he knew how to ask for help. He was a lucky man. Except for the fact that the woman he loved had kicked him to the curb.

"I told Renee I was in love with her," he said. "It didn't go well."

Drew motioned for him to come inside. "I'm sorry. I thought things were going good with her."

"I did, too. I tell myself it's because she's not ready, but what do I know?"

He followed Drew into the family room of the large house. His friend got him a beer, then joined him on the sofa. The game was on the big TV up on the wall but the sound was muted.

"Start at the beginning," his friend said.

Jasper told him about the one-sided conversation and how

Renee had accused him of breaking the rules. He didn't mention the heavy weight of sadness or how all his hope was gone.

"It wasn't supposed to get serious," he said. "She's right about that. I just thought things had changed. I guess they had, but only for me."

He thought about all the times she'd made it clear that she wasn't interested in getting involved. She never talked about getting married or having kids. Maybe she'd been telling the truth all along.

"I should have listened," he said. "I should have paid attention to what she was saying."

"It's not wrong to love her," Drew told him. "It's a gift."

"Renee's not big on gifts."

"Want to stay here tonight? We have a guest room."

"Thanks, but I need to get back to Koda." He'd promised his dog he wouldn't be gone all night. Plus, he knew there was no way he was sleeping. Not with a Renee-sized hole in his heart.

Renee couldn't remember the last time she'd felt so awful. Maybe after Turner had broken off his engagement to her, but she wasn't sure. Because as much as that had hurt, she'd known the reason had very little to do with her. Yes, her mother's ability was weird, but was it really a reason to dump and run? Or had Turner been looking for an out all along?

She'd never gotten the answer to that question and now, as she huddled on the floor in her bathroom, wondering if she was going to throw up her breakfast the way she'd thrown up her dinner the previous night, she knew that in many ways, this was different. Worse. Because not only was she desperately missing Jasper, she knew she only had herself to blame.

Last night she'd been able to get by on righteous indignation. The man had broken the rules. He taken their perfectly wonderful relationship and twisted it into something she couldn't recognize. He'd been wrong and horrible and how dare he tell her he love her! What was up with that?

But this morning there was too much sadness for her to be mad. She knew she'd done the right thing and now she had to deal with the painful consequences.

She leaned against the side of the bathtub and waited for her stomach to settle. It wasn't as if she could have responded any other way. She'd been burned too many times. Every relationship she'd ever had had failed.

Not with her mom, of course, but that was different. They were family. And her friendships here in Happily Inc were good. She loved working with Pallas and now they were going to be business partners. But her last serious boyfriend had lied about being married and there was Turner and her father had walked out on her and those kids in high school had treated her like a freak so it made sense that she wasn't going to accept that Jasper loved her.

Love was not in the cards for her. She'd made that decision and she wasn't changing her mind now. Her way was safer. Her way made sense. Her way sucked the big one, but life was pain.

She gave herself fifteen more minutes of waiting on her stomach, then got ready for work. No matter how bad she felt, this was the Scottish wedding weekend and she was going to make sure it was magnificent.

She arrived at Weddings Out of the Box in time to confirm the caterer was doing a great job setting up for the rehearsal dinner. After a quick pass to make sure everything put out the previous day was still in place, she retreated to her office to make her phone calls confirming everything from flowers to the cake delivery.

Normally her final to-do list only took her two or three

hours, but today she spent most of the morning working through it. She was slightly less nauseous than she had been, but much more emotionally devastated than she'd thought she would be. She could focus for the moment, then she remembered what had happened with Jasper and she got shaky again. She expected her heart to be battered but what was up with her inability to concentrate?

At noon she made sure the setup for the rehearsal dinner was complete. The caterer had also put out the tables for the reception. They would be decorated in the morning. She'd double-checked on all that she could. The cake would be arriving in the next thirty minutes and would be fully assembled by six that evening when it would be locked in the special cake-only refrigerated space. She was just wondering if she could keep down lunch or if she should simply skip the meal when Silver and Wynn arrived.

"Hi," Renee said, a little surprised to see them. "Everything okay?"

Silver shrugged. "I'm good. How are you doing?"

There was something in her tone. Something… "You know what happened?"

"Jasper stopped by to see Drew and Drew told me when Jasper left. You doing all right?"

"Sure. I mean it's sad and all, but I'm fine." Did that sound as normal as she hoped? Not that she was lying—not really. She was feeling all right, or she would be eventually.

Silver glanced at Wynn. Neither of them looked convinced.

"Did you guys have a fight?" Wynn asked.

"There was no fight. Jasper wanted to take things to the next level and I don't. It's no big deal."

"Are you sure? I thought you were pretty happy together."

"We were. He's great."

More than great. She liked being around him. He could be

annoying and bossy and determined to get his way, but when she explained the problem, he really got what he'd done and did better the next time. He admitted his flaws, he'd hung out with her mom, he was a fabulous kisser.

And caring, she thought, remembering how he was so considerate of Koda.

"I miss him, of course," she said, fighting a flood of emotion. "But that will pass." It had to. Time healed and all that. "I know I'm doing the right thing."

Wynn shook her head.

"What?" Renee demanded. "You think I should accept what he said? Just like that? Say sure and go for it? Trust him with who I am? What happens when he dumps me? What happens when there are forty-seven reasons why it won't work? I'm tired of having my heart broken all the time. I won't go through it again. I won't and you can't make me."

"You're scared." Wynn's voice was soft. "I get that. You've had to deal with some stuff in your life and you're scared and it's much easier to pretend you don't want what he's offering because if you do want it then you can be hurt. You can be broken and there are only so many times you can pick up the pieces."

Renee fought against tears. "I know and it hurts." She waited for her friends to hug her.

"Get over yourself," Wynn told her.

"What?"

"You heard me. Get over yourself. Jasper is a great guy and you're going to lose him because you're a coward. Girlfriend, you think you have regrets now? Wait until he's moved on and you wake up and realize you had a chance with him and now it's over. He's done with you and you're alone because you were too afraid to take a chance."

Silver's eyes widened. "Is that what you think about Jasper?"

"Me?" Wynn rolled her eyes. "No and no. Look, he and

I had a great time, but it was never going to be anything. I made sure of that with my rules about Hunter. He never loved me enough to fight and I never cared enough to bend. We let each other go without a backward glance. I don't regret Jasper but I do regret keeping myself so closed off all the time. Now it's been so long, I'm not sure I can find my way back."

Her voice softened. "Renee, don't give up on yourself and don't live with regrets. They hurt the most. You're stuck in the past when you have a wonderful man offering you the future. What more do you want?"

"I want to know for sure. I want to believe that it's going to be okay."

"It's not going to be okay if you just sit on your butt, feeling sorry for yourself. Success is about showing up. You're running in the other direction."

"That's easy for you to say. You don't know what I'm dealing with."

Wynn's expression turned sad. "We're all dealing with crap from our past. You think you're the only one? You're not."

"She's right," Silver said softly. "Look at what I went through with Drew. But I toughed it out and now we're married and it's great."

"Which is fine for you, but you can't make me do this," Renee shouted. "I won't let you. You don't understand. You can never understand."

She turned and made her way to her office. As she climbed the stairs, it occurred to her that she was spending a lot of time running from something rather than to something. But being a coward was easy and she wasn't sure at all that she had what it took to be brave.

Jasper hadn't known what to do about Hanna and Graham's wedding. Hanna had texted him twice, telling him what time the rehearsal started and inviting him to the Sunday morning brunch. He had already committed to attending the ceremony and reception, but with everything that had happened with Renee, he wasn't sure if he should go to any of it. Late Friday afternoon, he was still undecided, then figured what the hell. He would handle whatever happened. Renee wasn't the type to make a scene—not only wasn't it in her nature, she would never do anything to upset one of her happy couples.

Besides, he had a gift for Hanna and Graham—he was dedicating the book to them for letting him use their wedding as a backdrop for his story.

He unwrapped the pages he'd had mounted on poster board. The first one—the one that mattered most—had two dedications. *To R, with love,* followed by a paragraph thanking Hanna and Graham. The second one only had the thank-you.

He thought about bringing the first one and letting the truth hang out there. Except there would be questions and those questions would detract from the evening. Besides, he didn't want to embarrass Renee or make her feel bad. He only wanted to make her happy, to love her, to know they could be together always.

He grabbed the one with the single paragraph, told Koda he wouldn't be late and walked out to his truck. As he drove down the mountain, he realized he had no idea what was going to happen at the rehearsal and dinner to follow. He missed Renee more today than he had yesterday—which was not comfortable news. At this rate, within a week, being without her would be unbearable. He was already using the breathing techniques he'd learned in his therapy sessions and he was thinking maybe he and Koda should get in the motor home and go somewhere for a couple of months. Being on the road always made him feel better. He could get away from all the Renee-reminders in town and start his next book.

Only he didn't want to go anywhere. Not without her. He had it so bad, he would rather see her and feel the pain of not having her than be away from her. Which left him in an impossible situation.

He arrived at Weddings Out of the Box a few minutes before the rehearsal was due to start. A quick scan of the parking lot told him that Renee's car wasn't there. He knew she and Pallas had divided the duties—with Renee handling the rehearsal and wedding and Pallas stepping in for Sunday's brunch.

They must have switched things up, he thought grimly. Pallas was here tonight, when it was a smaller group. Tomorrow he would be easier to stay away from—and even if he wasn't, Renee would never disappoint Hanna.

Until that very second, he hadn't realized how much he'd been looking forward to seeing her. He loved her. There was no getting around that, he thought as he walked toward the building. He loved her and wanted to spend the rest of his life with her, and she wasn't interested. He couldn't figure out if she simply didn't share his feelings or if she was too scared to take a chance on him, but knew it didn't matter. In the end, they weren't together anymore and he was going to have to figure out how to deal with that and move on.

CHAPTER TWENTY-TWO

Renee spent a long, lonely Friday night home by herself. Fred and Lucille were some company but neither was much for conversation and after they got tired of playing with her, they went to sleep, leaving her alone with her thoughts.

Word of what had happened with Jasper had spread and Pallas had insisted on handling the rehearsal dinner so Renee didn't have to worry about running into Jasper at such an intimate setting. Although Renee appreciated the gesture, she couldn't help wondering if being busy would have been easier to deal with. Not that she would have enjoyed having to avoid Jasper at every turn. In fact there was no way she could have avoided him, and yet she really regretted not being at the rehearsal dinner, which meant what? She'd finally slipped into madness?

She spent a restless night and woke up before five on Saturday morning. After taking care of the cats, she left for work and got to Weddings Out of the Box well before seven. She reviewed Pallas's notes on the rehearsal dinner, then walked the venue and made sure everything was as it should be for the Scottish wedding.

The cake was safely assembled and in the refrigerated case. It would be wheeled out midmorning so it had time to come to room temperature. The bottom and top two layers were about three inches each with the middle layer twice as high. Blue, teal and magenta flowers cascaded down one side. Sprigs of heather would decorate the table. It was as beautiful as the pictures and Renee knew that Hanna and Graham would be thrilled.

She went into the groom's room and made sure all the tuxes were hanging in place. Graham's tux had been custom-made for him. The jacket lining had been printed with photographs of the happy couple from the time they met until their engagement photo. It was a wonderful surprise element that would be special to the couple. She remembered how they'd talked about having it done and how Jasper had encouraged them. He'd been right—the lining was perfect.

In the bride's room, Hanna's dress hung on the specially designed rack, leaving plenty of room for the train. Her shoes were there, along with makeup, and everything she would need for her special day.

The flowers arrived at eight. Renee confirmed the order, then helped the florist put the various bouquets in the bride's room and the boutonnieres in the groom's room. Three college-aged guys hung the floral garland in the main room where the ceremony would be, while two more students filled the shallow bowls with the clematis blossoms.

At noon Renee forced herself to eat a protein bar. She wasn't hungry, but knew she would need her energy for later. She drank a couple of glasses of water and told herself that eventually she would stop feeling as if she were slowly bleeding to death. That once she got through the brunch tomor-

row, she would retreat to her apartment and spend the next
two days seeing what she could do about moving on with her
life, but until then, she had to focus on Hanna and Graham.

A little after three, the activity began in earnest. Hanna
and her friends arrived. An hour later, Graham and his family showed up, including his twin sister who looked enough
like him to almost make things confusing. Hanna's parents
arrived separately, each with a spouse. The caterer was in
place, getting the food ready, while Silver had two trailers
parked by the reception area and was preparing for the post-
ceremony deluge.

Renee made a continuous circuit of the event space. She
smiled when she saw Hanna in her beautiful elbow-length
sleeve, off the shoulder, mermaid style, lace gown. Her hair
was up, her makeup perfect and the photographer was already
doing her thing. Renee confirmed the quartet were ready to
begin as the first guests arrived.

She kept busy enough that she only thought of Jasper every
thirty or forty seconds, which was better than it had been
that morning. She'd yet to catch sight of him, but she knew
he would be around.

At four thirty, guests began to fill the rows of white chairs.
At four fifty, the mothers were about to be seated. Hanna's
father was waiting for his daughter and a sense of expectation filled the space.

Renee went back to check on Hanna and found all six of
her bridesmaids milling in the hallway.

"What's going on?" she asked.

"Hanna asked for a few minutes to herself," one of the
bridesmaids said.

Renee went cold. No, no and no. Brides were never to be
left alone—too many bad things could happen.

She stared at the bridesmaids. "Do not, under any circumstances, come into the room. Don't let anyone else in, either. I'll handle this myself."

They all nodded.

She knocked once and pushed the door open before she heard a request for her to enter.

"Hanna, it's me," she called.

Hanna stood by the long vanity, staring at herself in the mirror. Her eyes were wild, her mouth twisted. She spun toward Renee.

"I can't do this. I won't do it. What was I thinking? I can't marry Graham. I need to get out of here. What did I bring? Do I need to pack?" Tears filled her eyes. "Renee, you have to help me."

Renee put down her tablet and poured a glass of water. She handed it to Hanna, then felt her forehead and the side of her face.

"Have you taken anything?" she asked quickly. "Valium, something else to help you relax?"

Hanna stared at her. "Of course not."

Her eyes weren't dilated and there were no other signs of drugs. As far as she knew, no one had brought alcohol into the room.

Renee pulled out a stool and positioned it so Hanna could sit down. "Drink some water," she said, seating herself across from the other woman. "Take deep breaths."

"I don't want to take deep breaths, I want to get out of here."

Renee waited. Hanna glared at her, but she sipped water and drew in a breath.

"Happy?" she asked, her voice both angry and panicked.

"Not yet." Renee kept her posture relaxed, her tone gentle. "Tell me what's going on."

"I can't marry Graham. Isn't that obvious?" The tears returned. "Everything is a disaster. Or it will be. Have you met my family? I don't even know how many of my stepbrothers and sisters are coming. I can barely remember who my parents are married to. I swear, they should wear name tags at all family events."

She clutched her glass in both hands. "That's going to be me," she said helplessly. "I'm going to have to divorce Graham and I don't want to."

"Do you love him?"

"Of course I love him. Now! But what about in two years or five years? What about when things go bad and I end up like my mother?"

She brushed away tears. "He says it will be all right but he can't know. Not really. It's too big a risk."

"Tell me about the first time you met."

"What? Now? No. Besides, I already did."

Renee waited.

Hanna glared at her. "Fine. We were standing in line for a movie. All our friends left so it was just the two of us. We introduced ourselves and started talking."

"Was it cold outside?"

Hanna smiled. "A little, but I didn't care. It could have been a hurricane and I would have stood there. I thought he was so good-looking and when he laughed at something I said, it was the best."

"Butterflies?"

"More than that. I was scared and excited and hopeful and happy. It was wonderful."

"When did you first know you loved him?"

Hanna sipped her water. "I thought it on maybe our fourth date, but I knew for sure after a month." She laughed. "I wanted to say something, but I knew that sort of thing scared off some guys, so I kept quiet until he said it first."

"Was it magical?"

"More than that. It was everything I'd ever wanted. He was amazing."

"Is he the best man you've ever known?"

The tears returned. "He is. He's kind and strong and he loves me with all his heart. I trust him completely." She stiffened. "What are you doing?"

"Trying to figure out if you're scared and reacting or if you really think you're making a mistake. There's a difference, Hanna. A big one. Weddings are a huge deal and it's not uncommon to have a mini freak-out. I have no problem with that. But if you really think you shouldn't marry Graham, I need to know that, too. Because what you decide right now is going to affect the rest of your life. If you call off the wedding, then realize you do want to marry him, Graham may be okay with that. But no matter what, the memory of what you did will be there, always. You can't take it back."

She leaned toward Hanna. "I will do whatever you want, and I will totally support your decision. I'm not judging. I'm making sure *you* know what you're doing."

Hanna put down the glass and grabbed Renee's hands. "Oh, no. I couldn't just leave him standing there. I couldn't humiliate him like that. You're right—he would always have to live with that. We'd be sitting together having dinner and he would remember. I don't want that. I love him. I don't want to hurt him."

"Do you want to marry him?"

"Of course." She started to laugh. "What have I been doing?"

"Like I said, having a little freak-out. It happens."

"I was so scared. I thought I was making a mistake. But I'm not. He's wonderful and the only bad thing would be not to marry him today."

Hanna stood and flung her arms around Renee. "Thank you for talking me off the ledge."

"You're welcome. Are you sure?"

"Absolutely." Hanna looked at herself in the mirror and shrieked. "My makeup! My dress."

"You're going to be fine."

Renee turned on the steamer, then brought in the bridesmaids. It took only about fifteen minutes to get Hanna bride-ready. Renee got everyone in place and, as the last note of bagpipe music faded, motioned for the quartet to start the processional music.

As the bridal party began the long walk to where Graham was waiting, Renee allowed herself to exhale fully for the first time in nearly three days. She hadn't just been speaking to Hanna back there, she'd been talking to herself. Because she was wrestling with many of the same fears as her bride.

What if it didn't work out? What if they weren't going to make it? What if, what if, what if. Her choices were simple—she could trust herself and Jasper to weather whatever happened and follow her heart, or she could spend the rest of her life being afraid. Because there weren't any guarantees or promises. There was her and the man who had told her he loved her.

She had spent years blaming circumstances or her mother for what had gone wrong—but what if the real culprit was her? What if she was the reason Turner had left? What if it was all on her?

With a little time and self-reflection she might get close to an answer, but so what if she was half to blame or 90 percent? The past was done—what did she want from her future?

Jasper, she thought with a certainty that filled every cell in her body. She wanted Jasper. All of him—the healed and the broken, the laughter and the pain, his past, her past, their future. She wanted him messing up and then growing from the experience. She wanted him busy with his writing, then hanging out with her. She wanted the man who spent time with her mother and came with her to get a cat and who brought her takeout when she was tired and hugged like he would never let go. She wanted to love him with the fearlessness he'd shown her. She wanted to be worthy and happy and giving and strong and she wanted to spend the rest of her life knowing he was exactly where she belonged.

And she couldn't tell him because Hanna and Graham were getting married and she needed to be doing her job.

Somehow she managed to get through the ceremony without bursting out laughing or yelling out his name. She watched as they exchanged rings and shared their first kiss as husband and wife. She got them back into the bride's room so they could have their first toast, just the two of them, then made sure the guests were moving out into the reception area.

When the photographer corralled the families for pictures, Renee ducked away and went searching for Jasper.

She found him in the back of the main building, standing by the empty white chairs. When he spotted her, she half expected him to walk away, but he stayed where he was, watching her approach.

He looked good, she thought happily. The dark suit, shirt and tie suited him. It was his sexy author look, and it worked for her in a big way.

"I don't have much time," she told him. "I have to get to the reception, but I didn't want to wait any longer to tell you that I'm sorry for what happened before, between us. I'm sorry for how I acted and what I said. I was caught off guard. That's information, not an excuse."

She paused, hoping he would say something, but he looked at her without speaking.

This was her moment to be brave, she reminded herself. She refused to lose out because of fear. Not anymore.

"A lot of things have gone wrong in my life," she continued. "Verity's gift has been a challenge from time to time, and while that's on her, my reaction to those circumstances is on me. I'm pretty sure I learned the wrong lesson. Instead of thinking other people needed to grow enough to accept her, I told myself to be scared. To hide, to not reach out to anyone. I was so afraid of being like her that I stifled any creative thought I had. I wasn't being my best self and when you came along, I didn't realize what an amazing opportunity I had until I messed up everything."

His dark gaze locked on her face, but he still didn't speak. Which made all this really hard, but she wasn't giving up.

Okay, this was it. She was ready to fling herself off the side of the mountain and hope he caught her.

"I love you," she told him. "With all my heart. I love you and I'm so grateful that you were able to see what we could be together. Even if it's too late and you're done with me, I still want you to know how I feel and I hope that you can—"

He pulled her close, breathed her name and kissed her. No, it was more than a kiss—it was a promise. She hung on to him, kissing him back, feeling at home in his embrace, knowing this was all she'd ever wanted.

"I love you, too," he said, pulling back enough to stare into her eyes. "It's not too late. It will never be too late, because I'm not going anywhere. I've just found you, Renee. I'm not letting go ever."

They smiled at each other, then kissed again. After a few seconds, he drew back.

"You have a reception to put on. Go back to work. I'll be waiting when you're done."

She nodded. There was so much to talk about. Them, their

future, where they were going to live and how they were going to have to introduce Koda to Fred and Lucille. But that was for later. He was right—she did have a reception to manage and a happy couple to watch over.

She raised herself on tiptoe and kissed him. "I do love you, Jasper Dembenski."

"I love you back, times a thousand. Now go. I'll be right here when you're done."

Three weeks later...

Koda stared at Jasper as if asking if this were really necessary. He was in his own home—shouldn't the other creatures be the ones on a leash? At least that was Jasper's interpretation of what Koda was thinking. If he really wanted to know, he was going to have to ask Verity to stop by.

They were in day two of what he liked to think of as the cat invasion. So far Koda had been accepting and the cats weren't overly freaked out.

Fred and Lucille had a small room of their own, so they could have privacy while eating and using the bathroom. The cats weren't allowed in his office, so Koda could have time away from them and relax. Renee was still concerned about the family blending but Jasper knew it was all going to work out.

They'd spent the past few days moving Renee into his house. They'd discussed getting a place in town, but she wanted to see if she could make the mountain retreat work. So far the late fall weather was cooperating, but the real test would be January.

He and Koda headed into the master bedroom where Renee was putting away her clothes. Knowing she'd moved in made him ridiculously happy, although he was trying to act as normal as possible. Thursday would be their first Thanksgiving together as a couple. Ed and Verity were flying in and they would all spend the day with Carol, her husband, Mathias, baby Devon, and Ed's brother Ted. Dinner would be at Carol and Mathias's house, with Koda getting a special invitation to join them.

For once, there were no Thanksgiving weekend weddings, so he and Renee would have several days together. They wanted to trade in her car for something with all-wheel drive, then spend the rest of the time together, just the two of them. Well, the five of them, if he counted the pets.

He had a special dinner planned for the Saturday after Thanksgiving. Not just the meal and the bottle of champagne he'd put aside, but also the ring he planned to give her when he asked her to marry him.

"You sure I can't help?" he asked.

She smiled at him as she carefully put folded sweaters on a shelf. "With my heart and my life, but not with my clothes."

He grinned. "Just asking."

"I appreciate that, but I'm good." She pointed to the door. "Go write. I know you're dying to get back to your new serial killer." She grinned. "Pun intended."

He crossed to her and kissed her. "I'm setting my timer for two hours. I want to spend the evening with you." And the night and tomorrow and all the tomorrows, but he didn't say that.

"I will start dinner at six and be waiting breathlessly for your return."

He and Koda started for the office. Fred and Lucille raced past, playing some chase game only they understood. He walked through the kitchen, where Renee's purse sat on the counter and her shoes in the middle of the floor. She had a messy streak he wouldn't have guessed.

Everything was different, he thought happily. Everything

had changed and very much for the better. He was one lucky guy and later, he was going to be the guy who got the girl. It was his own happy ending—and it was the best one yet.

★ ★ ★ ★ ★